Summons to the
Chateau d'Arc

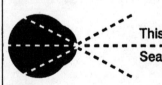

This Large Print Book carries the
Seal of Approval of N.A.V.H.

Summons to the Chateau d'Arc

Kay Cornelius

Thorndike Press • Waterville, Maine

Published in 2006 by arrangement with Tekno Books and Ed Gorman.

Thorndike Press® Large Print Clean Reads.

The tree indicium is a trademark of Thorndike Press.

The text of this Large Print edition is unabridged. Other aspects of the book may vary from the original edition.

Set in 16 pt. Plantin by Al Chase.

Printed in the United States on permanent paper.

Library of Congress Cataloging-in-Publication Data

Cornelius, Kay.
    Summons to the Chateau d'Arc / by Kay Cornelius.
        p. cm. — (Thorndike Press large print clean reads)
    ISBN 0-7862-8856-6 (lg. print : hc : alk. paper)
    1. Americans — France — Fiction.   2. Fathers and daughters — Fiction.   3. Administration of estates — Fiction.   4. Castles — Fiction.   5. France — Fiction.   6. Large type books.   I. Title.   II. Series.
PS3553.O65875S86 2006
    813´.54—dc22   2006014985

Summons to the Chateau d'Arc

Chapter One

Dreux, France — 1882

"*Attention,* Mademoiselle!"

I nodded to acknowledge the warning of the smartly uniformed conductor who had been so attentive during the journey from Paris, then turned to hand a coin to the smocked porter who set my luggage beside me on the platform.

"*Merci,*" I said. As long as I could reply "yes" and "thank you" to everything, all was well. But what would happen when I reached the chateau? I had been in France scarcely twelve hours, yet long enough to discover that my knowledge of the language had not prepared me for the rapidity with which it was actually spoken.

The porter scowled at the coin as if he expected more, then stepped back onto the train as it rumbled away, leaving me standing alone below a sign indicating I had reached Dreux, Eure-et-Loire.

I scanned the faces of the few people around me, wondering which of them might be there to meet me. But no one paid me the slightest heed until an old man in a dirty carriage robe approached, speaking rapid-fire French.

"I'm sorry, I don't understand — *Je n'ais comprende,*" I said.

The man gestured toward an open carriage bearing a sign I translated as "for hire." He reached for my portmanteau, but instinctively I held on to it.

"Ellen Edmonds?"

I turned as another man joined us. His clothing and bearing suggested he could be the Marquis d'Arc, and tentatively I spoke the name. But even as the words left my lips, I knew that this slender, dark-haired man must be years younger than the one who had summoned me to France.

At my words, his mouth twisted in a half-smile, but his blue eyes showed no amusement. "I am Philip Mailley, manager of the d'Arc lands. The Marquis asked me to fetch you."

He spoke in pleasant, British-accented English, but his tone sharpened as he said something in French to the man who had tried to take my luggage. The old man looked frightened and backed away, obviously mumbling an apology.

Philip Mailley then turned his full attention to me, his steady gaze moving slowly

8

from the top of my bonnet to the hem of my dove-gray traveling dress as if he had never seen anything like me before. His expression did not reveal if I met his approval, and without further comment he took my portmanteau and escorted me to an elegant enclosed coach while its liveried driver secured my trunk.

When he opened the carriage door, I saw it bore a coat of arms in which hounds bayed a stag. It was a scene I knew well — my mother had a brooch with an identical design. I hoped the coincidence was a good omen.

"Are you quite comfortable, Mademoiselle?" the driver asked in French as he latched the carriage door.

"*Oui, merci,*" I replied.

In his seat opposite me, Philip Mailley smiled. "So the American speaks French," he said in that language.

"Not as well as you speak English. Are you English?"

"No, Miss Edmonds. My mother was British, but I am a French citizen."

The driver mounted to his box, whistled to a matched pair of spirited bays, and the carriage jolted away from the Dreux railroad station. A few townspeople turned to stare as the carriage rattled past. With an ironic pride, I fancied they envied me and wished that they too could ride in luxury in this regal coach. As the carriage negotiated the narrow streets, I marveled at each shop we passed. I smiled at the miniature pig over the door of the *Charcuterie*. The fragrance of freshly baked bread from the *Boulangerie* competed with the rich odors coming from the adjacent *Patisserie* and reminded me it had been many hours since I had eaten a full meal.

"What marvelous shops!" I exclaimed, more to myself than to my silent companion.

"Most people regard Dreux as dull and provincial," Philip said as the carriage left its winding streets behind. "You'll find these shops really have very little to offer."

His implied criticism of my enthusiasm nettled me, but I resolved not to let this man spoil the moment I had anticipated for so long. In the comfort of the d'Arc carriage, I felt like Cinderella on her way to the Royal Ball. Not that I was going to anything remotely resembling a party. On the contrary, I expected to be considered as one of the household servants. Since private rides in the d'Arc carriage were a luxury I knew I would not often enjoy, I determined to make the most of this opportunity.

In this stage of the journey, we passed through a vast expanse of wheat fields stretching away to the horizon on both sides. Only occasionally did a narrow lane slice through the symmetry of the fields or a rare steeple or distant stand of trees mark what might be a small village. Blackbirds wheeled and cried against an almost cloudless blue sky.

Across from me, I was glad when Philip Mailley closed his eyes, sleeping or pretending to sleep. The way he had looked at and spoken to me made me believe he intended to make me feel uncomfortable. Instead, I relaxed my weary body against the plush upholstery and thought about the strange twist of fate that had brought me to the brink of seeing the castle I had dreamed about almost all of my twenty years.

Long before my summons to the Chateau d'Arc, Mama had told me of the French chateau set like a jewel before a dark lake and surrounded by vast lands. At first, I regarded it in the same way as the castles in fairy tales. In my young eyes, the chateau became a fabulous palace of splendor, far beyond the reach of a farm girl thousands of miles away. As I grew older, my mother spoke less often of the chateau, but its towers never left my private daydreams.

11

"Ellen, you are now the age I was when I went to France," Mama said on my eighteenth birthday. "You must travel while you are young."

She often spoke about my going to France, as if the only child of a poor woman who took in sewing to supplement her small Civil War widow's pension could afford to travel anywhere.

"I would like to see the Chateau d'Arc for myself," I said.

Dites-vous en Francais," she commanded, and for a time we conversed in the musical tongue she had been teaching me almost from my infancy.

Mama had learned to speak French while traveling in Europe as companion to an elderly widow. In Paris, they had been invited to a titled family's country estate near Chartres. The visit stretched into weeks, then months, as the elderly woman became ill and ended abruptly when she died. Mama returned home the month the fighting began between North and South and surprised everyone by marrying Lemuel Edmonds, whose hand she had rejected before going abroad. But she never forgot that she had once lived in France.

"It is time you went to the chateau," Mama declared one day when the illness that was to claim her life was far advanced.

"The chateau?" I repeated, thinking my mother must be in a delirium.

"There's a card in my desk," she gasped. "Write the Marquis d'Arc immediately —"

A fit of coughing seized her frail body and, without saying more, Mama sank into a coma from which she never emerged. On a raw March day barely a week later, she was laid to rest in the Edmonds family cemetery.

"The Edmonds family never liked me," my mother had remarked one day when she first became ill. "They blame me for Lemuel's death."

"That's ridiculous!" I protested. "What could you have done to keep my father from being killed in the War?"

"Nothing, of course," she said, but I sometimes felt that Mama kept something from me. Often I had studied the faded tintype of an unsmiling Lemuel Edmonds in his uniform, the look on his thin face suggesting he might have an argument with more than just the enemy. About all I knew of him was that he had joined the Army soon after marrying Mama and died near Gettysburg when I was little more than a baby.

Mama said Lemuel Edmonds had been a good man who deserved better. Sometimes the mere mention of his name brought on a spell of melancholy that lasted for days. I thought she must have loved him very much, and to avoid making her unhappy, I never questioned Mama about my father.

After the funeral, as I sorted through Mama's papers — mostly unpaid bills and a few orders for dresses her illness had prevented her from starting — I came across an exquisitely engraved ivory card in the bottom of her desk drawer.

Jean-Paul, Marquis d'Arc, Chateau d'Arc, Eure-et-Loire.

A chill ran down my spine as I recalled Mama's stories of her months in France, the highlight of her lonely life. I stared at the elaborate card and wondered why Mama had never shown it to me. She had asked me to write to him, but I did not know why. Nearly two decades had passed since my mother had been in France. The marquis, whom I pictured as an old man, might be dead and the address on the card was probably inadequate. I thought of at least a half dozen reasons to destroy the card and try to forget the chateau. But my memory of Mama's stories won out, and that very day I wrote the marquis a short note on black-bordered paper, using the best French I could muster, to inform him of the death of Sara Littleton Edmonds.

I lacked the French vocabulary to endow the news with the customary courteous flourish; anyway, I knew nothing more to say to a stranger half a world away. After I took my note to the post office in town, where the foreign address raised a few eyebrows, I put it from my mind.

With grudging charity, Aunt Irma invited me to share a room with my cousin Agnes, a plain woman five years my senior. I disliked giving up my precious privacy, but I had nowhere else to go. Mama's relatives had long since died or left the area, so I moved my few belongings and resolved to find some way to become independent as soon as possible.

Miraculously, the Marquis d'Arc had now given me that opportunity.

As the carriage continued on its way to the Chateau d'Arc, I opened my reticule and withdrew the letter that had summoned me to France. It was written in flawless English, and even though I already knew every word by heart, I read it again as a talisman for my impending meeting with the marquis.

Miss Edmonds —
  Please allow me to express my sincere sympathy on the occasion of the loss of

your dear mother. In our brief acquaintance, we learned she was kind and pleasant. I know you must miss her very much.

My daughter Lucy's former nurse is no longer able to carry out her duties. It is my hope that you will come to the Chateau d'Arc immediately and assume that post.

To cover your expenses, I have sent a letter of credit to the Merchants Bank in Albany.

The packet *White Swan* departs from New York City to Le Havre soon. I have taken the liberty of booking your passage.

We look forward to your safe arrival.

The letter was signed with a flourish — *Jean-Paul, Marquis d'Arc.* Viewing the signature, I tried to imagine what this man might look like. It was strange, but in all the stories Mama had told me about the chateau, she had said little about the family occupying it. She had lived there for only a few months and, as far as I knew, had had no contact with anyone from the chateau since leaving it. Yet the marquis' letter implied not only that he remembered my mother, but also that he must know something of my present circumstances.

The Marquis d'Arc's presumption I would agree to come to the chateau alarmed Aunt Irma. "This could be some kind of trick," she warned.

I shared her concern but, when I contacted the bank, I found that there was, indeed, a sum of money deposited for me, my name was on the *White Swan* passenger list, and I had only days to pack and say my farewells.

"Suppose I choose not to take the position?" I asked the banker.

He shrugged. "That is between you and this gentleman, Miss Edmonds. The sum provided is to be sent to the shipping line for your passage. Otherwise, my instructions are to return it."

"I see," I said, but I did not really understand why the Marquis d'Arc seemed so ready to invite a complete stranger into his home.

That he had used the word "nurse" made me wonder about Lucy's age. Had his daughter been a child, he would have spoken of needing a governess. Or were the terms perhaps different when translated into English?

I had many unanswered questions, but from the moment I first received it, I knew I would accept the marquis' offer.

I refolded the letter and put it away, then looked up to see that Philip Mailley's dark blue eyes were open and regarding me with frank curiosity.

"You have come a long way, Mademoiselle," he said. "I wonder why?"

I don't have to justify myself to this man, I thought. "Because the Marquis sent for me," I said.

"It might be better if he had not."

"Why do you say that?"

He shrugged. "You will know soon enough, in any case. Those are d'Arc lands on both sides of the road."

To my right the flat fields continued to stretch away to the horizon, but on the left a great masonry wall, at least eight or nine feet high, now ran parallel to the road. Mama had mentioned that the chateau grounds were walled, but I had not imagined such a massive buttress against the outside world. I felt a momentary uneasiness as I pondered what might await inside those walls.

Aware that Philip Mailley still watched, I smoothed my chignon, from which some of my rebellious, dark hair had become dislodged in the rigors of my long day's travel. I had been too keyed up to sleep the night

18

before and realized that my brown eyes were dark-circled. Not that I cared, of course; servants weren't supposed to be attractive, and it was of no importance whether Philip Mailley found my appearance pleasing or not.

Closing my eyes against my companion's appraisal, I summoned my image of the chateau, based on what Mama had said and on a few watercolor sketches she had made during her long-ago visit. Like all chateaux built at that time, the Chateau d'Arc was laid out on an east-west axis, facing south. The body of the chateau was a three-story rectangular brick building, with rounded towers at each corner that soared above the steep gables of the chateau's roof. The front and the back were exactly the same, except that the front opened onto an expanse of colored and patterned gravel, while the rear doors led to a grassy lawn on the verge of a dark lake.

A low, serpentine brick wall, inlaid in the same elaborate Italianate manner as the trim on the chateau itself, marked the graveled courtyard. The stable was to the right of the chateau, and beyond that was a small chapel my mother was told had once held a relic of the True Cross.

"There's nothing like it in this country,"

Mama had said when I questioned the pink color and the intricate patterns of the brickwork in her sketches.

"Was the sun setting when you did these?"

"No, Ellen. The chateau brick is just that warm pink color. Some day you'll see."

No, I won't, I had thought then, but now, incredibly, I was about to.

The driver slowed the horses, and the carriage swayed. I opened my eyes and leaned my head out of the carriage window. We were about to turn between matching pink brick towers to pass through a massive wrought-iron gate, opened wide to admit us. I still could not see the chateau, but I knew it sat at the end of a long poplar-lined driveway. I took a deep breath and tried to compose myself as the carriage approached the chateau and the fulfillment of my life-long dream.

"How eager you seem, Miss Edmonds," Philip Mailley said, and I felt my cheeks redden at his amused tone.

"I am quite naturally somewhat curious," I admitted. I turned from the window, thus missing my first long view of the chateau. But as the carriage circled halfway around the gravel drive, what I could see was even more imposing in reality than it had been in my imagination. When the driver helped me from the carriage, I stood on a large *fleur de lis* that formed the center of a design worked with varicolored, smooth gravel.

I did not have long to admire it, however. The carriage's approach had not gone unnoticed, and almost as soon as I set my feet on the ground, I was surrounded by a half-dozen barking hounds. One larger than the others growled menacingly and showed his teeth, as if he intended to bite me.

"*Allez-vous en!*" Philip called from behind me.

"These dogs look dangerous," I said, aware the large one had come even closer and still showed hostile intentions.

"Hercule is harmless, I assure you," Philip said. His tone suggested that he found my discomfort almost enjoyable.

Annoyed, I held my head high and pretended not to care that the dog continued to growl. "Perhaps, but he did not obey you."

At my words, Philip whistled and immediately all the hounds, Hercule included, gathered around him. He smiled and shrugged in a gesture I did not understand, then touched his hand to his forehead. "Welcome to the Chateau d'Arc, Miss Edmonds," he said. "May you find what you want here." With the hounds obediently trailing him, he moved away toward the stable.

What an irritating man, I thought. I was angry with myself that, despite his ill manners, I realized Philip Mailley was quite possibly the most attractive man I had ever met.

I had little time to dwell on the d'Arc estate manager, however, as the chateau's tall front doors opened. A liveried servant emerged to help the driver with my luggage.

"Bonsoir, Mademoiselle. Le Marquis —" he began, then broke off as he realized the marquis had followed him from the chateau.

"Miss Edmonds," a serious, dark man of middle years said, making it a statement. He bowed and bent over my hand, which I remembered to extend to him just in time to avoid an awkward moment. When he straightened, he looked at me so closely I began to blush. I had been brought up to believe it was rude to look directly at people, and his frank appraisal made me uneasy. First Philip Mailley had stared at me, now the marquis — was something wrong with my dress? Had my bonnet gotten askew?

Then it occurred to me that the marquis might be struck by my resemblance to my mother; I knew my small features and the oval shape of my face were similar to hers, although my eyes and hair were much darker, as Lemuel Edmonds' had been. I couldn't tell what he thought of my appearance, but for my part, the marquis looked somewhat younger than I had imagined him. A hint of gray at his temples lent a distinguished air, and while the fine lines around his eyes and mouth suggested he spent much time out-of-doors, his pale complexion denied it. His piercing eyes, a dark reddish-brown under heavy brows, were his most arresting feature, and I felt relieved when they finally finished their probing inspection.

"I trust you have had a pleasant journey?"

I nodded, finding myself suddenly wordless. The polite little speech I had rehearsed now seemed totally inappropriate. "Yes, thank you," I managed at last. I wished that my French were half as good as the marquis' English. Although he spoke my language with a distinct accent, each word was clear.

"Shall we go inside?" The marquis offered me his arm for the few steps that took us through intricately carved doors into the chateau.

The front hall itself is as large as our whole house, Mama had said, and when I saw its vast dimension, I realized she had not exaggerated. A parquet pattern in the wood paneling was repeated in the floor, and in the shadows two full suits of armor gleamed. Aware the marquis watched me, I tried not to appear surprised by anything I saw.

However, when we passed through double doors on the right and entered a huge sitting room, it was difficult not to gape at the room's dimensions. Mama told me the fireplace was massive; now I saw it could easily hold an entire tree, with room left to cook a side of venison on the racks above the fire. Even on this day in late May the room was cold, but the logs in the fireplace lay unkindled. Several great tapestries of hunting scenes covered the walls, reflected in the highly polished parquet floor. Ornate carved chests and a few silk-covered chairs were the room's only furnishings. Maroon brocade drapes half-covered the deep-set windows, which looked out on the front lawn and a sweep of grass leading to the stable. This grand salon was beautiful, but lifeless and overwhelming to one accustomed, as I was, to small, cozy rooms.

The marquis opened a door at the rear of the chamber and indicated I was to enter it. The contrast between this room and the one we had just left was so great I uttered an involuntary exclamation.

"The family salon might be more to your liking, I imagine," the marquis said.

"It's lovely," I managed to reply, not nearly doing justice to a room which called for superlatives.

The last rays of sunlight slanted into the tall windows, adding yet another pattern to the subdued hues of the thick Oriental rugs. Pale ivory silk covered the walls, and a fire blazed in the marble fireplace. Two couches were pulled up to the fire, a silver tea service on a table between them.

"Please be seated, Miss Edmonds. I thought we might have tea and speak together for a moment before you meet Lucy."

The marquis pulled a tasseled cord by the fireplace and sat on the couch opposite me. I sank into the down-filled cushions, deliciously unlike the stiff, horsehair-stuffed sofas in every front parlor I had ever seen, and resisted the urge to pinch myself. A small ormolu clock on the mantel chimed six times, and my stomach rumbled as if to remind me that, fairy-tale setting or not, it expected to be fed.

"My mother was so fond of the chateau," I said, hoping its master had not heard the rude evidence of my hunger.

He drew his dark brows together and I wondered if it had been an error to mention her. "Surely she could not have told you very much," he said. "She was here such a short time."

He made it sound like a question, and somehow I thought my answer had importance. "True, but I can see why the chateau impressed her. Perhaps you knew that she made some sketches? I am sure they helped her to remember it."

"Did you bring them with you?" he asked, and once again I had the distinct feeling I might have said the wrong thing.

"Yes, Sir, I did." *Everything I can call my own I brought here,* I could have added, but did not.

"I hope you will allow me to see them."

A young maid entered from another door, bearing glazed pastries on a silver tray. She poured tea into fragile porcelain cups and inquired in French how I took it. I managed to reply well enough for her to give me the requested dash of cream and single lump of sugar.

The maid curtsied and left the room, and for a moment the only sound was the ticking of the mantel clock.

"Perhaps you will be able to help Lucy improve her English," the marquis said at last. "I have not been able to interest her in the subject."

The hot tea and sweetness of the pastry, a raspberry tart, combined to make me feel almost comfortable. "Just how old is your daughter?" I asked.

The marquis took a sip of tea and set his cup down carefully before leaning forward to answer me. Again he seemed to be studying my face far more closely than politeness would allow, and I determined not to wilt under his scrutiny. For some time we stared at one another, until the marquis nodded slightly, as if he had assured himself of something.

"Lucy is several years your junior. She will be seventeen this winter."

I had expected her to be much younger, and I wondered how the marquis knew my age. A lucky guess, perhaps, made when he examined my face so carefully. But of course he knew I had been born after Mama left France. I had scarcely considered that question when the marquis raised another.

"Before you meet her, I must warn you that Lucy is —" He frowned and gazed into the fire, as if the English word he sought might be found there, then looked back to me, watching for my reaction as he finished the thought. "— afflicted, one might say."

"Afflicted?" I repeated, not quite understanding what he meant. *Is she half-witted?* I wondered.

With the remarkable facility he had for seeming to read my mind, the marquis shook his head and sighed. "Ah, Mam'selle, when you see her, you will understand. Lucy is intelligent, but she can be quite difficult. I hope you can get along with her."

"I shall try my best to do so, Sir." I hoped that my tone did not reveal my growing trepidation.

The marquis nodded and stood. "Enjoy your tea. I shall fetch Lucy and return presently."

While the marquis was gone, I took advantage of his absence to eat another of the remarkable fruit tarts. I also surveyed the room more closely. I noticed that another door at the far right of the room opened to the outside, and I guessed that it was the entrance the family preferred to the cold and formal front hall. *There must be dozens of rooms they never use,* I thought. I looked forward to seeing them all.

I had just finished my tea when the door opened and the marquis entered, pushing a wheeled invalid's chair.

"Miss Edmonds, may I present my daughter, Lucy d'Arc."

The girl regarded me impassively, and I

wondered what she thought of me. For my part, I would have guessed her to be older than sixteen.

"I am pleased to meet you," she said coolly in English more thickly accented than her father's.

The young woman was not unattractive, but it was obvious she had made no effort to enhance her appearance. Her rich honey-blond hair was pulled back tightly, emphasizing her high cheekbones and the sharp planes of her pinched face.

She has suffered a great deal, I thought, and the marquis looked at me almost as if I had expressed the words aloud.

"And I am pleased to meet you, Miss d'Arc."

I had stood to take Lucy's hand in greeting, and the marquis indicated I should be seated. He wheeled Lucy's chair to the end of the sofa closest to the fire, and poured her a cup of tea without asking if she wanted it.

"You have had a long journey," Lucy said. She spoke slowly, as if each word had to be considered, and with no real interest in what she said. Her ice-blue eyes watched me warily, however, betraying a curiosity her voice did not.

"Yes, but I enjoyed it," I replied, making

myself speak more slowly than customary. "You have a lovely home," I added, my gesture taking in the entire chateau.

"It is too old and too cold," Lucy said, unsmiling.

"There is nothing like it where I lived in America."

"There are many grander houses in France," Lucy said matter-of-factly.

"You two will have time to talk later," the marquis said, ending our pointless conversation. He rose and pulled the bell rope. "Miss Edmonds will want to rest and settle in. We dine at eight — Sophie will take you to your room now."

The maid reappeared and I followed her, nodding to Lucy and the marquis as I left. As the door swung shut behind us, I heard him speaking in French to Lucy, his tone surprisingly harsh.

"This young woman will not be sent away like the others, do you understand?"

I didn't hear Lucy's reply, but the marquis' words disturbed me. *What others?* I wondered. *And if I were sent away, what would I do?*

Sudden dread seized me as I followed Sophie down a long, central hall lined with what I supposed to be the d'Arc ancestral portraits. Their faces were unclear in the dimness, but I had the strange feeling that each inspected me as if judging my fitness to occupy their home.

A shiver ran down my spine as I walked through the drafty hall. I had not thought the chateau would be so cold, nor had it occurred to me that Lucy d'Arc might prove to be difficult. *This is the chateau of my dreams,* I reminded myself. The long journey had made me tired, that was all. Lucy would grow to like me — she had to.

I had nowhere else to go.

Chapter Two

The room to which I was led was on the
main floor, quite near the kitchen. I could
smell the savory odor of cooking meat even
after I stepped inside my small chamber in
what I guessed to be the servants' quarters.

Wordlessly, Sophie crossed the room and
opened the heavy rose-colored drapes, revealing a patch of green lawn bordered by
the thick woods to the left of the chateau. A
pitcher of water flanked a basin on the plain
table, the only furnishings in the room besides a single chair, a canopied bed, a small
chest, and a huge wardrobe that would
more than accommodate my meager belongings.

"Will you require help in unpacking?"
Sophie asked, gesturing toward my trunk.

"No, thank you," I said. I sensed that
Sophie, a fresh-faced girl about my age,
would resent waiting on me, another servant.

"Dinner is at eight," she said, then withdrew.

Resisting the temptation to lie down on the huge feather mattress, I took off my bonnet and began to unpack my trunk. As I did so, I considered what I should wear that evening.

"We dressed for dinner at the chateau as if dining out in Paris," Mama had told me. During her stay, she had alternated wearing her best blue satin gown and a black traveling dress. Her skilled needlework produced fichus and fancy collars from scraps of material, giving the illusion that she had many more clothes. Learning from her, I had added several accessories to my basic wardrobe. But for my first dinner at the chateau I set aside a plain, green dress of light wool, its only adornment the hunting scene brooch that Mama had treasured. I hoped to make a good impression on Lucy's mother and any other members of the household whom I had not met, as well as to reassure the marquis that my appearance would not embarrass him.

Having unpacked, I sponged my face and took down and rearranged my hair, twisting it into a figure eight against the back of my head. Mama had dressed it more elaborately, but this was the best I could do without help. I decided not to pin on Mama's gold watch, but I wound it and set it on the table so I could keep up with the time while I rested. At a quarter until eight, I slipped the dress on and smoothed it out, pleased to see that its long journey in my trunk had not wrinkled it badly.

Somewhere within the recesses of the chateau, a clock struck eight times, and with a deep breath I touched my brooch for luck and walked toward the room Sophie had pointed out as the family dining room. To my surprise it was empty, and when I abruptly turned to go back toward the family salon, I ran headlong into a figure standing in the hall.

A man's hands took both my wrists and held them for a moment. Startled, I let out a wordless exclamation and he dropped them and spoke rapidly in French.

"You must be the new one," I caught, but before I could ask who he was, the marquis came out of the family salon and spoke sharply to him.

"Miss Edmonds, I must apologize for Jacques. He is fond of startling people."

"I can apologize for myself, thank you," he said, speaking English in the same heavily accented manner as Lucy. "I am sorry if I caused you discomfort, Miss — ?"

"Edmonds, Ellen Edmonds," I supplied without waiting for the marquis to make the formal introduction.

"Yes, of course. Lucy's new companion, here all the way from America."

In the dim light of the hall, all I could tell about Jacques was that he was taller than I, but when we went into the gas-lit family dining room, I saw he was blond, with light blue eyes and heavy eyebrows. His mouth seemed to be curved into a perpetual, sardonic half-smile. When the butler pushed Lucy's chair into the room, I noticed she and Jacques bore a striking family resemblance. Neither had the dark coloring of the marquis, but I assumed Jacques to be his son.

"And here is Madame Albert," the marquis said when an elderly, somewhat plump woman entered, dressed in black and leaning heavily on a cane.

She barely glanced at me as the marquis introduced us, and I was relieved to see her take a seat at the opposite end of the table.

"The witch is angry because you are taking her place," Jacques whispered across the table, a smirk on his face. "She will try her best to chase you away."

Lucy's chair had been wheeled to my left at the foot of the table. Hearing Jacques, she scowled. "And how many have you chased away, my dear brother?"

"No more than you have sent packing yourself, *ma petite.*"

From his place at the head of the table, the marquis frowned his displeasure at them and rang a small silver bell. I waited for him to speak, but apparently he had merely been signaling the kitchen staff we were ready to be served.

"Is this everyone?" I asked, noting the five of us were scattered around a table that could have seated a dozen. I had half-expected to see Philip Mailley, but as the first course arrived, he had not made an appearance.

"Whom else would you like?" Lucy asked, and, unaccustomed as I was to her rapid French, there was no mistaking the hostility in her voice.

"Miss Edmonds has had a long journey and I am sure she is tired," the marquis said in French. "You will keep a civil tongue in your head tonight, young lady."

Lucy's face reddened, but she made no reply.

On the other hand, Jacques seemed grimly amused. "We are not accustomed to visitors, Mam'selle. You may find our manners are sometimes lacking."

"A condition which the young lady can help us mend, I am certain," the marquis said, nodding in my direction.

As dinner proceeded through soup, fish, and beef dishes, I spoke only to answer the marquis' questions about my voyage.

When the marquis' attention was temporarily distracted by Madame Albert, Jacques leaned across the table, his eyes frankly appraising my bodice.

"That is quite an unusual piece of jewelry, Mademoiselle. I would not think that such exquisite items would be available in America."

I felt my cheeks grow hot. "It was my mother's. I do not know where she got it," I managed to say.

"The scene looks quite familiar, does it not, Lucy?" Jacques asked, a question that his sister pretended not to hear.

At the head of the table the marquis stood, signaling the end of the meal. "Perhaps Miss Edmonds would like to hear you play," he said to Lucy.

Her face darkened and she gripped the arms of her chair. "Perhaps she would not," she said ungraciously.

Taking the hint, I said I was tired and would like to retire early.

"Lucy will want her breakfast at nine o'clock, sharp," Madame Albert said suddenly, speaking directly to me for the first time and still frowning as if my presence irritated her.

I nodded at Madame Albert and turned to Lucy. "Shall I bring you a tray?"

Lucy cast a baleful look at Madame Albert, then glanced back at me. "Sophie will attend to it," she said. "You may come to my room at ten."

"I'm afraid I don't know where your room is," I confessed.

Lucy seemed annoyed. "Can you find your own?" she asked, and I nodded.

"It is next to yours." Lucy nodded to the butler, Henri, who had stood quietly in the doorway throughout the meal, and he came over to push her chair away from the table.

"Shall I take you to your room?" I asked.

"That will not be necessary, Miss Edmonds," the marquis replied for her. "You are to be Lucy's companion, not her servant."

Madame Albert made a derisive noise, and Jacques seemed similarly affected, but neither said anything, nor did I.

"You are welcome to join us in the family salon," the marquis said, as if to reinforce his statement that I was to be regarded as more than a mere servant, after all.

Was his invitation just a formality? Suddenly I felt much too weary to care. In any case, I had no desire to see more of Jacques or Madame Albert that night.

"Good evening," a new male voice called from the doorway, and I looked up to see Philip Mailley.

How long has he been listening to us? I wondered, but apparently no one else seemed to think it was unusual he should appear just as dinner ended.

"What happened, Mailley? Did the stable air get too rich for you?" Jacques said, his tone taunting.

An angry flush appeared on Philip's face, but he ignored Jacques and addressed the marquis. "Is there anything you require of me this evening?"

"I think not, thank you. But perhaps you will accompany us to the family salon?"

"Yes, Mailley, do come. We might be able to persuade Lucy to play for you."

Now it was Lucy's turn to blush. "I am not in the mood to perform this evening," she said to Jacques.

Aware that the scene might become unpleasant, I stood. "Please excuse me, but this has been a most exhausting day. I really should like to retire early."

"Yes, Mam'selle, do take all the rest you can. You'll need it," Jacques said, too low for the marquis to hear.

"Then good evening. If you need anything, please ask," the marquis said. His tone was considerably sharper when he addressed Jacques. "Are you coming, Jacques?"

"I thought I'd see Miss Edmonds to her room first." Jacques glanced at me to see my reaction.

"That won't be necessary, thank you." I looked him straight in the eye, and he smiled as if my refusal pleased him. I lacked experience with men, but I had no intention of allowing Jacques to intimidate me.

"Until tomorrow, then," Jacques said, making it sound more like a threat than a farewell.

Philip bowed slightly and stood aside as I passed him, his expression amused. "Good night, Miss Edmonds. I hope you sleep well."

Risking rudeness, I did not reply.

When I returned to my room, I found my bed had been turned down. An oil lamp glowed dimly on the bedside table, and I realized that the brilliant illumination of the family dining room did not extend throughout the house.

I pulled on my ruffled white nightgown, one of the several that my mother had made before she became ill. Thinking of her fingers patiently working the tiny stitches, my eyes filled with unexpected tears.

Here I am, Mama.

I was in the grand house that she had loved, and although I had yet to see most of its rooms, I had to admit that the Chateau d'Arc was not what I had expected. I hadn't imagined it would be so dark and so cold, and I wondered what could have been so different when my mother was here.

Not only was the house not what I had envisioned; the d'Arcs were not the fairy-tale family I had expected. So far, the marquis had been genuinely cordial, but everyone else seemed to believe I should have stayed in America. Was that what Philip meant when he implied I shouldn't have come?

I thought of Jacques' warning about Madame Albert and dismissed it. The old lady might resent my presence, but I doubted she would actually do anything to me. *Jacques likes to startle people,* the marquis had said, and, knowing that, I felt I could handle him well enough.

Lucy d'Arc was a different matter, however.

What on earth have I gotten myself into? I asked the mirror as I brushed my hair, but my reflection granted me no answer.

★ ★ ★

I awoke to a knock at the door and at first could not recall where I was. My eyes opened to the dark rose of the canopy above my head and, at the window, the morning sun made a halo around the drawn drapes.

This is the Chateau d'Arc, and I am really here at last. I stretched and felt relief that my dark thoughts of the evening seemed to have vanished along with the night.

"Entrez!" I called.

Sophie entered, bearing a silver tray. *"Bonjour, Mam'selle."*

I sat up on the side of the bed and regarded the pot of tea and plump croissant on the tray. There was no butter, but a dollop of marmalade resided in an exquisite crystal bowl. Both the food and the way it had arrived surprised me.

"Would you prefer something else?" Sophie asked, and I shook my head and assured her as well as my French would allow that the breakfast was perfect.

"Thank you for bringing it, but I thought I was to take breakfast in the family dining room."

"The Marquis asked me to serve you this morning. Miss Lucy will see you when you have finished."

"Tell her I shall be there soon."

I was surprised to see the hour was so late; by the time I had finished my breakfast, it was nearly ten o'clock.

I put on one of my two daytime dresses, a serviceable navy blue serge which could be comfortably worn in all temperatures, and plaited my hair into braids which I then crossed and pinned atop my head. I fancied that the style made me look older, as well as adding an inch or so to my height.

I opened my door and almost ran into Madame Albert, who stood in the hall as if she had been waiting for me. I greeted her and started to move toward Lucy's room, but she laid a restraining arm on mine.

"Why did you come back?" she asked, speaking so softly that I could scarcely make out the words.

"Come back?" I understood the French words she had spoken, but not their meaning.

"Was it not enough that you destroyed Madeline? Must you also destroy her children?"

"I do not understand," I replied. The old woman's eyes burned with hate, and I pulled free of her and all but ran the few steps to Lucy's door.

"Come in!" Lucy called.

I pulled the door shut behind me and

43

hoped Madame Albert would not follow.

Lucy sat in an upholstered chair in a room that was twin to mine in size. Her draperies, a rich blue floral print, were opened to the morning light, and the room contained several chests, comfortable chairs, and, to my surprise, a sewing-machine.

"Good morning, Miss d'Arc," I said, nodding in what I hoped was a suitably respectful manner and hoping Lucy would not see my agitation.

"Sit down. I don't like for people to stand in my presence." Unsmiling, Lucy nodded toward the chair next to hers, where I sat at her bidding.

"I must have been very tired to sleep so late," I said.

"I take my breakfast at nine in the family dining room. Perhaps you will join me there tomorrow," Lucy said, making it more an order than a suggestion.

"Certainly. I am unaccustomed to being waited on," I said, speaking in English for the first time that morning.

"I do not like to speak English," Lucy said in French, her frown deepening.

"Your father wants you to learn to speak it well," I returned in English.

"And did he tell you why I must learn such a vulgar language, Miss Edmonds?"

"Does he need a reason?" I countered, trying to make my voice sound friendlier than I felt toward this strange girl at the moment.

Lucy's mouth twisted in a grim sort of smile. "The Marquis d'Arc does not need a reason for anything — you will soon find that out. For example, what reason did he have for bringing you all the way from America?"

I hadn't expected Lucy to raise the question I still wondered about myself, and she seemed almost pleased at my discomfort. "I don't know, but I presume it is because he cares for you and wants to please you."

Lucy's sudden laughter startled me, but it was not the laugh of one truly amused. "That is because you do not know him as I do. You will see."

Someone rapped lightly on the door, and I opened it with dread, expecting Madame Albert. Instead, as if speaking his name had summoned him, the marquis stood in the doorway. He wore riding breeches and a light jacket, casual clothes that hung rather loosely on his large frame. *He has a poor tailor — or perhaps he has lost weight,* I thought, noticing the fit of his apparel with a dressmaker's eye.

"Good morning, young ladies. I trust that

you slept well, Miss Edmonds?" At my nod, he continued speaking. "Lucy, you might show your new companion around the house. I would oblige, but I must ride over to Brezolles."

"Where is Jacques this morning?" Lucy asked.

The marquis shrugged. "I have not seen him. I suppose he is still abed."

"My brother gets lazier with each passing day," Lucy muttered to herself. Aloud she said, "I cannot take Mam'selle Edmonds to the upper floors."

"That can wait," the marquis said. "Miss Edmonds will have little reason to be in that part of the chateau, in any case. Good day, ladies." With a nod, he turned and walked away.

"I used to love to go upstairs," Lucy said, a wistful note creeping into her voice.

"What happened to put you in that invalid's chair?" I asked, momentarily allowing my curiosity to overrule my manners.

Lucy's face reddened. "I do not care to discuss it," she said curtly. "Do you want to see the chateau or not?"

"Of course. Here, let me push your chair."

Lucy said nothing as I wheeled the heavy

chair into the darkness of the hall. Although Oriental rugs covered the middle of the stone floor, the corridor was dank and drafty, and I soon understood why Lucy had thrown a shawl about her shoulders before leaving her room.

"The chateau must be terribly cold in the winter," I remarked.

Although I couldn't see Lucy's expression, there was no mistaking the amusement in her tone as she replied to my somewhat unthinking remark. "I expect you will be gone by then, Mam'selle. Very few outsiders stay here long."

"How many others have had my post?"

"In the past year alone, four, I think. Two of them were incompetent, and the others — well, no matter."

I was curious about the fate of my predecessors, but I had some doubt that Lucy's version of why they had left could be trusted. "Which way should I turn?" I asked.

"That way," she said, waving toward the front of the house.

"Are these the ancestors?" I asked when we passed a row of huge portraits lining both sides of the corridor.

Lucy looked up as if she had never noticed them before and shrugged her slight shoulders. "They are someone's ancestors, I suppose," she said indifferently. "I have never cared much about dead people myself."

She's just testing me, I told myself, but I could be equally indifferent. "Neither have I, Mademoiselle. I am glad to see we have something in common."

"Stop here," Lucy said suddenly. To our right stood a pair of massive intricately carved doors, and at her bidding I opened them.

"Oh!" I exclaimed, that being the only reaction of which I was capable. I stood on the threshold of a huge marble-floored room almost totally devoid of furniture. A row of windows came nearly to the floor on the wall directly before me, while floor-to-ceiling mirrors covered the side walls. "The mirrored ballroom," I said. It was exactly as Mama had described it. I stepped forward, and on either side, multiple Ellens imitated my movement. "This room must be a copy of the Hall of Mirrors at the Palace of Versailles."

Lucy shook her head and spoke again, reverting to French as if my gaffe made it impossible for her to converse further in my language. "*Au contraire.* It is said that Versailles copied this room, instead. This chateau is much older, you know."

"No, I didn't." I turned from the mirrors to look at Lucy. "I know nothing about the chateau's history."

"Then why—" Lucy began, then checked herself. "It was built in the time of Henri II as a fortification and remodeled into its present form by Italian architects and artisans."

"Henri II?" I tried to recall my small store of French history. "Wasn't he in the sixteenth century?"

"Yes. The Chateau d'Arc has been continuously occupied for a third of a millennium."

"But not always by d'Arcs," another voice said.

I turned to see Jacques in the doorway, wearing a heavy, white sweater and riding breeches that must have been tailored to fit his well-muscled frame. There was no doubt that Jacques d'Arc made a handsome appearance — and was well aware of it.

"So you finally managed to rise before noon for a change, eh?" Lucy asked.

"Just because I do not care for breakfast, my sister fancies I sleep later than she does," he said, looking at me rather than Lucy. "And what about you, Mam'selle? Do you prefer to take your breakfast late, as well?"

"I cannot imagine what concern that is of yours," Lucy said, adding something else I was not quick enough to catch. I knew that eventually I would become accustomed to their rapid-fire delivery and their accent, which made even familiar French words incomprehensible. Then I would understand everything they said, but for the present I could not.

"That is your trouble, Lucy — you have no imagination!" Jacques returned.

"Miss Edmonds does not wish to hear us quarrel," Lucy said in English. "I am supposed to show her the chateau."

"You haven't been upstairs yet, have you?" Jacques hardly waited for me to shake my head before stationing himself behind Lucy's chair and turning it back toward her room. "That must be remedied immediately."

"Be careful," Lucy told Jacques, and I had the distinct impression that she wasn't talking about the way he guided her chair.

Jacques laughed without humor. "Don't worry, *ma petite*. I shall be the very soul of discretion."

"Do you need anything before I go?" I asked Lucy when she was back in her room. She pointed to a long bell pull in easy reach.

"If I do, I will call Sophie. You may leave me now."

"Lucy does not seem to want me here," I ventured to say to Jacques as we began to climb the wide staircase at the front of the main hallway, just behind the huge foyer that had so impressed me on my arrival.

"Of course not. My sister is badly spoiled and accustomed to having her own way. I suspect she fears you might actually try to improve her."

"How long has she been that way?"

"She has been spoiled all her life."

I bit my lip, realizing that Jacques knew quite well what I meant. "And how long has she been unable to walk?" I persisted.

My question coincided with our arrival at the main hall of the second floor of the Chateau d'Arc, and once again I shivered from the chill which seemed to seep from the walls, a cold so at odds with the bright sunlight outside. As on the main floor, this corridor was lined with paintings, but instead of portraits, some canvases depicted mythological subjects, while others showed elaborate hunting scenes.

Ignoring my question, Jacques stopped before a huge canvas depicting the last moments of a stag that had been brought to bay as several hunters stood by, ready to administer the *coup de grace*. "Rather grisly, is it not?"

Looking closely, I saw that the central figure, spear in hand, bore a striking resemblance to the marquis. The scene was familiar to me — it was the same design I had seen on the d'Arc coat of arms and, although much smaller, on my mother's brooch.

"Is that — ?" I began.

"It's the first Marquis d'Arc. He stocked the lands with so much game that every hunt brought good results. It originally hung in the grand salon, but the present Marquis exiled it to the second floor. You can see why I noticed your brooch," he added.

Jacques put out his hand and touched Mama's watch, which I wore above my bosom where the brooch had been the night before, and once more my cheeks warmed at his boldness.

"The Marquis does not hunt?" I asked.

"Not since — not for many years. These are his rooms." He waved toward a pair of closed doors on the right. "And down the hall is Madame Albert's suite."

"Madame Albert does not seem to want me here, either," I said.

Jacques tapped a finger to his forehead in

the universal gesture that indicates madness. "You must pay her no heed. That old woman lives in a world of her own."

"What about the others that came before me? What happened to them?"

Jacques shrugged and moved toward the staircase leading to the third floor. "They left," he said simply. "But not one of them was as pretty as you," he added with a roguish smile.

"I do not appreciate flattery, M'sieu," I said with as much severity as I could muster.

"And I do not give it, Mam'selle. Remember that."

We reached the third floor, which seemed to be an exact replica of the second, except that its walls contained fewer *objets d'art*. Seeing a large window at the end of the hall, I walked over to it.

"Nice view, *n'est ce pas?*" Jacques said behind me.

Uncomfortably aware of his presence and sensing he might intend to put his arms around me, I stepped away from him.

"Yes, it is." I could see the dark lake behind the chateau, bordered by thick woods. No other dwelling was in sight.

"And now for the best view of all." Jacques opened a door to the right, revealing a winding staircase.

"It's dark." I thought about the many spiders and other creatures which no doubt inhabited the place. My farm upbringing had not altered my instinctive dislike of them.

"That can be remedied. I shall fetch a light from my room."

Jacques crossed the hall and opened a door, revealing a table covered with books and papers. From it, he took and lighted a small lantern.

"Follow me," he ordered. I held my skirts high and tried not to think what might be underfoot.

The stairs had been hewn from stone and were slippery. I shuddered when the hand I put out to steady myself encountered the damp, cold wall. The steps wound upward in a looping spiral, and by the time I finally stood inside the southwest tower, I felt giddy.

The room seemed to undulate as I crossed it and looked out a window that had evidently not been cleaned in years. Fields stretched away in the distance, while the chapel and stable spread out beneath me. Far below us, a man walked across the open courtyard within the stable enclosure.

Jacques stood by my side, and once more his nearness made me feel uncomfortable.

"There is our stable boy," he said with contempt.

As we watched, the man brought his hands together and bent down. Suddenly dogs surrounded him, and I recognized Philip Mailley.

"Stable boy?" I repeated. "I thought M'sieu Mailley had charge of the estate."

"He would certainly like to own it all," Jacques said. Suddenly he sneezed, shielding his face with the sleeve of his full-cut shirt. "Come, Miss Edmonds. The air up here is unhealthy."

"What about the other towers?" I asked, but Jacques sneezed again and shook his head.

"Not today, Mam'selle. I can tolerate no more dust."

As Jacques started toward the steps ahead of me, I noticed among the jumble of items littering the tower floor what appeared to be a woman's portrait. The small painting was partially covered, but I could tell its subject was a female with blond hair and an emerald-encircled neck. I wanted to ask Jacques about it, but he had already started down the stairs, the light receding with him. I resolved to return to examine the portrait and see the other tower rooms later, alone.

"Did you notice the clock on the northwest tower as you came in?" Jacques asked on our way back down.

"That tower is taller than the others, isn't it?"

"Yes, and unsafe. Some shingles are missing from the roof, and a good many creatures have moved in."

"Creatures?" I repeated the word, thinking that perhaps my French was inadequate to make the translation.

"Birds of all kinds, and bats. The Marquis keeps saying he will attend to it, but so far nothing has been done. In fact, you ought not go to any of the towers. You see how unhealthy they are."

Perfunctorily I agreed, but privately I reserved the right to return for a better look at the portrait. Then a new thought struck me. With dozens of empty rooms in the chateau, why use a remote tower room for storage? It could not be easy to carry objects up the steep stairs. On the other hand, once there, no one would be likely to see them.

Back on the third floor, Jacques sneezed a final time, then extinguished the lantern and paused at his door. "Would you like to see my room?" he asked, his smile making it clear he knew I would not.

"No, thank you. I am surprised that you

choose to stay up here all alone," I added, thinking how removed this floor seemed from the rest of the chateau.

"Not exactly. Servants occupy some of the rooms. In fact, Sophie moved up here when you came and took her room. We manage quite well."

I am sure you do, I thought, and felt sorry for Sophie. I knew I would not relish sleeping near Jacques, and idly wondered if the rooms on this floor had locks. I had already discovered that mine did not.

"I should get back to Lucy," I said.

"So pretty, and so conscientious too!" Jacques took my elbow, but I hurried on ahead of him and descended both flights of stairs far more rapidly than prudence dictated.

Jacques caught up with me on the main floor. "There is no need to run away, Mam'selle. Despite what my sister may tell you, I do not molest young women."

I said nothing, nor did I look at him.

"You should have a tour of the grounds," he said at Lucy's door. "That is, if you really intend to stay."

The challenge in his tone was clear. I raised my chin and looked directly at him. "I shall remain."

Jacques' habitual half-smile deepened,

and he put out his hand to touch my cheek. Quickly I moved away, and he laughed. "I believe you might, at that. In that case —"

"Miss Edmonds, is that you?"

Lucy's voice called out, interrupting whatever Jacques might have been about to say. "Yes," I replied, and opened her door.

Jacques shrugged and turned away. "I shall see you later," he called over his shoulder.

But not alone, I thought. That much I had already learned about the Chateau d'Arc.

Chapter Three

Lucy was seated at the sewing-machine I had noticed earlier when I entered her room.

"Back already, Mam'selle? Jacques' tours usually last much longer."

"It was long enough for me to know that you have an impressive home."

"You will not think so, when you have been here longer," she said scornfully.

Ignoring her remark, I touched the heavy brocade material on which Lucy worked. "My mother would have loved to have a sewing-machine. What are you making?"

"The Marquis recently replaced the draperies in his room. I am fashioning a cloak from the old material, but it is almost too heavy for the machine to stitch."

I looked closer to see how the machine operated. A belt turned a wheel, which moved a vertically mounted needle up and down through the fabric as Lucy pulled it through. I was fascinated by the speed with which a length of material could be sewn together; a process that would have taken hundreds of tediously formed hand stitches.

I was even more puzzled when I realized that the power to operate this wonder came from Lucy's feet, rhythmically pushing on a treadle that turned the belt.

"What you are doing must require a great deal of strength."

Concentrating on maintaining her steady rhythm on the treadle, Lucy did not immediately answer. When the final few inches of material had fed under the needle, she straightened and deftly cut the threads with a small pair of scissors tied at her waist.

"I suppose you do not understand how I can do this when I must use a chair to get about."

"I didn't say —" I began, but she made an impatient gesture.

"No one says, but they all wonder. Sometimes, so do I."

Her tone was bitter, but whatever anger she felt was not directed at me, and I hoped to keep it that way.

"Your legs — was there an accident?"

Instantly Lucy's head came up and she looked at me with the same spiteful malevolence I had come to regard as her normal expression. "No, Miss Edmonds. What happened was not an accident."

She looked away and began trying to fold the bulky drape from which she had cut the cloak. I retrieved the top of the panel from the floor and helped her fold it, then at her bidding I placed it on a chair by the door.

"I wish you would call me Ellen," I said when it became clear that she had nothing more to say.

Lucy looked back at me and shook her head. "It does not matter what I call you or what you call me. Either you will leave as the others did, or you will stay. In any case, it does not alter the way things are."

"No, but it might make the time pass more pleasantly if you could look on me as your friend." I knew I was being presumptuous, and I steeled myself for an outburst. Instead, Lucy merely compressed her lips and shook her head, her expression more sad than angry.

"You understand nothing, Mam'selle. If I were you, I would leave this place and never come back."

"Why do you say that, Lucy?" I asked, her apparent candor making me bold enough to use her first name.

We looked at one another steadily, and it was Lucy who glanced away first. "Because it is the truth," she said in a low tone. "There is nothing for you in this house."

"You're wrong, Lucy — I am here to help you."

Lucy looked away and spoke in her usual voice. "It is time for luncheon. You may call Henri to push my chair."

Her tone gave me a challenge, which I accepted. "I will push it myself. I doubt Henri will mind."

"The Marquis might object."

"I do not fear him, either." I spoke lightly, but Lucy didn't return my smile.

"Perhaps you should, Mam'selle. Hand me my shawl. As you now know, the hall will be drafty."

The same party that had dined the night before, except for Jacques, was assembled for lunch when Lucy and I arrived, and I briefly wondered at his absence. Madame Albert frowned at me when we entered, as if I had deliberately made Lucy late, but she did not speak.

"I am glad that you are joining us today, Lucy," the marquis said by way of greeting. Then to me, "Did I not tell you that Henri would see to Lucy's chair?"

"I assure you I do not mind."

"That is not the point, Miss Edmonds. You are not expected to perform manual labor."

It was the closest the marquis had come to

reproving me, and I decided it was important that he should understand how I regarded my duties. "I have worked hard all my life, Sir. I do not find it difficult to help Mademoiselle Lucy."

The marquis drew his brows together, as if he disliked the mention of my past experiences. "That is kind of you, of course. But I did not invite you here to become a slave."

"Why did you bring her back at all, Jean-Paul?"

At Madame Albert's sudden question, everyone turned to stare at her. The color drained from the marquis' face, and for once he seemed at a loss for words.

"Madame, I believe you are unwell," Lucy said, her voice unfamiliarly sweet. "Perhaps you should let Sophie assist you to your room until you are better."

The old woman seemed confused for a moment, as she looked from Lucy to me, then back to Lucy again. "Madeline always knew what was best," she said vaguely.

The marquis recovered his poise and signaled to Henri and Sophie. No one spoke as they guided Madame Albert from the dining room.

"I am sorry for the disturbance," the marquis said when she was gone. "Do not heed anything Madame Albert says."

"She spoke of Madeline?" I said, making it a question.

The marquis' lips were set in a thin line as he looked at Lucy, then at me. "Madame Albert's mind is confused. We will speak no more of this."

There was an awkward moment; then Lucy addressed the marquis. "Where is Jacques?" She glanced at me almost as if we were conspirators. "It is unusual for my brother to miss luncheon."

The marquis drained his wine glass and signaled for the meal to be served before replying. "He rode into Dreux."

"Ah, yes, it's Market Day," Lucy said. "I had forgotten. We will not see him this evening, either, I wager."

I considered what Jacques might find to do in the town that Philip Mailley had called dull and provincial and decided it was probably better that I not ask, since my questions seemed to have a way of disturbing everyone.

"Have you been speaking English with Lucy, Miss Edmonds?" the marquis asked.

"We have made a start at it."

The marquis nodded and spoke in English. "That is good. My own English could stand some help, as well, Miss Edmonds. From now on, all conversation at the table will be in English."

"Would that not be rude?" Lucy said quickly. "Madame Albert understands no English."

"Why this sudden consideration for Madame?" the marquis asked. "The woman scarcely understands French these days."

Lucy flushed, but for once she remained silent.

"You do not need to worry," the marquis said calmly. "Madame Albert will be taking her meals in her room for a time. The stairs are becoming more difficult for her to climb."

The marquis' pronouncement sent a chill through my body. *He has the power to keep that old woman a virtual prisoner here, and no one would ever know,* I thought, then chided myself. It was not my place to question the marquis' decisions, at least as long as they did not affect Lucy or me.

"I enjoyed my tour of the chateau this morning," I said after a moment of awkward silence. "It's as beautiful as I had expected it to be."

The marquis looked pleased, and even Lucy seemed relieved I had changed the subject.

"You should see something of the

grounds this afternoon," he said. "Lucy generally rests after lunch. After she is settled, you may meet me in the family salon."

When we had finished the clear soup, dark bread, cheese, and fruit that comprised the noon meal, I pushed Lucy's chair back to her room.

"Shall I call for Sophie to help you get into bed?"

"No. Push my chair against the head of the bed and hold it steady. I can manage from there."

I did as I was told, and saw that Lucy could swing herself from the chair by grasping the massive, carved headboard and standing briefly, before turning and collapsing onto the bed.

She must have some strength in her legs, I thought. I didn't understand why she could not walk, and I resolved to question the marquis about her condition.

"You should go now," Lucy said. "It is not wise to make the Marquis wait."

As I went to my room for a bonnet, I thought it strange that Lucy seemed to dislike her father, when he was so obviously concerned with her welfare. I also thought it was odd that Lucy and Jacques never called him anything but "the Marquis," a title that seemed much too formal for family use.

Perhaps their customs are different from ours. In any case, it was certainly not my concern what his children called my employer.

"I should like to walk to the summerhouse today," the marquis said when I entered the family salon. "You won't need a wrap."

"I don't recall hearing about a summerhouse. Is it new?"

The marquis smiled, and again I noticed the unusual color of his dark eyes. "Hardly, Mam'selle — unless you consider over a hundred years as new."

The marquis opened the side door for me and, for the first time since my arrival, I stepped out onto the grounds of the Chateau d'Arc. The air was sweet, and instinctively I turned my face to the warmth of the sun.

The marquis was right — it was much warmer outside than inside the chateau. Pea-sized gravel crunched under our feet as we walked toward the front of the house. When we rounded the corner, I looked up at the northwest tower. The hands of the clock registered a quarter past three, the same time they had indicated on my arrival. "I don't suppose the clock works," I said.

"Surprisingly enough, it does sometimes

run. I have no idea why. At any rate, repairing it has not been my chief concern."

What has been, Marquis?

He turned to look closely at me. "Getting my children safely settled in life is more important to me than petty affairs of the estate," he said, and once again I knew an eerie feeling that he could read my mind.

"What sort of settling do you have in mind for them?"

The marquis shrugged. "I had hoped Jacques would take an interest in helping to run the estate, but he does not care for the land and he chose not to educate himself for any profession."

"And Lucy? What of her?"

We had come to the edge of the wood, and the marquis took my elbow to help me over a fallen tree. "Mailley should have attended to this," he said with displeasure. We walked on, and he pointed out a structure very similar to a peasant's cottage, complete with thatched roof, surrounded by tall trees. "There is the summerhouse."

Le Petit Maison I thought, and spoke the words aloud. "Mama mentioned there was also a 'charming little house.'"

"Of course she would have remembered it," the marquis said, more to himself than to me. Then he looked at me more closely.

"What did she say about it?"

"Nothing in particular — just that she had liked it. But then, she liked everything here."

The marquis opened the bottom part of the divided front door, then reached in and unlatched the top. We entered a fairy-tale cottage, where a stone fireplace dominated a large room with a bare, wide-planked floor. Pewter tankards gleamed on the fireplace mantel and a rough-hewn table in front of the fireplace was set with pewter dishes. Two other rooms opened on either side of the fireplace, and I caught a glimpse of a braided rug and a bright coverlet on a bed through the open door. The main room was sparsely furnished, but a wooden bench against the back wall had been strewn with pillows, and on this the marquis motioned for me to be seated.

"This is wonderful," I said.

"Yes, isn't it? At the time it was built, aristocrats liked to play at being poor farmers. There are buildings like this all over Europe, although this one is more simply furnished than most."

"Do you use it at all?" I felt more at ease in this cottage than I had in the chateau, and I sensed the marquis must feel the same way.

"Occasionally. Sometimes the chateau can be a bit —" He paused, as if searching for the right word. "— overpowering. Here one can get away from all of that."

We were silent for a moment, then I reminded him of the question he had not answered. "I asked about your plans for Lucy."

The marquis looked down at his hands. "Lucy has resisted all my plans for her, just as she has resisted everyone who tries to help her. I would like to make certain that no one can ever make her leave the Chateau d'Arc against her will."

I felt a chill of apprehension. "Leave against her will? I don't understand."

The marquis looked up, his face expressionless. "When I am no longer here to protect her, it could happen. For a sum of money, there are invalids' homes where she could be put for the rest of her life."

"She would not like that."

He nodded in agreement. "Lucy does not like anything just now, or pretends not to. I believe your own *joie de vivre* can be a positive influence on changing her outlook."

"I hope so." I hesitated a moment, then asked the question which puzzled me. "Marquis, what happened to Lucy that she is unable to walk?"

He rose and walked away to stand at the fireplace with his back to me for a moment. Then he turned and returned to sit beside me. "Lucy suffered a riding accident when she was ten. At first it was thought she would not live. She was unconscious for weeks, and when she finally awoke, she had lost the use of her legs."

"I see. How did it happen?"

"To this day I do not know — no one saw it. Lucy could ride as well as a man and take jumps most men would find difficult. Yet she fell on a level stretch of ground. When I found her, I thought she was dead."

"How awful!" I exclaimed, imagining the scene. Although the marquis had spoken almost matter-of-factly, I sensed it was his way of keeping his emotions in check. Even years later, the tragic accident must haunt him.

The marquis' eyes held mine as if he wanted to see my reaction to his next words. "Yes, it was, especially since it happened the day her mother disappeared."

I felt the color drain from my face. I had assumed the marquise was dead, and his words shocked me. Silence filled the room as I waited for the marquis to say more. When he did not, I spoke. "What happened to her?"

The marquis shook his head. "I do not know. I searched for Madeline, but apparently she did not intend to be found. There is still idle gossip about it."

Madeline. Hadn't Madame Albert said something about my presence hurting Madeline?

"That must have been difficult for Lucy," I murmured, aware that must be another reason for her bitter outlook. And now I was certain it was the marquise's portrait I had seen in the tower room.

"And for Jacques, too, of course. He has not been the same since that day."

Almost automatically I placed a hand on his. "And you, Marquis —" I began.

He pulled away as if I had struck him and stood again. "I deserve no sympathy, Miss Edmonds," he said harshly. "I was not entirely blameless."

"But your wife left you! Surely —"

"I do not wish to discuss the matter further."

I took a deep breath and dared his anger. "Why did you bring me here? You know nothing about me."

The marquis' expression softened and he took one of my hands loosely in his. His hand felt strangely cool. "You are wrong," he said softly. "I know more about you than

72

you realize. You are a great deal like your mother. You have the strength to deal with Lucy and not allow Jacques to bully you. They can both be difficult, but if you stand up to them, they will back down."

Like you, Sir, I thought, and once again he half-smiled as if he knew my mind.

"Yes, I admit I may appear to be the same way. But I do not lack consideration. Stay here with Lucy for one year. If you then wish to leave, your return passage to America will be provided."

Once again the marquis had answered a question before I could ask it. I withdrew my hand from his. "I suppose that is fair."

"More than fair, as you know," he said brusquely. "Come, it is time we returned to the house."

"What kinds of things can Lucy do?" I asked as we walked back. "Surely she could leave the chateau occasionally."

"Lucy dislikes going out in public because she imagines everyone stares at her. She spends too much time inside — and alone."

"There must be something that will make her want to get out," I said, as much to myself as to the marquis.

We reached the side entrance and the marquis stopped at the door. "I was right to bring you here," he said simply. "You are the right companion for Lucy."

But as I returned to my room, I wondered if I had been right to heed the marquis' summons.

As Lucy had predicted, Jacques did not appear for the evening meal, and, with Madame Albert missing, the atmosphere seemed more relaxed. The marquis conducted the dinner conversation in English, asking questions about my schooling until Lucy interrupted.

"That is quite enough about education. I can think of no duller subject."

"Perhaps that is because you have had so little of it," the marquis said, and for a moment I feared another scene. But Lucy did not pick up the gauntlet, and the rest of the meal passed in peace.

After dinner, I was surprised when Lucy asked Henri to wheel her chair to the intricately carved piano that filled one corner of the family sitting room.

"It seems we are to be favored with a concert," the marquis said.

"Hardly," Lucy replied, but almost immediately she began to play the haunting strains of "Clair de Lune."

"Mr. Debussy is one of her favorites," the marquis told me in a stage whisper.

"Be quiet or I shall stop," Lucy said sharply.

As her hands moved over the keyboard, Lucy's expression changed and softened. She played with her eyes half-closed, her face calm as she swayed slightly in time with the music.

I wondered where she had learned to play with such skill, but even after the last note had reverberated away into nothingness, I dared not break the music's spell to ask.

"That is all," Lucy said. "Did it put you to sleep, Miss Edmonds?"

"Hardly," I replied.

"Bravo!" a new voice called, and I turned to see Philip Mailley standing in the doorway. This evening he wore a white shirt open at the neck, revealing a dark thatch of chest hair I tried not to stare at.

"Come in, Mailley," the marquis said somewhat after the fact. Philip wheeled Lucy's chair to its usual place by the fire and helped her readjust her shawl.

"Good evening, Miss Edmonds," Philip said in English, then addressed Lucy in French. "As usual, you played brilliantly, Mam'selle."

"As usual," she repeated scornfully, then spoke to me in English. "Everything around here is 'as usual,' Miss Edmonds. Usually."

I detected no hint she had spoken in jest, but the marquis smiled ironically. "Lucy may try to deny it, but the truth is, she prefers the status quo."

"Prefers it?" Her chin came up in defiance. "What chance do I have for anything else?"

"I believe that we can find a great many things to do, Miss d'Arc," I said.

Lucy looked at me for a moment as if she would like to believe that I spoke the truth; then she shook her head. "You can find a great many things, Mam'selle, perhaps even what you came here seeking. But leave me out of your plans, please."

Philip Mailley smiled at her outburst. "Very good, Lucy. I am sure Miss Edmonds enjoys your temper outbursts almost as much as your piano playing."

I held my breath, waiting for either the marquis or Lucy to order him from the house, but Lucy had no reply, and the marquis spoke calmly.

"What brings you here tonight, Mailley? Is there some problem that cannot wait for tomorrow?"

"No, Marquis."

After answering the marquis, Philip glanced my way, as if he still hadn't satisfied his curiosity about me, and I wondered if the marquis had noticed. Obviously Lucy had, for she spoke before her father had the opportunity.

"Perhaps the problem is that M'sieu Philip has noticed that the American mademoiselle is pretty."

"Lucy! Remember your manners!" the marquis said sharply.

Philip merely smiled and bowed in her direction. "In any case, I enjoyed the music, Mademoiselle Lucy." He turned to the marquis. "I have finished the monthly accounts, Sir. When can you go over them?"

"Bring them tomorrow at ten. And see to that fallen tree near the summerhouse. It is a hazard."

Philip nodded. "Is there anything else?"

"Mademoiselle Edmonds will need a mount," the marquis said, then looked at me. "I presume you ride, do you not?"

"Yes, of course," I replied, knowing our farm horses were far different animals from those the marquis stabled.

Philip half-smiled, as if he knew my thoughts. "I shall see to it immediately, Sir."

He didn't see the angry look that Lucy flashed his way, but the marquis noticed it. "That is settled, then," he said with a gesture of dismissal.

"Good night, Sir, Mademoiselles." Philip bowed in our direction and departed, and for a moment no one spoke.

"Do you play the piano, Miss Edmonds?" the marquis asked.

"No, I'm afraid not. Mama sold her pianoforte after my father died."

"How old were you then?"

"About three, I believe. I still remember hearing her play."

"I commenced lessons when I was four," Lucy volunteered.

"You must have had an excellent teacher," I said.

Both Lucy and the marquis tensed, and once again I knew I must have said the wrong thing.

"My mother taught me," Lucy said in a low voice.

"And Father Campeau," the marquis added. "Our priest is quite an accomplished musician."

"Father Campeau gave up on me a long time ago," Lucy said matter-of-factly.

"He said he could teach you nothing new," the marquis corrected. "If you would only agree to —"

"I am weary of this discussion," Lucy interrupted, breaking into French again. "Call Henri. I wish to be excused."

A muscle twitched in the marquis' jaw, but he said nothing as he pulled the cord to summon the butler.

"I will be along presently," I said.

"Please don't bother. Sophie will assist me tonight," Lucy said.

"I shall see you at breakfast, then."

I realized Lucy was angry with me, without knowing quite why. I lingered in the family salon after Henri had pushed Lucy's chair from the room. "She does play extremely well," I said.

The marquis nodded. "Yes, when it suits her. But she has not played in public since —" He rubbed his forehead, then continued. "At one time I hoped she might find solace in her music, but that has not been the case."

"There has to be something that will reach her."

The marquis' eyes held mine, and I felt that he understood the compassion I was beginning to feel for his difficult daughter. "Find it, Mam'selle, and we shall all be eternally grateful."

As I walked back to my room, I thought of the marquis' intensity when he spoke of Lucy. As difficult as it might be, I vowed to try to justify the marquis' trust in my ability. He seemed to be a decent man who had had more than his share of heartache, and I wanted to help him through helping Lucy.

My chamber was unexpectedly dark, and clumsily I groped for the lamp and managed to light it, annoyed that Sophie had failed to do so. As its light pierced the gloom, I noticed a paper on my pillow. Opening it, I translated the words, printed in French in large letters: IF YOU VALUE YOUR LIFE, LEAVE THE CHATEAU D'ARC.

No signature, no clue to its writer. Except for the marquis, whom I trusted, and Jacques, who was absent, anyone at the Chateau d'Arc could have written it. *It must be the work of poor old Madame Albert,* I told myself. I knew she was more to be pitied than feared, but as I undressed, I wished I had some way to lock my bedroom door.

Jacques did not appear for breakfast the next morning, but when Lucy and I arrived for luncheon, he was waiting for us. He smiled at me as if we were old friends who had not seen one another for some months, but his words led me to believe he might know about the note.

"Well, Mam'selle, I see you are still with us, despite everything. Tell me, what has influenced you to stay — or should I ask whom?"

"I have a position here," I said, not returning his smile.

Jacques laughed. "A very upright one, I am sure."

The marquis entered at that moment. "What are you sure about now, Jacques? What grand scheme did you bring back from Dreux this time?"

Jacques' smile vanished and his tone was sullen as he spoke. "You may make all the fun of it you like, but there is a fortune to be made on the Bourse."

"If one had any money, that is," Lucy put in. "You ought to be in Paris looking for a rich bride, instead of idling away your time in the country."

Jacques' face grew dark. "And what ought you to be doing, pray tell?"

A sharp rebuke from the marquis silenced both. "A truce during mealtimes would not seem to be too difficult. If you cannot be civil, you may both leave this room."

"We are not children anymore," Lucy reminded her father.

"Then do not behave as if you are."

Jacques looked at me. "Did you never quarrel with your brothers and sisters, Miss Ellen?"

"I have no brothers or sisters, but I grew up with my cousins. I suppose we had our little fusses, but by the time we put away our toys, all that was past."

Jacques smirked at my shameless self-righteousness, but the marquis looked pleased.

"Well spoken," he said. "You both might learn from Miss Edmonds."

"And teach her a few things, as well," Jacques said, too low for his father to hear.

"I am not here to learn from you, M'sieu," I whispered back.

"Bravo, Miss Edmonds," Lucy said in the same low tones.

"Speak up," the marquis said. "What are you whispering about?"

Jacques smiled engagingly. "Why, nothing, Sir. We were just remarking on the excellency of our luncheon."

By the time I had been at the Chateau d'Arc a week, I felt quite comfortable around the marquis, although I felt I couldn't trust Jacques. Lucy had showed she could be civil when it suited her, and I was learning to anticipate her moods. Philip Mailley was a daily visitor. Noticing that Lucy seemed upset when he paid me attention, I usually made some excuse to leave the room while he was there.

On Sunday the entire household went to the chapel for Mass, the only time Lucy left the house. With the weather growing warmer daily, I decided to ask Philip to help me take Lucy on an outing.

I had planned to look for him after I settled Lucy for her rest on Monday afternoon, but when I left her sewing in her room that morning, Sophie met me in the hall with the news that the marquis, who had not been at breakfast, wanted to see me.

"Did he say why?" I asked, and the girl shook her head.

On my way to the family salon, I wondered if the marquis might have learned about my threatening note. I had crumpled it into a ball and thrown it into the trash, but someone might have found it and passed it on to him.

When I entered the room, the marquis put down some papers and stood. "Come in, Mademoiselle. I wanted to tell you I must go to Paris directly."

My first thought was that I did not want to be in the chateau with Jacques without the tempering influence of his father. "How long will you be gone?" I asked.

"Jacques is coming with me," the marquis said before answering my spoken question.

"We may stay a week, perhaps longer. If you need anything, see Philip Mailley."

"Is something wrong?" I tried without success to read his expression. I'd noticed the marquis seemed to have developed a bad cough, and I thought he might need the services of a physician.

"Much of my business is conducted in Paris, Mademoiselle. It is often necessary for me to be there for weeks at a time."

"Does Lucy ever go to Paris with you?"

"I told you how Lucy feels about being seen in public. She refuses to accompany me."

"If I could change her mind, would there be a place for us to stay in Paris?" I asked, an idea half-forming.

The marquis shrugged. "Of course. But I doubt you can persuade Lucy to travel any-where, even to Dreux."

"I should like to try."

"Then do so, by all means. But for now, I would like to take your mother's sketches with me and have them framed. Would you object to that?"

"Of course not. I'll get them now."

But when I opened my wardrobe and lifted the stack of petticoats under which I had placed them, I discovered the water-colors were missing. Thinking I might have moved them and not recalled it, I searched through all my belongings to no avail. *Someone took them,* I thought. *Madame Albert?*

The marquis didn't seem disturbed when I returned empty-handed. "No matter. I am sure they will turn up — I can take them on my next trip. But now, I have a surprise for you. Come along."

I followed the marquis to the stable, where the carriage that had brought me from Dreux was being prepared for his journey. Although I looked around for him, I didn't see Philip.

The stable was built of the same brick as the chateau and ranged in a square around an open courtyard. Some of the stalls had been enclosed for other uses and some were vacant, but a half-dozen riding horses occupied stalls in the area to which the marquis led me.

In the first was the most wonderful white horse I'd ever seen, and I said so. "Is he yours?"

The marquis reached out to stroke the horse. "Yes, Caliph is a full-blooded Arabian. I have not given him much attention lately."

"He looks dangerous," I said as the animal tossed its head and whinnied.

"He can be, Mademoiselle, if mishandled."

The next stall held another large horse, a sorrel stallion. "That one also looks fierce," I said.

"That is Boxer, Jacques' horse. Jacques does not like for anyone else to ride him."

"What about that one?" I asked, as a big bay in the adjacent stall snorted and tossed his head.

"That's Thunder, Philip Mailley's hunter. He fancies he can out-jump Caliph, but his bloodlines are inferior."

Whose bloodlines are inferior, Philip's or the horse's? I wanted to ask, but knew that would be impertinent.

We moved on to the next stall, where a silvery-gray mare pricked her ears at our approach.

"What a lovely animal," I commented and reached out to stroke her velvety muzzle.

"I am glad you think so. She is yours."

Impulsively, I seized the marquis' hands. "Thank you!" I exclaimed. "What is her name?"

The marquis' face reddened and he looked startled, then pleased, at my enthusiasm. "I am told it is Etoile."

"Star!" I translated and looked back at

the horse. "Well, Etoile, I hope you live up to your name."

"You must let Philip show you where it is safe to ride. I am sorry that I must leave before I could take you riding myself — and so soon after your arrival."

Reading the marquis' true concern, I tried to reassure him. "Don't worry, Sir. Lucy and I will be fine while you are away."

He regarded me intently. "I am quite sure you will, Ellen."

It was the first time the marquis had called me by my Christian name, and I wondered why it seemed so natural for him to do so. On the way back to the chateau, I also wondered why Philip, Lucy, and Jacques had all warned me that the Marquis d'Arc was a difficult man.

They are wrong, I thought.

Or perhaps I was.

Lucy wasn't surprised when I told her the marquis and Jacques were going to Paris.

"They do so quite often," she said. "I will ask the Marquis to bring back a bolt of black wool. Madame must have a warm winter dress."

"Tell me about Madame Albert," I said, searching for a subject Lucy might willingly discuss.

Lucy frowned. "There is nothing to tell. She has always looked the way she does now, but of course she is older and cannot get about as well, and her hearing is poor. It is tiresome to have to shout at her all the time."

"It is kind of the Marquis to allow her to remain at the chateau," I offered.

The closed look I was beginning to know only too well returned to Lucy's face. "I do not care to discuss Madame Albert further."

"As you like," I replied.

Sophie rapped lightly on Lucy's door. "M'sieu Mailley is here to see you," she called out.

"Tell him to come in," Lucy said.

I gathered the needlework I had just begun and started out as Philip entered.

"Don't leave, Mademoiselle Edmonds. I came to tell you the Marquis asked me to take you riding this afternoon."

"Riding?" Lucy's displeasure was evident. "And which of the plow horses have you chosen for her?"

Philip's voice remained calm. "The Marquis told me to find Mademoiselle Edmonds a mount, and I did. You know I would gladly do the same for you."

Lucy's face darkened. "Would you,

indeed?" She shifted her gaze to me. "Watch yourself, Miss Edmonds. The d'Arc grounds can be treacherous."

"I will meet you at the stable when Lucy takes her rest, then," I said to Philip.

He nodded assent. "As you wish, Mademoiselle." His tone made it clear he was the coolly impersonal estate manager carrying out his master's instructions.

I found my heart beating a bit faster in anticipation of riding with Philip Mailley. He hadn't gone out of his way to welcome me, but we were in similar positions of servitude to the marquis. Further, he seemed to have the marquis' complete trust. I was certain that Philip could tell me more about Lucy's tragic accident and the marquise's strange disappearance.

And although I chided myself it was so, I also had to admit that I found Philip Mailley disturbingly attractive.

Chapter Four

Lucy had little to say to me at luncheon or back in her room as I settled her for her rest, and I made no issue of her silence. She could pout all she liked, but her father had said Philip should take me riding, and I intended to go.

I changed into a serviceable shirtwaist blouse and my only riding skirt, dark-brown twill, and asked Sophie to watch out for Lucy. I felt a sense of anticipation as I let myself out the side door. The fair, cool day was perfect for an outing, the blue sky dotted with the kind of cottony white clouds that accompany fair weather.

Walking the path to the stable, I felt a surge of gratitude toward the marquis. No doubt he realized I couldn't be at my best with Lucy if I were unhappy myself. Perhaps he noticed that being confined to the chateau was beginning to affect my spirits. But with my own horse, I could get fresh air and explore my new surroundings as well. When I reached the stable yard, a curly-haired young groom dropped the bridle he was mending, scrambled to his feet, and bowed as if to a fine lady.

"Good afternoon, Mademoiselle. Your horse is ready," he said in words that hardly seemed to be French, he spoke so coarsely.

"Thank you. Is Monsieur Mailley here?" I asked, somewhat surprised that he was not waiting for me.

"He may have gone to his office, Mademoiselle. I'll fetch him."

I was watching the stable boy make his way across the courtyard when Philip Mailley suddenly appeared at my side, startling me.

"Good afternoon, Miss Edmonds. I see you are prepared to ride. Marc has saddled Etoile, but before we leave, you must first ride in the courtyard. You will want to accustom yourself to your new mount's gaits."

Although Philip hadn't said so, I gathered he also wanted to judge my equestrian ability. I rode well but without elegance, having learned bareback on farm horses. Aware that Philip would notice my clumsiness, I stiffened in self-consciousness when he handed me the reins and took my elbow to assist me into the saddle.

"Do not be afraid, Miss Edmonds," Philip said in English. "I chose Etoile carefully. She will do what you ask of her."

"I'm not afraid, but it has been some time since I have ridden — and never on such a fine horse," I said, hating the defensive note I heard in my voice.

"This one should be easy for you to ride. Walk about a bit to get the feel of the tack before you let Etoile trot. After that, you may canter a bit. We do not, of course, gallop in the courtyard."

I glanced at Philip, trying to decide if he intended to tease me, but his serious expression gave no hint of humor. *He sounds like a rigid schoolmaster,* I thought.

I nodded and concentrated on my riding as I entered the enclosed courtyard. Both Etoile and the oddly shallow saddle took some getting used to, but I managed well enough, although without much grace.

"Sit up straight and tighten the reins," Philip called when I began to post to the trot. He watched from the center of the stable yard, his arms folded across his chest, and turned to follow our progress as Etoile and I circled the courtyard. "Faster," he ordered after a while. I enjoyed Etoile's smooth, even canter, but after only two circuits of the courtyard, Philip signaled me to stop.

"Do I pass inspection, M'sieu Mailley?"

"Your riding is acceptable," he said, and I read his expression to mean I rode better than he had expected.

Philip took Thunder's reins from Marc and swung into his saddle with effortless grace. I envied the easy way he managed the huge bay and wished that Philip had a better opinion of me. Riding with someone who had been ordered to accompany me took away some of the pleasure, but not even Philip's indifference could keep me from looking forward to the afternoon.

"Where are we going?" I asked as we rode toward the village gate, Marc running ahead of us.

"Through the village and to a place where you can always ride in safety. Then back to the chateau grounds, where I must check on some wall repairs."

Marc reached the village gate just ahead of us and struggled with the massive iron frame, finally wrenching it open just in time for us to ride through, then closing it behind us.

"Is the estate completely walled?" I asked.

"No. The Marquis controls many hectares of open land beyond the village. But the forests are all within the walls."

The village through which we rode had evidently grown up around the edge of the chateau about the time it was built. All its houses were similar and seemed to share a common antiquity. The buildings were situated flush to the narrow road and their grounds were walled, so that only an occasional glimpse through an open gate revealed the jumble of flowers and vegetable gardens and outbuildings behind each dwelling.

The sound of running water signaled that we approached a stream, where several women knelt on a platform built over the water doing their laundry. They carried on a lively conversation, punctuated by the slap of wet cloth on the rocks, until we started across the bridge that divided the village into more or less equal parts. Seeing us, the women fell silent as they stared first at me, then at Philip.

"Bonjour, mesdames. Comme ça va?" Philip called in greeting.

The women bobbed their heads but made no reply. After we had crossed the bridge, they resumed their chatter and, even though I could not make out their words, I guessed they were about me.

"News of your coming reached the village long before you did," Philip said. "Now that they have seen you, the women will have a new topic for gossip."

"Why should I be of any concern to the villagers?"

"Everything connected with the Chateau d'Arc affects the village. It is both their livelihood and all they know."

"I thought such feudalism ended with the French Revolution. Are the villagers still serfs, then?"

"Serfs? Of course not. Technically they are free to go anywhere they please. But realistically, they are bound to this land by ties no government can impose. As for the Revolution, in the long run it only exchanged one set of masters for another. *Plus ça change, plus c'est la même chose.*"

"Do you really believe that things always stay the same, or is it just convenient to quote epigrams?"

"That particular epigram happens to fit. In any case, here change comes slowly, if at all."

We rode past a scattering of public buildings, the *Mairie*, the *Ecole des Garçons et Filles*, and the *Postes*; its front door draped with faded red-white-and-blue bunting.

"The post office is freshly decorated each Bastille Day," Philip explained to answer my questioning glance.

Except for a small *Boulangerie* and an even smaller *Alimentation General*, there

95

did not seem to be any shops in the village.

"Where do the people buy what they need?" I asked when we left the village behind and were surrounded by open land.

"They are remarkably self-sufficient, but what they cannot grow, barter, or buy here, they can usually find at the market in Dreux."

Philip's mention of the market reminded me of Jacques, and I tried without success to imagine him enjoying himself in a crowd of blue-smocked peasants. No doubt his activities in Dreux had some other connection.

"Those are sugar beet fields." Philip pointed to an expanse of land to our right where a half-dozen men and women wielded hoes. He did not need to tell me that the crop to the left was wheat, almost ready to be harvested.

"Does everyone in the village work for the Marquis d'Arc?" I asked.

"The ones who do not work the land make a living supplying those who do, so indirectly, at least, the village owes its life to the chateau. It has always been so."

"And always will be, it seems."

It had been an idle remark, but Philip frowned and shook his head. "Not if a certain person has his way," he said, his voice so low I scarcely heard the words.

"What do you mean?" I asked, and once more he shook his head.

"It is no secret that Jacques d'Arc does not share his father's love for the land. He would like to sell off a portion of the estate."

My gesture took in the vastness of the fields around us. "Surely there is more than enough here so a few hundred hectares would not be missed."

"So it seems to you, Miss Edmonds, and so even an English farmer might think, seeing the holdings in Britain are generally much smaller. But it is the forest within the chateau walls that Jacques wishes to sell. Or, barring that, he would harvest the timber and reduce the forest to rubble."

Knowing the rarity of virgin stands of timber in European lands, I could understand Philip's reaction to the destruction of the chateau's great forest. "But why would Jacques want to do that?"

Philip glanced at me and shook his head as if my ignorance amazed him. "Why else? For money. Young d'Arc wants to engage in speculation in business ventures. He has no money of his own and thinks he could make a great deal in a hurry if he had some capital to invest. Selling off part of the timber would give him quite a stake."

"The Marquis does not agree," I said. Now I knew at least one reason Jacques and his father seemed to be at such odds.

"He does not." Then as if he realized he'd said too much about his employer, Philip abruptly changed the subject. "We have gone far enough on this road for today. You may follow it safely for a number of kilometers anytime you please. Stay away from the fields, however, particularly after the harvest, when they will be filled with bird-hunters."

Having delivered those words, Philip wheeled and rode away, churning a cloud of dust. Coughing from its effects, I spurred Etoile to a gallop and pulled ahead of him, a situation Philip soon remedied.

"If you want to race, you ought to choose a better course," Philip said, quickly regaining my side.

I slowed Etoile to a trot, then to a walk as we re-entered the village.

"If there is anyplace to race around here, I'm game to try it," I said, meaning every word.

Philip shook his head. "Perhaps you are, Miss Edmonds, but I must decline the challenge. It is not the sort of thing which the Marquis would approve for either of us to do."

"I see. Does that mean that you fear the Marquis?"

I watched Philip's face for any indication that his real feelings might not match his words, but saw no evidence of evasion.

"I am not afraid of the Marquis d'Arc, but I work for him and therefore have a responsibility toward his welfare. I will not betray his trust."

He seems to be sincere, I thought, but the knowledge merely made me feel more confused. I didn't like the way Philip had of catching me off-balance and making me uncomfortable. I also disliked myself for allowing him to upset me. Yet in some perverse way, I still wanted to win Philip Mailley's approval.

"I have no intention of betraying the Marquis' trust, either," I said.

An expression I could not read passed over Philip's face. "First you have to earn it — as you most obviously have. You should know, Miss Edmonds, that the welfare of the Chateau d'Arc concerns me quite deeply. I am, in fact, as committed to this land as if it were my own."

Was his tone mocking, or was Philip sincere? Boldly I regarded him. "Perhaps you even covet it for yourself."

He glanced away, his face without expression. "No doubt you heard that from Jacques. He is rather fond of saying so."

"Is it true?"

Philip's gesture took in the chateau and its lands. "A man cannot covet what he already possesses. Jacques would never understand that."

I didn't ask Philip to explain what he meant, for somehow I understood. I had felt strangely connected to the Chateau d'Arc years before I had seen it. Even though it had not turned out to be as I had expected, something about the place called to me. Surely Philip, who had been here many years, must feel an even closer bond to the chateau and its lands. Otherwise, why would he continue to put up with the collective rudeness of the d'Arcs?

Philip gestured toward a path beside the creek and, when he spoke again, it was in his usual cool, impersonal tone. "There is a shorter way back to ride into the chateau grounds. Follow me."

A few hundred yards downstream from where the women still tended to their washing, the water had been stopped by an earthen dam, creating a lake behind the chateau. Sluice gates allowed a constant flow of fresh water to enter with a roar that made conversation impossible as we walked our mounts across a narrow path atop the dam.

Once on the other side, Philip nodded toward the lake. "The water is deep here and the banks quite slippery. You must never get too close. The far end, where the stream goes on its way to the Eure River, is shallow enough to allow safe bathing."

I looked out at the lake and unaccountably shivered. Its mirror-like surface was still and dark, broken only by a few water lilies and cattails around the edge and an occasional ripple as something moved within its depths.

"Where are the swans?" I asked, attempting to shake off the depression the lake had made me feel. "I thought all castles came equipped with swans."

Philip almost allowed himself to smile. "Once all sorts of waterfowl gathered around the lake, but their noise disturbed the Marquise. She ordered them removed, but white swans will soon swim here again."

I looked toward the chateau, already half-shadowed in the afternoon sun. Nothing stirred, and for a split-second I had the foolish sensation that it had fallen under some sort of enchantment and had been asleep for many years. Then a curtain moved at a window in the family salon and I could almost imagine that the marquise herself stood there and watched us with disapproval.

I shook my head as if to clear away my foolish thoughts. "Did you know the Marquise?" I asked, and once again Philip's countenance assumed a studied blankness.

"Why do you ask?"

"Something that happened long ago seems to bother Lucy. I thought it might have some connection with her mother."

"Whatever happened in the past, it cannot be undone. And it is none of your business, either."

Even though I sensed that Philip spoke more in warning than disapproval, I was disappointed. For Lucy's sake, I had hoped he would tell me more about the d'Arcs. To that end, I changed tactics.

"Lucy seems to like you m'sieu."

Philip shrugged, but he did not disagree. "I suppose she tolerates me as well as she does anyone, including herself. Lucy can be quite unpleasant — but of course you already know that."

"I think Lucy's temper would improve if she got out more. Perhaps you can persuade her to do that — she seems to pay more attention to you than she does to the Marquis."

Philip smiled without humor. "Lucy refuses to be easily influenced by anyone. She is capable of doing a great many things, but she is also very stubborn."

Just beyond the chateau, we came upon a small formal garden where four paths of raked gravel converged around a small fountain. Its clipped hedges were bordered by a variety of flowers, some familiar to me and others I had never before seen. I recognized peonies, dianthus, and camellias, and the sweet scent of heliotrope that floated on the light breeze that had sprung up.

"Surely Lucy would enjoy spending some time in such a lovely setting," I said.

"That is where you are wrong, Miss Edmonds. You see the beauty, but to Lucy these grounds serve only as a constant reminder of her accident," Philip said. Then as if he regretted having mentioned it, he quickly continued speaking. "But if some suitable outing can be arranged, I will do my best to persuade her to try it."

I wasn't yet quite ready to smile at Philip, but my "thank you" was spoken sincerely. I didn't want to risk losing his grudging offer of assistance by saying anything else, and he seemed quite willing to continue riding in silence.

Several hundred yards beyond the gardens, we entered a stand of hardwood trees from which all underbrush had been removed. Lush grass, greener than any I had ever seen, covered the ground like a carpet. I was about to ask Philip how it was mowed to such a precise length when we came upon a small herd of grazing sheep, some with spring lambs by their side. The little ones looked up when we approached and bleated anxiously, but their mothers did not seem to fear us. Their keeper, an old man with a grizzled beard, dozed with his back to a broad tree. We were almost upon him before he heard us and awoke. As he struggled to a standing position, his face blanched, his eyes widened in fright, and he made a rapid sign of the cross.

Philip spoke to him in French. "How does it go today, *grand-pere?*"

"All is quiet so far, M'sieu Philip." The man's voice trembled as if to belie his words.

Philip looked back at the sheep, as if silently counting them. "No more losses? Good work."

"As you directed, M'sieu Philip, I have kept the flock away from the deep forest. But soon they must cross it to go to the summer meadows."

Philip nodded. "I will let you know when it is safe to move them." Seeing that the

man continued to stare at me, Philip introduced us. "This is Mademoiselle Edmonds.
She has come from the United States to
attend Mademoiselle Lucy. And this is our
shepherd, Maurice Duval."

The man's face had regained some color
as he bowed again, but to my polite acknowledgment of our introduction he made
no reply.

"Let's move on," Philip said, and it was
some moments before he spoke again. "Old
Maurice is usually eager to talk, since he
spends so much time in solitude. But you
seem to have frightened all the words out of
him, Miss Edmonds."

I glanced at Philip and decided that this
time, at least, he was not patronizing me. "It
is hardly flattering to think that the mere
sight of me would be so frightening. I suppose the man must be unaccustomed to
seeing females."

"There is more to it than that. He would
not have crossed himself had he not been
afraid. In this remote area, the people are a
superstitious lot. Perhaps he thought he saw
a ghost — or maybe he suspects you are a
witch."

I smiled briefly at the thought that I might
be mistaken for any sort of supernatural
being. "There is another possibility. I have

been told that I am like my mother. M'sieu Duval is certainly old enough to have known her."

Philip turned and stared at me with unfeigned surprise. "Your mother?" he repeated.

"You did not know she visited here many years ago?"

Philip shook his head. "No. That must have been some time before I came to the chateau. Watch out — a few tree limbs hang dangerously low through here."

Reminded of Lucy's accident, I slowed Etoile to a walk and fell in behind Philip, considering his words. I had somehow assumed the marquis would have mentioned my mother to him, but obviously he hadn't. Philip's familiar relationship with Lucy had led me to believe he was on a more intimate basis with the d'Arc family than might actually be the case. Still, Philip had been at the chateau long enough to know more about the family history than I did. To get him to tell me what he knew I would have to make Philip like me, a task that now seemed quite formidable.

Soon we rode into a shade so dense that no sunlight ever penetrated the thick leaves. Here no shrubs or grass grew, and we made our way silently over a forest floor carpeted with years of layers of fallen leaves. It was cooler in the deep shade, but the strange chill I felt had little to do with the temperature. *There is something evil here,* I thought.

"Have you ever heard of the Druids?" Philip asked.

"I believe they worshiped trees in England."

"Not only in England — Dreux means 'city of Druids.' The oak tree was especially sacred to them."

I could imagine ghostly figures clad in white robes conducting mysterious rites at this very spot and, recalling that human sacrifice had been at the heart of their worship, I shuddered. "I suppose their religion has been dead for many years," I said.

Philip shrugged. "Maybe. But every time I ride through this particular oak grove, I feel some sort of presence. I wonder what strange sights these old trees might have seen."

"I don't think I want to know." I felt relieved when we began to climb a slight rise and left that part of the forest behind.

A few minutes later we came to the chateau wall and rode along beside it until we came to a place where a large, T-shaped crack ran from about the middle of the wall to the bottom. It had been patched with mortar, but a few of the displaced stones still lay in a jumbled heap at the base of the wall.

"What happened here?" I asked.

"Something hit it from this side, evidently with great force. A boar, perhaps."

"A pig?" Trying to imagine an animal that could do such damage to a thick wall, I shook my head.

Philip had dismounted to examine the wall more closely; now he remounted and once more regarded me with what I thought of as his schoolmaster look, brows drawn together, his dark blue eyes commanding my attention. "A wild boar is not like a domestic pig, Miss Edmonds. It is a dangerous animal with a bad temper, perfectly capable of charging a wall — or anything else."

I recalled Philip's conversation with the old shepherd and felt uneasy. "Such as the sheep?"

Philip nodded. "Yes. Here, hunting is not only a sport; sometimes it is a necessity. Obviously, it is time we had a boar hunt. In any case, it is unsafe to ride into the deep woods alone."

"I have no desire to do that," I said, irritated at the way Philip seemed to assume I totally lacked common sense. "I gather that

Jacques is somewhat interested in hunting, but the Marquis doesn't care for it. Do you suppose he will join this hunt?"

Philip's curt tone told me I had once more said something that displeased him. "That is up to the Marquis, Miss Edmonds. I do not presume to know his mind."

Philip urged his horse to a rapid walk and I followed suit, trying to stay beside him. Despite Philip's rebuff, I refused to let the subject drop. "I've heard the accident that crippled Lucy was connected with a hunt. I suppose hunting will always remind the Marquis of that tragic day."

"Whatever you hear, pay no heed to gossip." Philip spoke with the tone of a teacher addressing a particularly trying student. I felt tempted to tell him the marquis had been the source of my knowledge, imagined Philip's reaction, and then thought better of it.

"I know gossip is often inaccurate. But I'm also convinced that something connected with her accident still haunts Lucy, something other than her physical injury. Surely you must also know that, being so close to her."

Philip reined in so suddenly that Thunder shied sideways and bumped Etoile, who half-reared and whinnied in protest.

Philip's mouth twisted and his voice was flat and cold. "What may have happened in the past and my relationship with Mademoiselle d'Arc are not your concerns, Miss Edmonds. Everyone knows why you came here — your pious show of affection for Lucy fools no one."

If Philip had struck me, I could not have felt more shocked. My mouth fell foolishly open before I recovered enough to speak. "What on earth are you saying?"

Philip regarded me with the same kind of frank appraisal he had given me at the Dreux train station. "You are not stupid, *ma chere*. You merely weaken your effect when you try to pretend to be."

"My effect? What effect?"

"Come, Miss Edmonds. You must know that beauty such as yours has the power to make an unsuspecting male quite weak."

I felt my face redden. Philip had insulted me, but rather than attempting to defend myself, I decided to play the vain and calculating opportunist he seemed to think I was. I leaned closer to him, tilted my chin, and looked at him through half-closed eyes, a strategy I had seen other women use to great advantage. I spoke softly. "Do I make you feel such weakness, M'sieu?"

Even though I knew it was the kind of

remark better spoken behind a half-closed fan in a dim drawing room than in the light of day, I had not anticipated that Philip would find it amusing enough to laugh out loud.

"Are you trying to make me feel weak, Mademoiselle?"

My *femme fatale* pose faded quickly into righteous indignation. "Of course not! I have no desire to make anyone feel weak. And just what is it that everyone except me supposedly knows about why I came here, anyway?"

Philip's sudden smile exasperated me even more. "I see you do have some spirit, after all, Miss Edmonds. That at least makes you a bit more interesting than Lucy's other companions. It is presumed you came here for the same reason they did, and you are also expected to leave as they did, having helped neither Lucy nor yourself."

"I know nothing about what anyone else might have done. I was summoned here to care for Lucy at her father's specific request. And as for leaving — I don't intend to do that."

"I am sure that none of the others planned to leave, either. Nevertheless, not one stayed more than a few months. What makes you think you will be any different?"

"For one thing, I'm sure I can help Lucy, which no one else I've met seems to have done. Jacques told me she was spoiled, but if she is, it's because everyone finds it easier to give in to her than to make her help herself."

Seeing Philip seemed unimpressed and wanting to make him see Lucy's situation as I did, I continued talking without pausing to weigh my words first. "Lucy has gotten into the habit of being disagreeable, but she does not truly like the way she is. I believe I can find a way to overcome Lucy's low opinion of herself. But apart from that, I have a good reason to remain. Perhaps unlike the others, I really have nowhere else to go."

As soon as the words were spoken, I realized my unbridled tongue had given Philip, who already seemed determined to dislike me, a potential weapon against me.

His eyes searched my face as if testing my sincerity. When after a long moment he spoke, his voice was quiet. "Then perhaps the stakes are somewhat higher for you than they were for the others, Miss Edmonds. But you should know that the game you are playing can be very dangerous."

"Helping Lucy is no game to me, I assure

you. And how could that possibly put me into any danger?"

"Meddling into things you do not understand can be very perilous. So can trying to divide a father and his son."

Philip's mouth was set in a line of righteous disapproval, and I saw my honest bewilderment over his charges had done nothing to change his mind about me. I doubted that reasoning would work, either, but I had to try.

"How could I do anything more to divide the Marquis and Jacques? They seem to have been doing a pretty fair job of that on their own, long before my arrival."

Philip's voice was distant. "I think you know exactly what I mean, Miss Edmonds. Decide which man you want and go after him, by all means. But do not be surprised if you lose them both."

I could scarcely believe Philip's words, and I had to take a steadying breath before I could force myself to speak again. "You are quite wrong, M'sieu Mailley. I did not come to the Chateau d'Arc with any such purpose in mind. I certainly have done nothing to invite Jacques' attentions, nor do I regard the Marquis in any way except as my employer."

Philip raised his eyebrows. "I expected

Jacques to pursue you — he has always liked a pretty face. But the Marquis has never paid much attention to any of Lucy's other companions. He certainly never offered to give any of them her own horse."

"I asked him for nothing."

"Perhaps. But I happened to be passing by the stalls when he showed Etoile to you. You were both too occupied to notice me, but I saw the way you looked at him and reached for his hand. Really, Miss Edmonds, you were not very subtle —"

My open hand connected with Philip's left cheek, making a satisfactory smacking sound and checking his distasteful words. When I tried to take it away, he seized my wrist in his powerful grip and glared at me. Etoile sidestepped nervously, pulling me farther from Philip and causing me to cry out in pain. Almost before I could realize what was happening, Philip slid from Thunder's back and, still grasping my wrist, used his left arm to pull me from my saddle. He whirled me around and pinned me against the broad trunk of a linden.

He breathed rapidly and his voice rasped as he spoke. "American women must be among the most stupid in the world, *ma chere*. How many times do you have to be warned? Anyone else would already have given up and left by now. I mean what I say. Every moment you stay at the Chateau d'Arc only increases your danger."

"If you say I am in danger, M'sieu, perhaps it is of your own doing. But I also mean what I say. I will stay."

I glared at Philip and wrenched my wrist from his grasp, but immediately he grabbed my upper arms and pulled me toward him. For an instant, I was certain he intended to kiss me, yet I could do nothing to hinder him.

We stood a heartbeat apart, both breathing as if we had run a great way. Moving slowly, Philip dropped his hand from my left arm and brought it toward my face. I stood frozen, expecting that he would either strike my cheek or stroke it, and powerless to prevent either.

I half-closed my eyes and held my breath in anticipation, but then Philip muttered something in French, dropped his arms to his sides, and took two steps back, putting distance between us. He shook his head, as if trying to awaken from a dream, and when he spoke, it was with icy control.

"Very well, Miss Edmonds. Stay if you will, but at least you have been warned."

Unexpectedly, Philip put his hand to his cheek and smiled in a way I found to be far more infuriating than his anger. "We must start back now. It is unwise to be in the deep forest after sundown."

As if nothing had happened between us, Philip helped me to remount, his touch on my arm light and impersonal. He rode ahead and I followed silently, my mind churning with his accusations. I certainly hadn't set my cap for any man; surely my behavior had been blameless. As for any danger in connection with my desire to help Lucy — the very idea was ludicrous. The note warning me to leave hadn't been repeated, proof that it had meant nothing, and except for my mother's missing sketches, nothing else unusual had occurred.

No, I decided, Philip Mailley must have noticed that Jacques seemed to be interested in me and thought I'd encouraged him. As for seeing me with the marquis, I couldn't imagine that my genuine expression of pleasure over my gift would lead Philip to think I was romantically interested in my employer, unless —

I could not finish the thought. Philip disliked me too much to be jealous of any man who might show an interest in me. However —

I recalled Jacques' scornful words that

Philip Mailley would like to be the master of the chateau himself, a charge that Philip hadn't really denied. If Philip married Lucy and something should happen to both the marquis and Jacques, then Philip would have the power and position Jacques said Philip wanted. But somehow I had not thought, even given his evident dislike of Jacques, that Philip would stoop to using Lucy to his own advantage.

Or would he? I sighed and acknowledged I still had much to learn about the inhabitants of the Chateau d'Arc.

Back at the stable, Philip let Marc assist me from Etoile and looked on as I patted her soft muzzle.

"I'll see you soon, my Etoile," I murmured. "I expect to be around here for a long time," I added for Philip's benefit.

Marc took Etoile's halter and I turned to walk away, but Philip put a detaining hand on my arm and spoke with quiet authority, his eyes holding mine. "What you do with your personal life is none of my concern, but what you do with Lucy does matter to me. As long as it appears you are really helping her, I will stay out of your way. But the second you hurt Lucy, I will do everything in my power to see that you leave the chateau immediately."

I returned the intensity of his gaze. "Are you threatening me, Philip Mailley?"

He dropped his hand from my arm, curled it into a loose fist, and took a half step backwards.

"No more than you threaten me, Miss Ellen. Adieu."

Philip turned abruptly and walked away, calling out an order to Marc. I stood for a moment as though rooted to the spot; then I turned and began to walk back to the chateau in the lengthening afternoon shadows. The puffy white clouds I'd admired earlier had turned dark, and a subtle smell of rain hung in the air. I suddenly realized that I felt very weary.

I had intended the afternoon's ride to be a pleasant diversion which might provide new information about the d'Arcs, but instead it had only served to show me how misunderstood I really was, and to repeat another senseless warning of danger. And what did Philip Mailley mean when he said I was threatening him? It made no sense. Hearing the cry of birds, I looked up at the tallest tower just in time to see the clock's hands move ever so slightly. So the tower clock was running again, as the marquis said it sometimes did for no discernible reason.

Strange things seem to happen all the time at the Chateau d'Arc. I would have to accept that and not allow it to daunt me.

I had absolutely no romantic interest in either Jacques or his father, but I would be more careful to avoid any action that Philip or anyone else could take as such evidence. And even though Philip Mailley had been no help, I intended to find out more about the marquise. I refused to accept Philip's dire predictions of danger. No doubt he too had his motives — and sooner or later, he would give himself away.

I did not intend to go anywhere — and I could wait.

Chapter Five

I didn't see Lucy when I came in, and by the time I had changed my clothes, she was already in the dining room. She did not look particularly happy to see me.

"Is Philip coming for dinner?" Lucy glanced at the door as if she hoped to see him enter.

"Not to my knowledge," I said. "Are you expecting him?"

"Sometimes when the Marquis and Jacques go away, Philip comes for dinner."

"I'm sure you welcome his company."

Lucy's face colored, and I realized my remark had been thoughtless.

"You have said nothing about your outing, Miss Edmunds. Was it all you expected?"

I shrugged. "I hardly knew enough about the chateau lands to have any expectations, but what I saw was certainly impressive."

Lucy nodded. "That is a safe enough word, I suppose. Where did Philip take you?"

"We rode through the village and beyond it for some distance, came through the back way to the forest, and looked at a wall that had been repaired. Then we returned."

"You were gone a long time." Lucy's tone suggested I could have deliberately omitted something from my account.

"The chateau grounds are huge — if we had tried to ride around the walls, I daresay we would still be out there. I saw only a small part of it today, but it was lovely."

Lucy raised her head as if she needed to see my expression when she spoke. "What do you think of Philip, Miss Edmonds?"

Her question surprised me, and I hesitated a moment before replying. "I don't think Mr. Mailley likes me very much," I said, honestly enough.

Lucy's lips parted and she sighed, perhaps in relief. "He does not like many people. Pass the bread, please."

After dinner, we adjourned to the family salon, where Lucy bent over some sort of sketching, and I turned the pages of a book from the chateau's extensive library. We passed a few minutes in what I felt to be a companionable silence, then Lucy spoke.

"How far did you ride past the village?"

What an odd question, I thought, but then Lucy was an expert at asking such questions. "I have no idea — a few kilometers perhaps, past some sugar beet and wheat fields."

Lucy shook her head. "Ah, Miss Edmonds, you will see such fields in any direction you ride. But on down the road from where you were today is a sight most people say is truly worth seeing. It is not part of the d'Arc land, but I thought perhaps Philip would show it to you."

I had no idea what Lucy was talking about, but she seemed pleased that Philip had not shown me this extraordinary sight, whatever it was.

"Well, I must say that I saw nothing at all remarkable on that road, but he told me that it would be a safe place to ride. Perhaps you will go with me sometime and show it to me."

Before Lucy could reply to my suggestion, we heard a male voice in the hall, then Philip strolled in. He had changed from his riding clothes but was more informally dressed than normal for his after-dinner visits. I was torn between relief and disappointment that his face bore no sign of having been soundly slapped a few hours earlier. I was glad I didn't have to mention the incident to Lucy, but I also wanted Philip to remember I would always fight back when I was cornered.

"I heard what Miss Edmonds just said, and it sounds like a good idea, Lucy. Marc can take you out in the pony cart."

Caught between her pleasure in seeing Philip and her distaste for his suggestion, Lucy merely shook her head. "It bounces too much. Besides, I am far too old to ride in a pony cart."

Philip seemed amused, but he didn't challenge Lucy's statement. "The cabriolet is being repaired, and the Marquis took the big carriage to Paris, so that leaves only the pony cart. Perhaps if I padded the seat —"

"No!" Lucy interrupted. "Forget I said anything. Anyway, when I go out again, I intend to be on my own horse."

Philip and I exchanged surprised glances over Lucy's head. She spoke as if she had never been offered a horse at all, which I knew wasn't the case.

"That could be arranged, I suppose," he said, his tone suggesting that the matter was of no consequence to him one way or another. "I saw some fine animals at Dampierre, where I found Miss Edmonds' horse. Of course, they have no doubt all been sold by now."

"That would be for the better, M'sieu Mailley," I said with disapproval, following

Philip's lead. "Riding would be far too dangerous for Mademoiselle Lucy even to consider."

"At any rate, it is not her decision to make. Until the Marquis returns from Paris and grants his permission, nothing can be done, so it is a moot point." Philip spoke directly to me, as if Lucy were not even present.

"It is not a moot point — whatever that means," Lucy said, speaking English as we had been. She made a fist and struck the arm of her chair with a resounding thump. "Take me out on Miss Edmonds' horse and I will show you that I can still ride."

"Is that possible?" I asked Philip, and I was not just talking about the marquis' permission.

"I think it might be, although of course we must not be in a hurry about the matter."

"Then I will write the Marquis tonight and you can take the note to him tomorrow," Lucy said.

Her jaw was set in her familiar stubborn determination, but her eyes shone with unusual excitement. I had never seen her so animated, and it was obvious that Philip had also noticed the change in Lucy.

"You know I cannot leave the chateau, Mademoiselle," he said. "I am in charge, and I must stay. You can post a letter to-morrow and have a reply in a few days."

Lucy's mouth was a straight line of resolve. "I do not wish to wait that long. Send the Marquis a telegram — surely you can find someone to go to Dreux."

Philip rubbed his chin as if giving the matter great thought. "I am not sure about that, Lucy. A messenger would have to be hired to deliver the reply."

"Then do it! I know the Marquis always leaves money with you — and he would want you to do this service for me."

Philip looked at Lucy, then at me, pretending to be unconvinced. "How about it, Miss Edmonds? Should I do as I am asked or follow my own best judgment? I will accept the verdict of Mademoiselle Lucy's new companion."

Lucy made a rude noise. "Phau! What does Miss Edmonds know about anything? It is not her place to forbid me to do things I can do perfectly well."

"I'm not so certain of that," I said, speaking the truth. I knew Lucy had not been on horseback since the riding accident that had put her in an invalid's chair. The last thing I wanted — for my sake as well as hers — was for her to be hurt in my care.

Lucy turned to me with a supplicating

look that would melt a stone. "At least let me try. All afternoon I thought of how you and Philip were out there in the sunshine, and here I was, always alone and bound to this hateful chair . . ."

Her voice wavered, then stopped, as if she regretted the frank confession of her need.

"All right, Lucy." I moved to her chair and put my hand on her shoulder. "If M'sieu Philip is agreeable, then I will make no further objection."

Lucy looked up at Philip, her eyes pleading. "I really want to do this, Philip. Please?"

Philip shrugged and spread his hands in defeat but did not look pleased. "It is against all common sense and my better judgment, but I suppose putting the matter before the Marquis can do no harm."

"A good suggestion," I said.

Lucy tore a page from her sketchbook and handed it to Philip. "Write down what I tell you," she said with the air of one long accustomed to having her bidding done.

"Very well, Lucy," Philip said. "But you would be more likely to persuade the Marquis to agree with your request, if you would wait to ask him in person."

Lucy waved her hand impatiently. "Just write. I know what I am doing."

Once more Philip and I exchanged a brief glance, like conspirators in some grand scheme, before he returned his attention to Lucy. It was hard for me to pretend to disapprove of Lucy's request — and even more difficult to remember that I should dislike Philip.

After many revisions and amendments, Lucy was finally satisfied with her message to the marquis and Philip left, promising to see that it reached the telegraph office in Dreux at first light.

This has been an interesting day, I thought on the way back to my room from Lucy's. Although my encounter with Philip had been disturbing, he now seemed ready to cooperate with me, at least as far as Lucy was concerned. And perhaps one day he would even tell me what he knew about the marquise.

I had nearly reached my room when I heard a noise that seemed to be coming from within it, and I stopped at the door, uncertain if I should enter. I had no lantern, and the dimly lit hall shed no light into the room when I opened the door. But after a moment during which all was silent, I gathered my courage and walked inside.

The first thing I noticed was that my

window, which I knew had been closed earlier, was standing open. The draperies, swelled by the night breeze, had taken on the appearance of ghostly apparitions performing a minuet.

The next thing I saw, after I managed to light my lamp, was the note on my pillow. It was in the same place that the first one had been, and was very much like it.

YOU HAVE BEEN WARNED. IF YOU VALUE YOUR LIFE, YOU MUST NOT REMAIN.

I sat on the bed and looked at the paper for a moment, trying to still the racing of my heart. I shivered, then realized the room had become quite chilly from the open window. I was certain whoever had left the note must have fled through the same window, and I leaned out, looking for any clue which might have been left behind. The dim moonlight revealed no details, but when I lowered the lantern as far down as I could, I made out a faint track in the dewy grass.

Without pausing to consider the folly of my action, I climbed out of the window, as I imagined my intruder must have, and followed the tracks that he had made.

He, I thought. Surely only a man could have opened the heavy window from the outside. Madame Albert had neither the strength nor the agility to perform such a feat, and once again Jacques was nowhere around.

Philip must have done it, I thought numbly as the tracks disappeared in the gravel path in front of the chateau. I looked toward the wing of the stable where Phillip Mailley lived and recalled his insistent warning that I was in danger. Yet tonight, I had felt that we were working well together on Lucy's behalf.

Did the man want to be rid of me badly enough to try to frighten me into leaving the Chateau d'Arc? It was hard for me to believe my presence could threaten him, yet he must still think that it did.

Shivering in the night air, I returned to my room the way I had left it, closed the window behind me, and picked up my hair-brush. I recalled that Philip had said something about the stupidity of American women. Despite what he might think, I would not be so easily frightened away. This time I would keep the note and show it to the marquis at my first opportunity. Then Philip Mailley would see who was really the stupid one.

But suppose Philip didn't write the note?

I paused, my breath and hairbrush both held motionless.

He must have done it, I told myself, but my pale reflection did not appear to be convinced.

Lucy awoke in good spirits the next morning, but with every hour that passed without a reply from the marquis her initial exhilaration gradually gave way to her usual irritability. I felt almost as much suspense as Lucy did. Although I was almost certain the marquis would agree to buying Lucy a horse — something he had apparently always been willing to do — I feared he would insist that Philip wait until he returned to oversee the purchase. By then, Lucy might have changed her mind, especially if she spent much time thinking about the horseback ride that had left her crippled.

I found myself returning to the grand salon several times the next day, looking for Philip, who was nowhere to be seen, and watching the driveway for any sign of an approaching rider. Lucy refused to lie down after our luncheon but stationed herself in the family salon to await her answer.

"Something must have happened to the telegram," Lucy said when the mantel clock chimed four times. "Ask Philip to come here — he must go to Dreux immediately and send another message."

"I am certain the reply is on its way," I told her, but Lucy refused to be placated.

"Must I send Sophie after Philip, then?"

Reluctantly, I arose. "No, of course not. But M'sieu Philip will only tell you the same thing."

Lucy stuck out her lower lip and shook her head. "Then I will hear it from him, not you. Hurry, go on," she added when I still made no move toward the door.

"Very well, I shall try to find him," I said, knowing I'd have no peace until Lucy got what she wanted.

I was certainly not eager to see Philip again, yet I thought perhaps he might say or do something to let me know that he had been in my room the night before. Apart from that, I knew I must tolerate the man for Lucy's sake, at least until I could speak to the marquis about him.

"M'sieu Philip is in his office," Marc told me before I could ask. He added something else in a French patois spoken too rapidly to understand it all. I gathered the boy meant that he had a chore to perform that prevented him from escorting me to Philip himself.

"Thank you, Marc." I smiled and nodded, then for the first time I crossed the stable yard and made my way through a narrow passageway to the wing where the estate's affairs were managed. To the left, a chorus of barks attended me from the kennels where the hunting dogs were kept. *They need a good run,* I thought. Perhaps they would be getting one soon enough. To the right, the top part of a divided door was open to reveal a large room containing several tables strewn with a variety of ledgers and writing implements. A huge mahogany secretary's desk dominated the rear wall, located at a right angle to a fireplace bearing the blackened evidence of much use.

Without any suspicion I might be trespassing on forbidden territory, I entered the empty room. Thinking that the partly open door to the left led to another part of the office, I pushed it open and took a step forward.

To my shock, I realized two things at once: I had entered Philip Mailley's private apartment, and he stood with his back to me, naked from the waist up.

"Hurry up with that water, Marc," Philip called when he heard my footsteps. He did not turn around, and I had a moment to study the contours of his broad back.

I had seen my uncle's hired hands working shirtless during the summer harvest, so the sight was hardly novel. But I had

132

to admit I liked watching Philip's muscles move under his smooth skin as he bent to remove his slippers. *He doesn't look at all dangerous now,* I thought, and once again I wanted to doubt he could have been responsible for my warning notes.

Considering Philip's state of undress, I intended to leave quietly before he spotted me, but his expression when he turned and saw me watching him was almost worth my own embarrassment at being discovered spying on a half-naked man.

"*Sacre bleu,*" he muttered, then reverted to my language. "Can I have no privacy at all in my own home?"

"It is the same in the chateau," I said. I watched his face closely for any admission of guilt. "My room has been entered more than once without my invitation."

Philip raised his eyebrows and smiled slightly. "But not, I hope, while you were bathing, Miss Edmonds?"

He is insufferable, I thought, but at the same time I was relieved he didn't seem to know what I meant. I also noticed he made no move to cover himself with the shirt that lay on a chair beside him.

"You aren't bathing, either," I said. I wanted to study Philip's bare chest with the same intensity I had given his back, but I pretended to be indifferent to the sight and looked at my surroundings instead. "You have just this one room?"

It was a large chamber, crowded with enough furniture to fill several rooms. Except for a stack of papers, books, and magazines which covered most of a dining table and threatened to slide off onto the bare, planked floor, all was neat and orderly.

"It is sufficient — I seldom entertain, particularly when I bathe."

Philip threw the shirt around his shoulders but made no move to button it. The hair on his chest was a lighter shade of brown than that on his head, and I wondered if it would feel as silky as it looked. Then I realized how inappropriate the thought was and, somewhat belatedly, I blushed.

"Lucy wants to see you," I said, forcing my gaze to his face. "She's concerned that she has had no reply from the Marquis."

"I told her it might be tomorrow before any answer could arrive."

"She doesn't want to wait that long. She thinks you should go to Dreux yourself and re-send the message."

Philip lifted the shirt from his back and began to put his right arm into the sleeve.

"What do you think, Miss Edmonds?"

"I think if you do not see her, she'll just send me back here again."

Philip sighed. "All right, tell Lucy I will be there soon. But I would like to bathe first, since the water seems to have arrived, finally."

"I am sorry, Sir," Marc said from behind me. "The fire kept going out."

The boy struggled into the room, sloshing water from the two large buckets he carried. Setting them down, he knelt and reached under the canopied bed in the corner for a shallow copper tub like the one Sophie filled for my baths.

Neither of us spoke as Marc poured the steaming water into the tub, then handed Philip a linen bath towel and a chunk of soap.

"Enjoy your bath, Sir."

As he left, Marc gave me a knowing grin. I realized he had probably tried to warn me that Philip was in no state to receive visitors and now misunderstood my presence. I would have to let him know he was wrong before the chateau gossip created some sort of romantic intrigue between Philip and me. For the moment, however, I hadn't finished with Philip.

"You may as well come for dinner," I said

from the doorway.

Ignoring my presence, he had removed his shirt again and seemed on the verge of undoing his trousers, but I stood my ground and waited for his reply to my invitation.

"Your hospitality overwhelms me," he said dryly. "I should remind you, however, that you are not yet chatelaine of the chateau."

Had I been nearer, I would have been sorely tempted to apply my hand to his face again, but I didn't trust myself to go any closer, nor could I even look directly into his eyes. Instead, I addressed the top of his head.

"And I should remind you, Sir, that you are not yet its owner. Lucy will expect you for dinner."

Philip's laughter followed me out of the room and into the estate office and echoed in my ears as I hurried across the courtyard, but I did not look back.

Marc, who seemed to have an uncanny way of disappearing when he was most wanted, was nowhere in sight at the stable.

Oh, well, I thought on my way back to the chateau, *Marc is just a child. He probably has no intention of saying anything about Philip and me, and even if he did, what harm could possibly come of such a wild tale?*

As if thinking about him had conjured him, Marc suddenly appeared on the chateau path, pointing to something behind me with great excitement.

"A rider, Mademoiselle!" he cried, and I turned to see a lone horseman making his way down the chateau drive at a full gallop. *The messenger from Dreux,* I thought, but as he drew closer, I realized I was mistaken.

"*Bonsoir, Mademoiselle.* The prodigal has again returned."

"You weren't expected back so soon," I said.

Jacques dismounted and handed Marc the reins. "Here, boy, attend to this nag, will you? It was the best Sully's stable had for hire — the man has no shame, offering such a beast for real money."

Marc led the horse away and Jacques turned and, with his hands on his hips, stared at me as if he had never seen me before. "Did you miss me, Miss Edmonds?"

I resumed walking toward the chateau and attempted to sound polite. "You were hardly away long enough for Lucy and me to realize you were gone," I replied, truthfully enough.

"How flattering," Jacques said. As we

walked, he shrugged out of his traveling cloak and shook off some of the dust, muttering an oath under his breath. "The train was slow, then there was not one carriage or decent horse for hire in the whole town of Dreux. A man with a good livery stable could make some money there."

"Then perhaps you should open one," I said, knowing quite well Jacques had no money of his own. His scowl was my only answer.

"Is that the messenger?" Lucy called out when I opened the door to the family salon.

"I suppose you might say so," Jacques said, entering the room at my heels.

Lucy's face fell. "I was expecting a telegram from the Marquis," she said.

"Is that any way to greet your long-lost brother? Besides, I brought several notes from him — let me see, where did I put them?"

Jacques made a show of looking in his pockets, then shook his head. "They must be tucked away somewhere — I'll bring them to the dinner table. Where is Henri?" he added, after a pull on the bell cord yielded no immediate results.

"Tell me what the Marquis said," Lucy begged, but Jacques merely shrugged.

"Alas, I cannot. I was not at the house

when the telegram came, and the Marquis had already written and sealed the notes before I saw them."

"He must have told you what they said," Lucy began, but was interrupted by Henri's arrival. "Good evening, Henri. Bring some hot water to my room — and set another place for dinner."

"Two more places," I added. "M'sieu Philip is joining us this evening, as well."

Jacques scowled. "Who does he think he is, sniffing around here when the Marquis and I are gone? That fellow needs to be put in his place."

"I invited him," Lucy said quickly. "You know Philip often dines here when you are gone. Someone has to attend to our safety."

Jacques laughed without humor. "*Certainment.* By all means, send the fox to tend the chickens. I will see you at dinner."

"I wish the Marquis had just sent a telegram," Lucy said when her brother had made his exit.

So do I, I thought, but held my tongue. There was already too much animosity in the d'Arc family; I had no desire to foster more.

Philip arrived at the family salon before Jacques, more elegantly dressed than I had seen him. In addition to a dark jacket and dove-gray trousers, he wore a cravat over the collar of his completely buttoned shirt. When he bent to kiss Lucy's hand, I detected a faint, spicy scent. Bay rum, perhaps, or whatever concoction a Frenchman might apply after shaving.

"Oh, Philip, the messenger turned out to be Jacques, but he refuses to tell me what the Marquis said."

Philip nodded as if the news did not surprise him at all. "Yes, I thought the Marquis might send Jacques back, but I did not expect him until tomorrow."

"After reading your message, the Marquis wanted to come back himself," Jacques said, entering the room in time to hear Philip's last remark. "Unfortunately, his pressing business engagements prevented him from doing so."

"Is there a note for me?" Philip asked.

"Yes — and for Lucy and Mademoiselle, as well. All of that can wait until after supper."

Lucy squared her chin. "I want my letter now."

"And so do I," I said and reached out my hand.

Jacques cringed in mock horror. "You remind me of vultures after a dead creature.

I wish someone would consider my words half as important."

"Thank you, dear brother," Lucy said with heavy sarcasm as Jacques extended the paper to her, then pulled it back, making her reach for it again. Once again Jacques offered it, then withdrew it.

"Give her the letter, Jacques." Philip's blue eyes were as cold as his voice, and they never left Jacques' face until Lucy had her letter in hand.

Jacques' face was suffused with anger. "You do not tell me what to do, Mailley."

"Stop it!" I cried, and both men turned to regard me with surprise. "What would the Marquis think, to see you squabbling like little children? Surely you have better things to capture your interest."

"Miss Edmonds is right," Philip said.

"But you are not, Mailley," Jacques said.

Henri appeared in the doorway to announce dinner, then came forward to wheel Lucy's chair into the dining room.

Philip stepped behind the chair before Henri reached it. "Never mind, I have it."

"The man is so gallant," Jacques muttered, but only I was close enough to hear him.

When we had taken our places at the table, Jacques handed Philip and me our messages. "I hope these will not interfere with your dining pleasure."

Lucy had already broken the seal on her note and begun to read it. I watched her face, but couldn't tell what she thought of its content. Philip was likewise absorbed in his note from the marquis.

"If you'll excuse me, I'll read mine too," I said.

Jacques raised his wine glass in a mock toast and grinned. "I am always willing to excuse you, Mademoiselle. Pray read what the Marquis has to say — while I drown my own sorrows in this excellent Vouvray wine."

The marquis' bold handwriting reminded me of my summons to the chateau and assured me the note was not a forgery. I wouldn't put it past Jacques to attempt some sort of trickery, but this letter, at least, seemed to be genuine.

"Dear Ellen," it began. The marquis' use of my first name in writing brought a fleeting pang of alarm that he presumed an intimacy that I had not invited, but as I read on, my fears were allayed.

The news that Lucy wants to ride once more is staggering, and I cannot tell you how pleased I am to hear it. Yet

142

this is not a matter to be undertaken lightly, particularly given her health. I have been in consultation with a new physician who takes an interest in cases such as hers. If she is willing, I would like for you and Jacques to bring Lucy to Paris in a few days. In the meantime, she may go out in the pony cart, but not on horseback.

Although she has not said so, I think Lucy is growing to like you, and please know that I am in your debt for your fine work with her.

I shall look forward to seeing you in Paris soon.

"Good news, I presume?" Jacques said, and I looked up to see that the others had also finished reading their notes.

"The Marquis has invited us to Paris," I said.

"Ordered us, you mean," Lucy said. Although she sounded cross, it was a much milder statement than I had expected.

"Do you know about the hunt?" Philip asked, and Jacques nodded.

"The Marquis wants the matter taken care of as soon as possible. That is why I came back."

"What hunt?" asked Lucy.

"A wild boar from the stock imported by the first Marquis d'Arc seems to have gone on a bit of a tear. Therefore, it must be dispatched before it does any more damage," Jacques said cheerfully.

Lucy made a face. "Those ugly beasts! I hope you do not intend to make us dine on it."

"We shan't even dine tonight, if we keep talking like this," I said. Assuming the role of hostess, I rang the bell to signal Henri we were ready to be served.

"Tell me about the plans for the hunt," Lucy said to Philip, but Jacques interrupted before he could reply.

"There is nothing to tell yet. I would rather talk about what is happening in Paris."

When Lucy didn't respond, Jacques turned to me with a smirk. "I am sure Mademoiselle here would rather hear about the City of Light, *n'est ce pas?* Do you know it at all?"

"I stayed there one night on my way here from LeHavre," I replied. "I can tell you about the boat train and my small room in the *Hotel Belle Fleur.*"

"Well, do not expect Philip to enlighten you," Jacques said. "He has never been an intimate part of Parisian society."

"Or wanted to be," Lucy said.

Philip remained silent, and I was glad when the main course arrived and the conversation turned to the subject of food. Only there, perhaps, might the four of us find safe ground.

After we had dined, the men retired to the library, I supposed to discuss the impending hunt, and Lucy seemed rather restless as we returned to the family salon.

"I would enjoy some music," I said.

"I am not in the mood to make it," Lucy replied. She picked up her sketchbook and rifled through its pages, then threw it down. "These are all terrible," she said, and began to tear pages.

"Stop!" I cried. "Put it away for awhile and, when you are in a better frame of mind, you might decide they have merit after all. Let me see what you have done."

Reluctantly Lucy gave me the sketchbook. "Look if you must, and laugh. You will see that they ought to be destroyed."

Slowly I turned the pages. What I had supposed to be pencil drawings of the chateau or its inhabitants were actually sketches of a variety of costumes. Some bore labels like "morning gown" and "ball gown," while others were half-done, and several had been scribbled over. The last page contained an unusually draped gown with a fitted bodice. Beneath it Lucy had written: "For Ellen."

Touched, I looked up at her. "I am afraid I'm not up on the latest fashions, but I recognize good designs when I see them. These are lovely."

Lucy shook her head. "As you say, you know nothing about it."

"That is not true. I have seen similar work in books my mother sent all the way to New York City to get. She told me they came from Paris. When we go there, you will be able to see what the ladies of fashion are wearing —"

"I have not said that I am going."

I bit my lip and chided myself for my clumsiness. Knowing her contrary nature, I should have let Lucy broach the subject first. "Of course not, and I think you are wise to wait," I lied. "The Marquis will be back home in a few weeks. If you still feel you want to ride at that time, he might be willing to listen to you."

"I do not intend to wait that long. Philip can go ahead and find me a horse, anyway. The Marquis does not need to know about it."

"Neither do I." Standing, I handed her

the sketchbook. "Too bad you'll never know if these have any merit."

"Where are you going?" Lucy asked when I moved toward the door.

"To bed. Sophie can help you tonight."

"Why are you so angry with me?" Lucy asked, and I realized I had rarely let Lucy see that I too could show my temper.

I returned to my place on the sofa next to her chair and spoke calmly. "I'm not angry with you, Lucy, but I am a little disappointed. I should like to see something of Paris myself."

"It is too big."

I smiled. "That is what you said to me about the chateau the day I came," I reminded her. "What else can you tell me about Paris?"

Lucy half-closed her eyes and leaned back in her chair. "There was a park near the house, and nearly every afternoon there would be a puppet show or someone would play tunes. In the center of the park, there was a carousel that made music as it turned. And Mama—" She broke off and sat up. "It has been a long time, and this is wearisome. I would like to retire now."

I didn't call Sophie, but pushed Lucy's chair to her room and helped her prepare for bed. I even assumed the task of brushing

Lucy's heavy, honey-blond hair. As I counted the one hundred strokes it must have each night, I felt her gradually relax. Her face in repose showed her features at their best; with a touch of color in her cheeks and her hair properly dressed, Lucy would be beautiful.

Like her mother. I wondered if Lucy realized how much she resembled Madeline d'Arc. The knowledge that I was like my mother had come to me only after a number of other people had told me so, but it had pleased me to know it.

At any rate, Lucy both remembered her mother and seemed to be disturbed by her memories. The marquis had given me a part of the story, but I sensed there was much more to it than he had told me. Philip, if he knew, had refused to tell me, and Jacques would be no help at all.

But there was one person who might give me the clue I needed to help Lucy throw off her painful past, and she was right there in the chateau.

I set down the brush and helped Lucy to her bed. "Have you seen Madame Albert lately?" I asked idly.

"No, but Sophie tells me she is well."

"Did you say you were going to make her a dress? Perhaps she can be brought down to be fitted for it."

"Oh, I have her measurements — unless her figure has changed. I suppose I could check them before I cut into the material."

"That might be a good idea. Good night, Lucy."

I left Lucy's room with a firm step and new purpose. We would be in the chateau for a few more days before going to Paris, as I now felt certain we would. In that time, I would pay a visit to Madame Albert. In the way of the old, she had probably already forgotten she had once threatened me. I hoped to persuade her to tell me more about her beloved Madeline. In so doing, she might reveal something useful.

I paused at my door and listened, but heard nothing. Inside, the room seemed undisturbed, but as a precaution I dragged a chair to the door. It would not prevent someone from entering, but it would at least alert me to any intruder. Although I doubted I would have any more unwanted visitors that night, it was still a long while before I fell asleep, and then to troubled dreams.

Chapter Six

The next day I found myself caught up in an unexpected flurry of activity that accompanied the boar hunt. I had presumed that Philip and Jacques, perhaps accompanied by one or two others, would simply go into the forest, find the boar, and kill it. Instead, once the word got out the marquis had authorized a hunt, the chateau began to fill with men from several nearby estates, all intent on having a good time while performing a service for a neighbor.

With the marquis away, the servants needed direction, and it fell my lot to see that rooms were prepared for the hunters' use and that enough food was on hand to feed them all. Leaving Lucy to her own devices, I made several trips to the second story, selecting the best of the chambers and having the rooms hastily cleaned and aired.

I had just left fresh linens in one of the last of four rooms that had been opened for the hunters when I sensed I was not alone. I turned to see that Jacques had come into the room and now leaned against the door, smiling at my startled reaction.

"Mam'selle Edmonds has been very busy today," he said.

"There is much to do. How many more hunters are expected?"

"As many as arrive — perhaps ten in all."

"To kill one boar?"

"One extremely mean and nasty boar," Jacques corrected. "The more hunters we have, the sooner the job will be done."

"Then I should open more rooms." I started toward the door, but Jacques did not step aside.

"There is no hurry. They will not need beds until tonight."

I reached for the door latch, but Jacques quickly stepped in front of it, so that my hand brushed his waistcoat instead. Taking advantage of the brief contact, he seized my arm and attempted to pull me to him.

Something in his eyes made me know that this time he wasn't merely engaging in a mild flirtation, and I knew a flicker of fear.

"Let me go!" I put my free hand on his chest and pushed hard, catching him off-balance. I fumbled for the door latch, but Jacques recovered in time to put his hand on mine and keep me from opening it.

"*Bien!* I like a woman with some spirit,"

he said, and I longed to wipe the smile from his face with my hand. That his words echoed Philip's angered me even more.

"If you don't let me go this instant, you might see more spirit than you'll like," I said.

"*Je ne comprende pas,*" Jacques said. "In any case," he continued in his heavily accented English, "that pretty mouth of yours badly needs kissing."

"And you badly need some manners!"

In reply Jacques twisted my arm and pressed me against the door with such force that I almost lost my breath. Against his strength I could do little, but despite the pain in my wrist, I continued to struggle. Soon, anger began to replace my initial fear.

"Let me go, or I'll create a scene."

Jacques looked amused. "Yes? And just who will witness it, *ma cherie?* Everyone is quite occupied below, talking about every hunt they have ever seen. No one will hear you."

I knew he spoke the truth, and when he began maneuvering me toward the bed, I also knew I had to do something to stop him. Jacques bent his face to mine so closely, I could feel the warmth of his breath. But just before his lips could touch mine, I screamed as loudly as I could, then screamed again.

Uttering an oath, Jacques drew back, instinctively covering an ear with one hand. I took advantage of his lessened grip to wrench away from him and run to the door. With a push of the door latch I propelled myself into the hall — and directly into Madame Albert.

Jacques was close on my heels, but he stopped short when he saw we were not alone.

"Well, Madame! And how are you this fine day?" he said loudly. He bent to kiss the old woman's wrinkled cheek, but her expression did not change. She paid me no heed at all.

"Is my Jacques being a naughty boy again?" she asked in a tone appropriate for a young child.

"I am afraid so, Madame. Will you forgive me?" Jacques knelt before the old woman with his hands clasped in supplication, his lips curved in a boyish smile.

"You know I will, as always, my sweet child." Madame Albert did not exactly smile, but for a moment her face softened and she looked almost pleasant.

"Come, Madame, let me accompany you to your room, where you must stay for a while. The house is going to be filled with visitors, and you should stay out of their way."

When Jacques took Madame Albert's arm, I slipped away and walked downstairs. Finding Sophie, I instructed her to bring up enough linen for several more beds. After making certain that Jacques had left the house, I went back to Madame Albert's room.

"Entrez," she called when I rapped lightly on her door.

Hoping she could understand my French, I greeted her politely as I entered her cluttered room.

The old lady sat in a massive, upholstered chair near a window overlooking the formal garden. She gazed at me as if she had never before seen me, and I decided it would be better to let her speak first.

"Who are you?" she asked after a long moment of silence.

"Mademoiselle Lucy's companion."

"Come closer — I cannot see you," Madame Albert commanded.

Her eyes narrowed as I approached, and she furrowed her brow as if trying to remember something. "You are not French."

Her tone made the words an accusation, and I nodded. "That is correct, Madame.

I am an American."

"American?"

I saw no glimmer of recognition in her black eyes. Whoever she had thought I was before and been so angry with had apparently been forgotten. Relaxing a bit, I looked around the untidy room. Several small portraits stood on a dresser, and I walked over to inspect them.

Madame Albert said something I did not quite understand, and I turned back to her. *"Comment?"*

"Have you seen Madeline today?" she asked, this time slowly enough for me to hear each chilling word.

"No, Madame," I replied, truthfully enough.

She frowned. "She has not been to see me lately. Tell her I must speak to her immediately, Mademoiselle."

I nodded. "Yes, I will. You have been with the Marquise for many years, have you not?"

"Many years?" Madame Albert sounded almost angry. "I was there when she was born, and a more beautiful infant you will never see."

"What was she like?"

Madame Albert closed her eyes. "A fair babe, with golden hair halfway down her back, and so good — she never cried, not once."

"And now?"

Madame Albert's eyes flew open, then narrowed as a subtle change came over her countenance. "Now she is a beautiful woman, of course. But why are you here?"

"I am Lucy's companion," I repeated.

"Lucy? You speak nonsense. She is my charge. Not as lovely as her mother, and quite strong-willed, but in many ways they are quite alike."

I nodded, not knowing what else to do, then glanced back at the jumble on Madame Albert's dresser. Amid a discarded fichu and a pair of gloves, I caught a glimpse of something quite familiar. Casually I moved the fichu aside to reveal the missing watercolors my mother had done of the Chateau d'Arc.

"Where did you get these pictures of the chateau?" I asked, but when I picked up the top one, I was appalled to see it had been ripped in two.

Immediately a closed, secret look came over her face, and Madame Albert stood, then swayed and put a hand out, as if fighting for balance. Afraid she might fall, I went to her, only to have her push me aside.

"You witch," she rasped. "You tried to

trick me, but now I see who you really are."

"I am Ellen Edmonds, Lucy's companion," I said as calmly as I could. "We met when I first came to the Chateau d'Arc."

Madame Albert stood still for a moment, her brows furrowed, as if she were trying to take in my words. Then a look of pure hatred filled her face, and she spoke such a rapid spate of French that I could make out only a few words, none of them kind.

"Go away!" she screamed, and that I understood quite well.

Hastily I retrieved Mama's destroyed sketches and fled from the room, Madame Albert's invective following me all the way. Just as I closed the door behind me, something crashed against it, followed by the sound of shattering glass.

I was still trembling when I reached my room, where my mirror showed a wide-eyed, disheveled young woman.

I am not afraid of Madame Albert, I told myself, but I was not quite convinced. Old and infirm though she might be, the woman had for some reason chosen to hate me. She had evidently taken Mama's sketches, then torn them in a fit of anger against some imagined wrong Mama did to her years ago.

I must show these to the marquis, I

thought, but I had no place to hide them in my room. They would be safe in Lucy's room, but I couldn't let her see me in such a state. By the time I had rinsed my face and put a few drops of water on my brush to help coax my hair into place, I felt much calmer.

The door to Lucy's room stood ajar, and I entered, expecting to find her rising from her rest. Instead, I was greeted by the sight of Philip standing in the middle of her room, holding a pair of Lucy's shoes. In his tight-fitting English jodhpurs and an open-necked shirt, he made a handsome but incongruous picture.

"She is not here, Mademoiselle," he said.

"So I see. But why are you?" The sight of Philip threatened the composure I had so recently fought to regain, and I spoke more crossly than the situation warranted.

"If Lucy is to ride, she must have the proper footwear. I intend to take these slippers to a bootmaker I know. He can have riding boots ready for her in a fortnight."

"Where is Lucy?" I accepted his explanation, but I felt belated guilt that I had left her alone all day.

"She is sketching in the family salon, I believe. By the way, you should say nothing about the boots — I would like to surprise her with them."

"I won't tell her, but she may want to wear those slippers. How long do you intend to keep them?"

"Not long. I have some errands in the vicinity of the bootmaker's shop this afternoon. He'll take the measurements and return them to me immediately."

"I suppose that will be all right."

"Thank you for saying so, Miss Edmonds," he said, and I knew he was making fun of me. "What is that?" He pointed to Mama's sketches.

"My mother did these when she was here, but apparently Madame Albert took them from my room and tore them. I intend to show them to the Marquis when we go to Paris."

"That is unfortunate," he said. "I did not think Madame Albert would be happy to have you here."

"Why not?"

"Your presence reminds her that she is no longer capable of caring for Lucy, for one thing. When do you plan to leave for Paris?"

"As soon as you can kill that boar, I suppose. How long will it take?"

"I am no fortune-teller, Mademoiselle. We start tomorrow at first light. With luck we will find him the first day, but if not, we will keep on until we do."

159

"We'll need more stores, if the hunt lasts more than a few days."

Philip nodded. "I will see to that part of it. Is there anything else?"

I drew a deep breath. "Yes, there is. I would like a lock for my bedroom door."

"A lock? Do you think that is sufficient to protect you, Miss Edmonds?"

The way Philip looked at me made me want to believe he knew nothing about my threatening notes.

"It would keep out Madame Albert. She must have taken the sketches from my room. I just found them by accident a few minutes ago."

Philip shrugged. "You will have to take the matter of a lock up with the Marquis. I have no authority to alter anything in the chateau. As for the sketches, you can probably expect more of the same as long as you stay here. Now, if you will excuse me, I have work to do."

"Will you come to dinner tonight?" I called after him.

He stopped at the door and turned toward me. "Is that an invitation?"

"I thought you might need to discuss the hunt with our visitors," I said with as much disinterest as I could muster under the steady gaze of his dark blue eyes.

"Yes, I will do that. Until this evening, then."

To my chagrin, I looked forward to dinner with a great deal more anticipation than the situation actually warranted.

The marquis had chosen his staff well. The servants worked efficiently and actually seemed to enjoy preparing to serve a large number of visitors again.

"In the old days, fourteen for dinner was nothing, Mademoiselle," Henri confided when I told him how many places to lay at the table.

"You have been here a long time, then?"

"Eighteen years, Mademoiselle Edmonds."

So, Henri would not have known my mother, but certainly he must have taken orders from the marquise. I hadn't thought to question him. "What was the Marquise like?" I asked.

Henri stiffened slightly as if I had violated some unspoken code. I knew servants gossiped among themselves quite readily, but apparently Henri didn't feel I was a part of their circle.

"She was a beautiful woman, Mademoiselle."

"I have not seen a portrait of her. Is there one?"

"There was, but I believe it has been stored. Please excuse me now, Mademoiselle. I must speak to the cook."

I sensed that Henri would have invented an errand, had one not existed, to keep from discussing Madeline d'Arc. All I knew about her so far was that she had been a beauty. I paused before a cloudy mirror in the hallway outside the family salon and regarded my own reflection. Despite Philip Mailley's comment about my effect on men, I doubted anyone could actually think of me as beautiful. My features were even, true enough, but my hair seldom remained in any sort of style and my figure was far too spare to suit the fashions of the day. My small waist didn't require corseting, but my bosom, while adequate, was not ample, nor were my hips. The ball gown Lucy had sketched for me, with its skillful draping, would flatter me, but the plain dresses and skirts and shirtwaists I wore every day had been designed for utility, not beauty.

"You must not ask who is the fairest of them all — she is there in front of you," Jacques said, entering the hall from my right.

Embarrassed that he had caught me looking so intently at my reflection and wary of his intentions, I quickly turned from the mirror. "I must see to Lucy," I said, and brushed past him before he could move to block my way.

"Wait a moment. You must not be angry because I find you so beautiful."

Jacques' smirk told me he had no intention of apologizing for his behavior, especially since in his eyes, he had done nothing wrong. To him, it was my fault I had attracted him, my fault I had very nearly been assaulted. But the fault would be mine if I failed to tell Jacques what I thought about him.

"You're not worth my anger, M'sieu, but if you ever try to force yourself on me again, the Marquis will know about it."

The smirk faded from Jacques' face, replaced by a scowl. "I thought you were more sensible than that, Mademoiselle. Do you believe for a moment the Marquis would listen to your absurd charges? You are in no position to threaten me."

I held my ground, my chin firm. "We shall see about that in Paris, perhaps."

Jacques smiled without humor. "One thing more, *cherie*. Do dress nicely for dinner tonight — our guests will expect it. And be sure to wear that charming brooch."

"I shall wear what I like," I said over my shoulder, as I entered the family salon and slammed the door behind me. Lucy looked up from her sketching, her eyebrows raised in an unspoken question which I didn't answer.

"I hope you won't be too tired at dinner, since you missed your usual rest today," I said, striving to sound normal.

Lucy shrugged and resumed sketching. "I do not plan to be at dinner tonight."

"But you are expected to greet our guests."

She pursed her lips. "Our guests, Miss Edmonds? Are you a d'Arc now, too?"

My face colored. "Of course not. But I've been involved in preparing for these people and I know the Marquis would expect us all to welcome them."

"And you will tell on me if I do not behave," Lucy said, sounding so much like a child I almost laughed at her.

"I am sure that won't be necessary. Anyway, Philip will be present too, and he expects you to join us."

Lucy made a face. "Phau! Have you ever heard men talking about their hunting prowess? It is disgusting."

"Perhaps they'll wait until after dinner to speak about hunting," I said.

"Not likely. The men come here to hunt and to drink too much, not necessarily in that order. Women will not be welcome."

"Perhaps you are right, but courtesy demands we be at the evening meal tonight. After that, we'll see."

Lucy nodded. "All right, if I can be seated before they are admitted, I shall dine with the hunters tonight. But you'll see I am right."

I decided on the same dress that I'd worn my first night at the chateau; with an intricately woven lace collar to add elegance, it would serve. Jacques had told me to wear Mama's hunting-scene brooch, but I had no intention of doing so. From my small store of jewelry, I chose a circle pin set with garnets, then realized the brooch was not in the case. *Madame Albert again.* At that point I was more annoyed than frightened at the thought that the old woman could apparently come downstairs and rummage through my belongings at will. She had taken Mama's sketches, and I felt certain she also had the brooch. *The old woman is a nuisance, but nothing more,* I told myself, and I refused to allow her to spoil my evening.

The dining room was barely recognizable when I pushed Lucy's chair into it a few minutes later. Fourteen places had been set around the table, with room for even more. Each place had gold service and bread plates, three wineglasses, and a full complement of forks and knives and spoons for the various courses that would be served. A huge épergne on the sideboard contained roses from the chateau garden, their scent wrapping the room in subtle fragrance.

"Everything looks lovely, Henri," I told the butler.

He bowed. "*Merci,* Mademoiselle. Shall I announce dinner?"

"If all is ready, please do so."

"Yes, we might as well get on with the horror," Lucy said glumly.

"I've never seen that dress," I told Lucy. "It becomes you quite well."

Lucy looked down at her pale green silk gown as if she hadn't seen it before. "I made it last winter for want of something to do. It's almost too snug for me now."

With her hair dressed in soft curls around her face and a touch of rouge on her cheeks, Lucy looked lovely, and I found myself wondering if the marquis would be struck by her resemblance to his late wife.

The murmur of conversation grew louder as the men made their way from the grand salon, where they had been partaking of pre-dinner drinks, and through the hall to the dining room. I remained seated as they entered and Jacques made the necessary introductions.

"Monsieurs, may I present Mademoiselle Edmonds, Lucy's companion. She is from America."

I felt relieved that Jacques made no other comment about me or the fact I wasn't wearing the brooch. As each man passed my chair, Jacques supplied his name, and in turn the gentlemen bowed and kissed my hand.

I nodded to acknowledge each introduction. I met another marquis, a judge, a doctor, an attorney, a priest, and several other men identified only as neighbors. The last to enter was Philip Mailley, who pointedly declined to join the others in kissing my hand. He kissed Lucy's hand, however, adding to the color already in her cheeks.

Henri had assisted me with making the place cards, so each guest had the seat dictated by society's protocols. In her place at the foot of the table, Lucy was flanked by the Marquis de Chelley, a lean, dour man who said little, and a much plumper but no more animated Judge Perrault. I was seated to the right of Jacques, who had taken the place of his father as host. On my right was the priest from Dampierre, a man who looked as if he would feel far more comfortable at a hunt than a formal dinner. The men had all obviously partaken generously of the offered aperitifs, and all were eager to discuss the coming hunt.

"You say this animal broke through the wall, Mailley?" asked the merchant seated beside Philip in the least desirable location.

"Not all the way through it, but enough to do a great deal of damage."

"It has killed several lambs, as well," Jacques put in. He buttered a radish and bit into it with a loud, crunching noise.

"Could we not speak of something less bloody?" I tried to say, but something about the French words I chose must have been wrong, for everyone, including Lucy, convulsed with laughter.

"Mademoiselle does not want the dinner conversation to turn on hunting," Lucy said when she had regained her speech.

"Ah, but what else is there to speak of in this place?" the doctor asked. He had a very red face and very white whiskers, and I was reminded of an illustration of a man named Micawber I had seen in a book by Mr. Charles Dickens, the English writer.

"What is the plan for tomorrow?" the other marquis asked, and I sighed, resigned to the inevitable.

Although he hadn't been directly addressed, Philip replied. "I have divided the deep forest into sections, and after dinner you will draw for them. I propose to put out six two-man teams, each with three hounds and a yap. One man of each pair should have a longbow and the other a lance."

"I brought my short sword," the judge said.

"So did I," echoed the doctor.

"Those are excellent weapons, gentlemen, but extremely dangerous to use with boar."

"Phau!" exclaimed one of the neighbors, who went on to relate a particularly bloody encounter with a boar in which the beast had been killed by a single thrust of his well-aimed broadsword.

When Henri entered with a side of rare beef, I saw Lucy turn pale and wished we had offered a less sanguine dish. I made another effort to divert the men's talk.

"What kind of animal is a yap?" I asked. Immediately all eyes turned to me, and another wave of laughter swept the room.

Philip didn't laugh, however, and he answered my question. "A yap is a small dog who barks to let the hunters know when the hounds have found a boar."

"The hounds can also bark. Why would

you need another dog?"

"Because, my dear Mademoiselle, the hounds are too busy attacking the boar to speak about it," Jacques said. "If the yap did not let the hunters know the boar had been found, the dogs would be ripped to shreds."

"I should like to be excused," Lucy said in a thin voice, and immediately Philip rose from his seat and rolled her chair away from the table.

"Please excuse us, gentlemen," I murmured and hurried to join Philip and Lucy in the hall.

"I told you how it would be," Lucy said accusingly.

"I'm sorry, Lucy. The men were quite rude."

Philip looked at me without smiling. "They were being themselves, Miss Edmonds. It is the way hunters are."

"If so, it's a brutal way to be."

"Men are brutes, anyway," Lucy said, as if to herself.

It was the first time I had heard her say anything about men, and I wondered where she had gotten that notion.

"Yes, *ma petite*, I fear you are correct," Philip said. "And now I must return to the other brutes. Everyone will retire early tonight to be ready for the hunt tomorrow. It would be best for you to stay inside until we have finished."

"Especially because of the reckless way some of these men hunt," Lucy said. "Believe me, Mademoiselle, talking is their best skill."

"You are too hard on them," Philip said. "They will do what they came here for, I am certain. Wish us all luck."

"You will need it," Lucy said.

"Who is your partner?" I asked.

Philip's mouth tightened. "Jacques, of course. We have hunted together many times."

"He is the worst one of all," Lucy said with disdain.

Philip and I exchanged a brief glance over Lucy's head and at that moment I felt a strange kinship with him, almost as if we shared the same thought.

Be careful, my eyes said.

I will, Philip's eyes replied.

"Come to see me after the hunt," Lucy said. "I do not plan to join that group for dinner again."

"And you, Miss Edmonds? Was the dinner talk too rough for you as well?" Once more Philip's tone challenged me.

"As long as the Chateau d'Arc needs a hostess, I am available," I said.

171

Philip did not smile. "Yes, I am sure of that. Good evening, ladies."

Back in my room, as I prepared for bed, I thought it seemed odd that Jacques and Philip would willingly do anything together, especially something as potentially dangerous as a boar hunt. For Jacques, being careful did not exist, and I knew Philip would tolerate nothing from him.

Wild boars might be dangerous, but enemies like Jacques and Philip, armed with crossbows and lances and alone in the deep forest, could be far worse.

This place seemed to be filled with menace.

I would be glad when the boar hunt was safely completed.

Chapter Seven

True to Philip's words, the hunters must have risen well before dawn, for it was still dark when I awoke to the sounds of their departure. Curious to see the start of a mounted boar hunt, I put on my riding skirt and boots and threw a warm shawl around my shoulders against the heavy morning dew before I took the path to the stable. A wispy morning fog hung on just above the ground and muffled every sound. Yet, even from the chateau I could hear the hounds baying and the hunters' shouts as they cinched their saddles and checked their weapons. So busy were the men that I was able to walk undetected to the rear of the stable, where I used an upturned bucket as an impromptu platform from which to view the proceedings.

My first impression was that these boar hunters did not stand on ceremony. The marquis and his groom were similarly garbed, the judge wore trousers which had long since seen better days, and the doctor seemed to be mounted on the sort of horse I had previously seen used for plowing.

Despite a great deal of milling about and what seemed to me to be total chaos, the men eventually sorted themselves into their small groups. The hounds were likewise divided, each pack roped together. The yap dogs' shrill barks pierced the morning air with such a din that I thought that every boar in Eure-et-Loire must surely hear them.

"Attention, s'il vous plait!" Philip Mailley cried, and even the dogs grew quiet for a moment.

I was too far away to hear every word Philip said, but from his gestures I understood that he was sending them off at intervals rather than all at once. One by one the groups formed, waved to the others, and rode off in the general direction of the deep woods. Finally only Jacques and Philip remained, with only Marc left to wave them farewell.

"Do not forget about Boxer's hoof, M'sieu Jacques," Marc called out, along with a string of other words that I could not quite understand.

"I am not worried about it," Jacques called back before the excited dogs began to make all conversation impossible. Then he

174

and Philip rode out of the stable yard to join the hunt.

I stepped down and walked over to Etoile's stall, where I patted her muzzle and fed her a bit of sugar I had saved for that purpose.

Marc had watched until the riders were out of sight before returning to the stable. Upon seeing me, his face brightened.

"You are up early, Mademoiselle," he said with a sweeping bow.

"I wanted to see the hunters on their way."

"I wish I could go with them." Marc looked toward the forest. "I am old enough."

"How old are you?"

"Fifteen, Mademoiselle. Almost sixteen."

Not much younger than Lucy. Yet in every respect, Lucy seemed years older than the d'Arc stable boy. "How old must one be to hunt boar?" I asked.

Marc shrugged in the Gallic way, arms outstretched, palms up. "It is up to M'sieu Philip. But M'sieu Jacques hunted boar at fourteen years old."

So Jacques was probably hunting the day of Lucy's accident. But surely Lucy would have shown more signs of being upset if her injuries had attended a boar hunt.

"Do you know if Mademoiselle Lucy ever

hunted?" I asked, or tried to; my words seemed to puzzle Marc.

"*Comment?*" he asked.

"Mademoiselle Lucy," I repeated. "Hunt the boar?"

Marc shook his head. "It is not possible, Mademoiselle. The boar hunt is not for women and children."

"It is dangerous?"

Marc bobbed his head so emphatically his curls bounced. "Yes, Mademoiselle. We shall probably lose several hounds."

He looked so solemn that I had to stifle a most inappropriate smile. "I hope not," I said, then bade the boy a good day and started toward the chateau. On the way I looked in the direction of the deep woods and wondered how Jacques and Philip were faring in their quest.

"Would you like to go out this afternoon?" Lucy asked me as soon as I entered her room later that morning.

"Out where?" I asked, surprised.

"To see a sight that Philip did not show you. And to get away from the hunters and their talk for a while."

"They have already left and should be gone all day, unless they happen to find the boar sooner."

"How do you know they are gone? Did you see them off?"

Lucy's tone sharpened, as if she suspected I might have deliberately done something that excluded her.

"They did not see me, but I watched them leave. All the hounds were barking and all the men were talking. Such racket will probably frighten the boar away."

Lucy drew her brows together. "If you must speak English, at least use words I can understand. What is 'such racket'?"

" 'Racket' is loud noise," I explained.

"There will be none of that on the hunt. When the dogs go into the deep forest, they never bark. The hunters are quiet as well. That is why they will all talk so loudly when they come back here."

I had been standing with my back to Lucy, opening her draperies, but now I turned to face her. "You seem to know a great deal about the boar hunt. Did you ever go on one?"

Lucy's face showed no emotion, but the emphatic shake of her head and the manner in which she quickly changed the subject told me I had touched a sensitive area.

"Will you agree to go out this afternoon, Miss Ellen?"

"Will you agree to ride in the pony cart?" I countered.

Lucy frowned briefly, opened her mouth as if to protest, but settled for an affirmative nod of her head. "But I refuse to let Marc drive us. You can handle the cart alone, *n'est ce pas?*"

"I have driven my cousin's pony cart. Yours should not be much different."

"Then it is settled."

I had expected that preparing for the impending outing would occupy Lucy's attention throughout the morning, but I was wrong. As soon as we had finished breakfast, taken on trays so as not to interfere with the table settings in the dining room, Lucy said she had an errand for me.

"Go to Madame Albert's room and ask her to come down here. I want to make sure of her measurements before I make the pattern for her winter dress."

"Do you think she is able to use the stairs?"

Lucy laughed. "Of course. She often wanders around downstairs when the Marquis is out of the house. Now that he is in Paris, she has probably been up and down every day."

"But she has not been joining us for meals," I said.

"It is not the Marquis' wish," Lucy said stiffly, and I silently translated her true meaning. It was not Lucy's wish, either. Otherwise, she would have had the old lady at our table in a trice.

"If you don't mind, I have a few letters to write," I said, stretching the truth a bit. I had no reason to write to anyone in America, having already informed Aunt Irma of my safe arrival and having received no reply in return, but I had no idea how much the old woman would remember of our last encounter, and I did not want to upset her in front of Lucy.

Besides, it would give me a good chance to search Madame Albert's room for my missing brooch. "I'll ask Sophie to bring Madame Albert to you."

Lucy shrugged. "As you wish, but before you write your letters, tell Marc to have the pony cart ready this afternoon. I think we should go around three o'clock."

I nodded. "Very well. I will find Sophie now."

The maid was on the second floor, collecting used linens from the guest rooms. She was quite willing to leave that task and promised to deliver Madame Albert to Lucy immediately.

I made a show of going back to my room,

but instead hid in the dim recesses of the hall until I saw Madame Albert actually enter Lucy's room. Then I returned to the second floor and entered Madame Albert's chamber, feeling somewhat like a thief myself. I had never felt comfortable going through anyone else's effects, and even though the situation justified it, I did not relish the task of examining Madame Albert's personal possessions.

However, I wanted the brooch back, so I began as methodical a search as was possible in the jumble of Madame Albert's room.

Taking care to replace items where I had found them, I went through every drawer and table top in the room and even checked the few dresses that hung in her clothespress. Nowhere was the brooch to be found.

It has to be in here somewhere, I told myself. I lifted upholstery cushions. I knelt and looked under the furniture, where the undisturbed dust told me nothing had been placed there recently. I even ran my hand under Madame Albert's feather mattress, feeling for a telltale touch of metal, but I found nothing.

Finally, fearful of being found in Madame's room if I stayed longer, I let myself out and walked through the front hall and out the main doors to the stable. I supposed I would have to resign myself to the loss of my mother's brooch. I had so few of her things that it was a hard loss.

Marc was putting fresh straw in the stalls being used by the hunters, but when he saw me he dropped his pitchfork and bowed. It was no easy task to explain to him exactly what I wanted him to do, since my halting words for "pony cart" did not seem to match anything in his vocabulary. But when I located the cart itself, I was able to make him understand that Lucy wanted to me to drive her somewhere in it that afternoon.

"Mademoiselle Lucy wants to go out?" he asked as if the idea strained his credulity.

"Yes."

"But I must stay here," Marc said. "The hunters —"

I interrupted and assured him I could drive the cart myself, then held up three fingers to indicate the time we would be leaving. "Bring it to the door of the family salon," I added.

"It will be done," Marc said, then added something else with too many unfamiliar words for me to comprehend.

"*Merci beaucoup,*" I said, hoping my smile would convey my thanks even if my words were inadequate. "How do you think the hunt is going?" I said as I turned to leave.

"It is too early yet to know, but you should have no fear. M'sieu Philip is a good hunter."

Without looking at him, I knew Marc was smiling, and once again I debated if I should try to correct any mistaken idea he might have about Philip and me. And once more I decided there was no harm in it. At any rate, I doubted Marc would understand everything I said, which could only make matters worse.

By the time I returned to Lucy's room, Madame Albert had left and Lucy sat at a makeshift desk, entering figures in a small notebook.

"Did you get what you needed?" I asked.

"Yes, although Madame was certainly tiresome and in a sour mood today. I am not sure I will make her a dress, after all."

"Are those her measurements?" I asked as Lucy closed her notebook.

"Yes, and others for whom I sew. Some day I might take yours," she added, her eyes averted.

"Marc will have the pony cart ready at three," I said as if I had not heard her. For

Lucy, even a vague promise that she might sew for me was a great concession, but I did not want to seem either grateful or impressed.

She nodded. "He had better."

Lucy decided to take a brief rest after luncheon, but when I came back to help her dress, I found her with something new to wear.

"Where did you get this?" I asked, holding up a split riding skirt very much like my own.

"I made it, of course. Where else would I get it?"

Although her cross words attempted to mask it, Lucy's pride in her accomplishment was quite evident.

"You don't really need a riding skirt for a pony cart," I observed.

"But I will need it when I get my horse. Come, Miss Ellen, help me into it."

"Miss Ellen?" I repeated. "You might as well call me Miss Edmonds, if you won't call me Ellen."

Lucy gave me an appraising glance out of the corner of her eye. "I cannot imagine what difference it makes what we call one another."

I smiled faintly. "The first time you said

that to me, you added I would soon be gone.
Do you still think so, Lucy?"

If I'd expected any change in her position,
I would have been disappointed.

"That remains to be seen, does it not?
Now braid my hair, and be quick about it."

I was glad the servants were all suitably
occupied as three o'clock came; it gave me
the opportunity to take Lucy outside
without having them stare at her. I told
Sophie where we were going, and she laid
aside her silver polish long enough to help
Marc and me lift Lucy into the cart, which
he had all but driven into the family salon.

I climbed into the cart and took the reins
and whip from Marc. He showed me where
the brake was located, said the pony was
named "Dapple," then left me to slap the
reins and make a somewhat jerky start to
our ride. As he had done when Philip and I
rode out, Marc went on ahead of us and
opened the village gates.

"How will we get back inside?" I asked
him as the heavy metal latch clanged shut
and I saw that it could not be opened from
the outside.

"Go to the main entrance, Mademoiselle.
The gateman will open that gate for you.
With all the hunters here, the gates must

remain closed at all times."

"Otherwise we might witness the spectacle of having the hunt move outside the walls and down the main road," Lucy said.

"You don't mean that," I said.

"It could happen. Anyway, I want to hear no more talk of the hunt."

This afternoon the sun was not quite as warm, and no village women had gathered at the wash house by the creek. However, as I drove through town and the pony's hooves struck the cobblestone and echoed off the walls, I had the distinct feeling that eyes watched us from behind almost every window.

"The villagers are a curious lot," Lucy said in English as a stout woman stopped by the side of the road and bowed as we passed.

"*Bonjour, Madame,*" we said together, returning the woman's greeting.

"Are you comfortable?" I asked. I was afraid the jolting of the cart on the rough stones might hurt Lucy, but I need not have worried.

"I would be more so if you would whip up the pony a bit. Have you never driven a pony cart before? It rides much better at a trot."

Obediently I touched the whip to the back of the plump, well-named dappled brown pony, and obligingly he broke into a trot. After an initial lurch, he settled down to a steady gait, and once we were away from the village's cobblestones, I saw it was, indeed, a much smoother ride.

"This cart is very nice," I said. "It doesn't even seem to be too small for us."

"It is not as comfortable as the big carriage, nor as interesting as riding horseback," Lucy said. "I do not intend to get into this cart ever again."

I tried to picture Lucy on horseback, galloping with the wind blowing through her honey-blond hair, and admitted that it made an appealing picture. Perhaps that was why she was so determined to ride again.

"The wheat looks about ready to be harvested," I commented as we reached the first billows blowing in the slight wind.

"How would you know?" Lucy asked.

"I lived on a farm in America. My uncle always grew wheat."

"And did you work in the fields too, Ellen?"

Trust Lucy, I thought. Naturally, she would make her first use of my given name the occasion of a rude remark. Thinking she expected me to show anger, I merely shook my head, smiling slightly as if I thought her remark was meant to be amusing.

"How much farther are we going on this road?" I asked when I was certain we had passed the point where Philip and I had returned to the village.

"You will know when we get there," Lucy said. "Keep driving."

We came to a farmhouse on the right, built with a central courtyard around which the stable and other outbuildings were arranged. A blue-smocked old man smoking a pipe waved as the pony cart passed his gate, and we both waved back.

"Slow down now," Lucy ordered a few moments later. "Keep your eyes on the road ahead."

I was about to ask her why, but just then we topped a slight rise, and the vision hovering on the horizon drove everything else from my mind. I could only stare in silent wonder at the apparition that had magically appeared before us. Seemingly set in the midst of waving wheat fields, a huge cathedral shimmered in the soft afternoon sunlight like an enchanted mirage. From my studies, I recognized its unmatched pair of spires and even fancied I could make out a round, centered stained-glass window. All alone on its vast prairie of waving wheat, the cathedral was an ethereal vision, yet it seemed tantalizingly close.

"Chartres Cathedral," I murmured after a moment. "It is so lovely!"

Lucy's voice was uncharacteristically soft. "Yes. I have missed seeing it lately."

"I thought the cathedral was in the center of the town. How then does it seem to rise from the flat wheat fields like that?"

"I suppose you could call it an optical illusion. Actually, the cathedral is situated on the highest hill in Chartres. From this viewpoint — and this alone — it appears to float over the fields, especially just before the wheat harvest."

"Thank you for sharing it with me, Lucy. It would be a pity to be so close to such a wonder and not see it."

"The Marquis will probably want to show it to you himself — if he should bring you here later, he will be angry I spoiled his surprise."

"I doubt he has any such plans," I said with some asperity.

"Jacques would never bring you here. He does not waste time on things of no material worth."

And what about Philip? I wondered, but dared not ask. We had been only a few kilometers away when Philip had turned back. *Why had he not let me see this sight?*

"You and Jacques do not seem to be much alike," I observed.

Lucy shrugged. "On the contrary, we are perhaps too much so. Anyway, this is all I have to show you. We can go back now."

"Don't you want to ride on a little while longer?" I felt certain Lucy was enjoying herself, despite her attempt to sound as if she were not.

"No. I want to get back inside before the hunters return to the chateau."

Somewhat clumsily I managed to turn the pony cart, almost bogging down in a beet field to the right in the process, and soon we were back in the village.

"How do we get to the chateau gate?" I asked.

"Straight through the village and take the right-hand fork in the road."

We passed more houses exactly like the ones at the other end of the village, then came to a division of the road. The signposts indicated that Dampierre was to the left and Brezolles and Dreux to the right.

"Philip will probably buy my horse in Dampierre," Lucy said. "I shall be glad when this boar business is over and he can start looking for it."

"Suppose the Marquis doesn't approve?"

Lucy shrugged her slight shoulders. "I

will have to go to Paris to get his approval, but it is a formality. Philip knows it too."

Does he? I wondered.

"Here we are at the chateau," Lucy said.

I stopped the pony cart in front of the tall, elaborately-worked front gates until the gatekeeper ambled out of one of the round, pink towers to open it to us.

He bowed deeply and smiled at Lucy, revealing a gap where several teeth had once been. *"Bonsoir, petite Mademoiselle,"* he said. His bow to me was perfunctory, as was my return greeting to him. I was already enjoying the sight of the Chateau d'Arc at the end of the long sweep of lawn and drive leading to it.

"The chateau looks calm and peaceful today," I said, as much to myself as to Lucy.

"It is hardly that, Ellen."

And this time, Lucy sounded quite sincere.

The hunters began to return late that afternoon. From the windows in the grand salon, I saw them ride in, not in pairs as they had gone out, but in two groups of four or five. Two of the men carried something heavy on a canvas swung between their horses, and I made out the gleam of curved tusks as they dumped their burden in the stable yard.

I didn't see Jacques or Philip, however, and when the first hunters entered the chateau, I attempted to find out what had happened to them. I could not understand their reply, but gathered nothing was amiss.

Finally, my dinner partner from the evening before came in and, after he had downed some spirits, he was able to tell me the boar had been found and killed, but something had happened to Jacques' horse, and he and Philip had fallen behind.

"Are they all right?" I asked.

"Of course, Mam'selle. They will be on directly."

I left the men to their drinking and went to the stable, where Marc and the grooms some of the men had brought with them were caring for the horses. Averting my eyes from the bloody carcass that had been the object of the hunt, I sought out Marc.

"I want to ride out to meet M'sieu Jacques and M'sieu Philip," I told him.

"But, Mademoiselle —"

"Saddle Etoile for me immediately," I ordered in my sternest voice, and somewhat reluctantly, Marc agreed.

I could not explain my actions to myself, much less to anyone else, but something compelled me to go looking for Philip.

"You had best stay out of the deep woods, Mademoiselle," Marc warned when he helped me mount.

"I will," I promised. "Anyway, it is still a long time until dark."

I rode past the place where Philip and I had seen the flock of sheep, but found no one there. I had no idea where the men were, but I figured if I rode at a right angle to the deep forest, I could intercept them as they came out.

A path of sorts led through the scattering of trees that preceded the deep woods, and I rode along it for a few minutes, pausing occasionally to listen. But only the sounds of the forest broke the stillness — the call of a bird, the rustling of leaves as a squirrel retreated before my intrusion.

At the edge of the deep forest I turned Etoile toward the north, feeling a bit foolish to find myself in the midst of the d'Arcs' boundless acreage with no clear idea of why I was there or what I would do when — or if — I found Philip and Jacques. Neither would welcome my presence, I knew; the intelligent thing would be to turn back. Yet some compulsion made me keep riding, and when I saw a clear trail leading into the deep forest, I turned into it.

I came upon a thick stand of oaks and,

while they weren't the same ones Philip and I had ridden through, I again felt something strange and unnatural might once have taken place here. Despite a sense of urgency to remove myself from the place as fast as I could, I slowed Etoile to a walk and kept an eye out for the overhanging limbs that could well knock me from my saddle.

I had just bent as low as I could to avoid such a branch when the strangest sound I'd ever heard sent a cold shiver down my back. Etoile shied, and I had all I could do to keep her still while I waited for the sound to be repeated. I looked in all directions, but saw nothing except the impenetrable layers of forest and underbrush that made up the deep forest.

The sound came again, beginning on a low note and rising gradually to a high-pitched whine, a snort ending in an almost-scream. I resisted the urge to scream back and urged Etoile to turn around. For the first time, she refused an order and stood absolutely still, even when I smacked her flank as hard as I could with my open hand.

"Come on, my pretty," I murmured in her ear as I stroked her neck. "Whatever that is won't hurt you."

I convinced neither of us, however. Seeing Etoile was unlikely to carry me back to the chateau, I slid off her back and tried to pull her around by the reins. I was thus engaged when she whinnied and reared, her forelegs barely missing my face. I let go of the reins and she wheeled and galloped away, leaving me alone in the deep forest.

I felt more annoyed than afraid as I began to retrace my path. But soon the strange sound sounded even closer, and I heard something crashing through the under-brush, coming from behind me. I wanted to turn and see what it was, but I dared not.

I began running and felt the sting on my arms and legs, repeatedly cut by under-brush. Fear proved stronger than the pain, and I kept going until a stitch in my side bent me double and I was forced to lean against the trunk of a broad oak to recover my breath. In that vulnerable position, I peered around the side of the tree and saw the bulk of a huge animal charging toward me.

My first thought was that I was having a waking nightmare — the hunters had killed the boar. But then I made myself look at the creature again and, although its eyes burned red in the twilight shadows and the earth shook with each pounding step, it had no tusks, and I realized it was not a boar.

The boar's mate, I guessed, out to revenge his death. Or perhaps just angry and confused. I did not want to wait to find out its intentions, yet I doubted I could run again.

I eased around to the side of the tree and tried to melt into it, hoping the animal had poor eyesight. It stopped and its snout probed the earth as if trying to pick up my scent. If ordinary pigs could detect buried truffles, I had no doubt this wild sow could find me with no trouble. The question was, what would happen then?

I didn't want to find out, so when the animal's head jerked up and it seemed to be looking directly at me, I took off at a run again, this time at an angle to my previous path. At first all I could hear was my labored breathing and the steady drum of the sow's feet in my pursuit. Then another sound intruded, and I heard a dog bark nearby.

The yap, I thought, and prayed the hounds would follow and do their work swiftly.

All at once the forest exploded with action as the sow squealed, several hounds loped into view and began to chase her, and the yap danced around, keeping up a furious barking. I stopped running and sank to my knees while the drama of the hunt played itself out only a few feet away.

I knew the hounds must be tired, especially if they had already taken part in one kill that day, and I wondered if Philip and Jacques would arrive in time to prevent their massacre. The sow might not be as large as the male boar, but she was no less determined to live, and the guttural shrieks she uttered as she fought the hounds made me shudder in horror.

I'd just decided I was alone in the forest when I heard a horseman approaching, not at a full gallop, but riding faster than prudence would dictate through the jumble of trees.

He was almost upon me before I could tell it was Philip, but he was looking in the direction of the fight, not at me. Swiftly he dismounted, and armed only with a broadsword, he waded into the snarling dogs.

"Enough!" he commanded, and two of the hounds obeyed and backed away from the sow. The third hound, the one Philip had called Hercule, hung on to the boar until Philip slapped him with the side of the sword. In one swift move, Philip turned the sword and thrust it deep into the sow's chest. Blood spurted out and covered Philip's jacket, but he paid it no heed as he withdrew the blade and wiped it on the animal's heaving flanks. After one spasmodic twitch, the sow lay still.

I rose from my vantage point and walked toward Philip on legs that wobbled. "Congratulations," I said.

Philip's face was a study in surprise. "Ellen? Are you all right?"

I put a hand up to my face and brushed back my hair, which had come loose from my chignon, and observed that my wrist was bleeding. As from a great distance, I watched a few drops of blood fall on my shirtwaist, and I suddenly felt dizzy. "Yes," I tried to say, but instead I moaned and pitched forward, forcing Philip to support me.

I was aware that the blood on his jacket was staining my shirtwaist, but I didn't care. It felt good to be in his arms, and for the moment, at least, I felt safe.

Philip's lips murmured against my forehead and cheeks, but he did not attempt to kiss my lips, even when I turned my face up to his in shameless invitation. With a groan Philip pulled back and looked down at me, his eyes dark.

"You could have been killed," he said roughly. "What on earth possessed you to walk into the deep forest in the midst of a boar hunt?"

"I didn't walk." I made no effort to move

away from Philip's loose embrace, even though my dizziness had passed. "The hunters said the boar had been killed."

"The male was, but we knew his mate might be nearby."

"Where is Jacques?" I asked, and immediately Philip took his arms from my body and stepped back.

"Here I am, Mam'selle," Jacques said, joining us as if on cue. He was leading his horse, which had apparently gone lame. "It seems I missed a good kill."

Philip's lips compressed to a thin line. "You can thank Miss Edmonds for that. She managed to flush the sow for the hounds."

Jacques' appraising glance took in my bloody clothing and scratches and he smirked. "A hunting bitch, indeed."

I thought he had spoken too softly for Philip to hear, but the way Philip wheeled and grabbed Jacques by the collar of his jacket made it clear he had heard only too well.

"You owe an apology to Mademoiselle Edmonds for that remark."

"What we say to one another is none of your business, Mailley!"

The men glared at one another, a silent tableau in the lengthening shadows of the deep forest, until the tension grew unbearable.

"I would like to leave now, please," I said loudly.

Both men turned to look at me as if they had forgotten I was there; then Philip released his hold on Jacques.

"Where is your horse?" Philip asked me.

"Probably back at the stable now, having a good laugh at abandoning me here." I hoped my light tone would ease the tension, but it was evident that neither man wanted to forget the enmity felt toward the other.

"Very well, then. You can sit on Thunder and I'll lead him," Philip said.

"I don't have to be led," I protested.

Jacques laughed. "All women have to be led, *cherie*."

"Not by you, however," I said.

Philip glared at me. "We waste time. We must get back."

His arms circled my waist and he lifted me up on Thunder's back. He called the hounds, took hold of his horse's bridle, and started the long walk back to the stable.

"What about that?" I asked, pointing toward the bloody corpse on the forest floor.

"It will be attended to later," Philip said.

"Yes, Mam'selle," Jacques added. "It is

as dead as it is going to be."

And so, in a rather strange procession, the last of the boar hunters made our way back to the Chateau d'Arc from the eternal twilight of the deep forest.

Chapter Eight

Jacques stayed at the stable to see to Boxer's hoof, leaving Philip to bring me back to the chateau. My bedraggled appearance occasioned some untranslatable comments among the boar hunters, and their laughter told me that was probably just as well. Lucy's reaction was predictable; she glared at Philip and me and withdrew to her room with a muttered threat to tell the marquis about my foolish escapade.

For his part, Philip turned me over to Sophie and hastened to rejoin the other hunters, and I saw him no more that night.

From my room I could hear the hunters talking loudly at dinner, then their noisy farewells as they took their leave shortly afterward.

The next morning I awoke stiff and sore, my arms bearing several angry, red marks which long sleeves and the judicious use of face powder would conceal. I was relieved Lucy chose not to quiz me about my private boar hunt, but instead ordered me to help Sophie pack enough clothes for a week in Paris.

"Is that not a rather short visit?" I asked.

"Not to me. But if we need anything else, we can always find it there."

For a price, I thought. The marquis had never mentioned giving me a salary and, until now, I hadn't been anywhere to spend it if he had. But being penniless in Paris was quite a different matter, and I resolved to speak to him about it at my first opportunity.

In a few hours all was packed, and Jacques, who had slept late, finally appeared and announced it was time to leave.

"I must return the nag of a horse I got in Dreux," Jacques said. "I will meet you at the station."

When we appeared outside with the luggage, Philip strolled over to say goodbye.

"I see you have a few souvenirs from your boar hunt to carry to Paris," he said, eyeing the scratches I had not completely concealed.

"Yes, I may be scarred for life," I said lightly, then regretted my words when Lucy overheard me.

"You must never jest about such things," she told me. Then she addressed Philip.

"Let me know when you find my horse."

"As soon as I have the Marquis' approval, I shall begin to look, but you may be back home before I can find one. It's possible all the good Dampierre horses have been sold."

"You might as well begin looking right away. The Marquis will certainly give his permission."

Philip nodded. "Perhaps, but I will wait until he does so."

"I wish the Marquis had let us have the big carriage," Lucy complained as Philip effortlessly lifted her into the estate's supply wagon, once more displaying his impressive strength.

"This will get you to the train station just as well."

I had half-expected Philip to drive us to the station, but he stood back and waved farewell as the regular teamster took the reins and we jolted away. Philip walked back toward the stable, soon lost to sight behind the screening trees along the drive.

Although blankets had been spread over hay to cushion our ride, it was far from comfortable, as Lucy frequently pointed out. When we reached the train station, I saw the old hack driver that Philip had chased away, and thought that in some ways it seemed that I had been at the Chateau d'Arc for months, rather than weeks. But in other respects, I was still — and would no doubt always be — a stranger there.

The far more comfortable train journey from Dreux to Paris passed relatively quickly. My pulse quickened when a scattering of dwellings began to thicken, and soon the train made its way through the heart of Paris to the Gare St. Lazare.

The marquis' carriage waited to take us to his townhouse, located just off the Boulevard Haussmann, and it was all I could do to keep from hanging out of the window as it proceeded leisurely through the city. This first week in June, daylight lingered a long time, and even though it was past our usual dinner time when we reached the four-story mansion in the middle of a long street lined with identical houses, sunset was still hours away. Everything seemed suffused in a soft glow and touched with pale blue or light gray in the afternoon light.

"I can see why Paris attracts so many painters," I said. My few art lessons had convinced me I lacked my mother's talent, but I understood why any real artist would want to attempt to capture the elusive quality of the city.

"Indeed, Paris attracts all sorts of scum,"

Jacques said, apparently unimpressed by the beauty around us.

"Yes, my dear brother, you certainly keep coming back here, do you not?"

I shook my head at Lucy's caustic comment and wished the change of scene might also soften their attitudes toward each other, but I knew that was highly unlikely. Then the carriage door was opened, and a servant in the d'Arc livery helped me out.

I had expected to see the marquis, but as we entered the huge foyer, only the staff greeted us. There seemed to be almost as many servants at the townhouse as we had left in the chateau, including a ladies' maid to attend Lucy in Sophie's place.

"Your rooms are ready, Mademoiselles," the housekeeper said. She was a tall, spare woman who wore rimless spectacles and carried a huge ring of keys at her waist.

"I must have the yellow room, Madame Leclerc," Lucy said.

"Of course, Mademoiselle. I did not forget."

The butler opened a wide door in the rear of the hall to reveal a small elevator, barely large enough to accommodate Lucy's chair. It was one of the few elevators I had ever encountered and the first I'd seen in a private home. I realized maintaining his townhouse must cost the marquis almost as much as running the chateau. Everything in the house, from the carpets on the floor to the paintings on the walls and designs on the ceilings, had apparently been chosen at the same time by someone whose tastes ran to the Baroque. Madeline d'Arc, perhaps. In any case, a woman had definitely made these choices.

When I reached Lucy's third-floor room, I understood why she liked it. In addition to being decorated entirely in butter-yellow silk, the room had its own balcony where she could sit in the sunshine and enjoy the view overlooking a nearby public garden.

"It all looks the same," Lucy pronounced, and I wondered how long it had been since her last visit to Paris.

Madame Leclerc bowed stiffly. "No one else has used it, *petite Mademoiselle*. Nicole will help you unpack. Let her know if you require anything further."

"Miss Ellen is my companion. She will unpack my things," Lucy said in her most regal manner.

Madame Leclerc's eyes flickered, but she merely nodded in acknowledgment of Lucy's order. "Very well. Mademoiselle Edmonds' chamber is across the hall. Dinner is at nine."

"So late!" Lucy complained when the others had withdrawn.

"That leaves time for you to rest before dinner. Perhaps that is what the Marquis had in mind."

Lucy made a rude noise. "Believe me, Ellen, he arranges his dinner hours to suit himself, not me. We always dine in the dead of the night in Paris. That is one reason I prefer the chateau."

I turned back the yellow satin coverlet, revealing lace-edged linens, and helped Lucy remove her traveling dress.

"I am a little tired," she admitted when her head touched the bolster. "Tell the Marquis I am unable to come to dinner tonight."

"We shall see," I said. "Rest while I unpack your things."

Lucy's even breathing told me she had fallen asleep by the time I had put away her clothes and set her gleaming silver comb and brush on the marble-topped cherry wood dresser.

I closed the door quietly behind me and went to my own room, which was a soft blue. Although not as light and airy as Lucy's, it was by far the loveliest chamber in which I had ever been allowed to sleep. It had no balcony, and its lone window overlooked a small rear garden and the roofs and chimney pots of the adjacent buildings, which probably made it undesirable to most of the marquis' guests.

Did Mama ever stay in this house? I knew she and her employer had met the marquis in Paris and then gone on to the Chateau d'Arc, but I doubted they had actually spent time at the marquis' townhouse.

I unpacked my things and rang the bell for Nicole to bring me a basin of water, taking off my traveling dress while I waited. When a knock sounded at the door, I merely called for her to enter.

And so it was that the Marquis d'Arc found me with my hair down around my face and clad only in my chemise. It would be hard to say which of us was more embarrassed, but the look on the marquis' face went beyond that, almost to fear. Instead of turning red, his face blanched, and he looked almost exactly like the shepherd who had crossed himself on seeing me.

I reached for my peignoir and he began to back out of the room.

"I thought you were the maid," I said.

"Please excuse me," he said at the same time.

I tied the peignoir around my waist and gestured for him to stay. "Lucy is asleep now. She asked me to tell you she did not feel like coming down to dinner."

The marquis had recovered his color, but his face still seemed haunted by something he had seen in mine. "I am not surprised at that, of course, but you may tell her that from now on I expect her to be present at all meals."

I nodded. "Lucy seems quite serious about wanting her own horse. Perhaps her manners will improve, at least until she gets her way."

The marquis smiled faintly. "The trouble is, she usually gets her way in any case." He turned as the elevator door opened and Nicole appeared with a basin of water. "I shall see you at dinner then, Ellen. Welcome to Paris."

If Nicole thought it strange that the marquis should be conversing with and addressing me so informally, she kept it to herself. I judged her to be no older than seventeen or eighteen, and I wondered if she had been hired just to serve Lucy.

"Have you been here long?" I asked.

"A few months, Mademoiselle. I am with Madame Jourdan."

"Madame Jourdan? I do not know that name."

"She will be at dinner tonight, Mademoiselle. Shall I dress your hair?"

I almost told her not to bother, then thought better of it. Few times in my life might I ever have this opportunity to be waited on, so I should take advantage of every moment.

"Yes, thank you, Nicole. What do you suggest?"

The hairstyle Nicole coaxed into my rebellious hair looked grand, I thought — too grand for my simple gowns. Not even my best lace collar could approach the elegance suggested by the piled-up curls Nicole had produced. Still, I was no more than a family servant, and to presume otherwise by overdressing would be even worse.

Promptly at nine, the butler brought the elevator to the third floor and escorted me into it. He turned a lever, and we began a somewhat jerky descent.

"I shall use the stairs from now on," I said when the elevator shuddered to a stop on the main floor.

"As you wish," he said, pointing a white-gloved hand toward the right. "The others are waiting."

For a moment I thought the butler was actually going to announce my name, but he merely bowed to the assembled diners, then stood back to allow me to make a dramatic entrance. The marquis, distinguished in black dinner clothes, rose and took my hand, leading me the rest of the way into the room.

I was dimly aware of a massive, lace-covered table, around which some half-dozen diners were seated. Except for Jacques, all were strangers.

"Ladies and gentlemen, this is Lucy's companion from America, Mademoiselle Ellen Edmonds."

Heads nodded and all eyes followed me as the marquis led me to my place and the butler pulled out my chair and placed a huge napkin in my lap.

When I was seated, the marquis named each person in turn. I nodded to a stout, middle-aged couple having some connection with managing the marquis' affairs; a doctor whose name I missed and his somewhat frumpy wife; Jacques; and, seated to my right at the opposite end of the table in the traditional hostess chair, a striking woman with a cloud of unnaturally-colored red hair.

"Madame Jourdan," the marquis said.

"So you are the American," she said in a low, throaty voice. "Please call me Mignon, my dear."

I found it hard not to stare at her as the meal proceeded at its leisurely pace. Mignon Jourdan wore a black satin dress, cut in a V shape at the neck and revealing an alarming portion of her ample bosom. Her waist was corseted to slenderness, giving her an exaggerated hourglass shape.

She is older than she tries to look, I judged. Skillfully applied cosmetics high-lighted her pale gray eyes and lent color to her cheeks, but her neck bore telltale wrinkles not even her diamond choker could conceal. She had a brilliant smile, which she turned on me several times during the course of the dinner.

"I have never been to America," she said in the pause between the removal of the fish and the serving of the veal. "Do tell me all about it."

With her question I could not possibly answer, Madame Jourdan made me feel gauche and awkward. "It is a big country," I said lamely.

Madame Jourdan took a sip of Madeira, her eyes watching me over the rim of her glass. "And what part of that big country is your home?"

"I lived in New York," I said, deliberately choosing the past tense of the verb.

"Oh, really? Such a great city, I hear. It

must be very entertaining."

"I am sure it is, Madame, but I grew up in the state of New York — on a farm."

The woman drew her brows together and shook her finger at me. "Mignon, you must call me Mignon, my dear. I want us to be friends, you see."

Why on earth would you want that? I asked myself.

From time to time, I looked over to see Jacques avidly listening to our conversation, but the marquis was talking to the doctor and did not seem to notice what transpired at the other end of his table.

"It is a pity Lucy could not join us for dinner," Mignon said over our Charlotte russe and champagne. "It has been far too long since I have seen the child."

"If you still think of Lucy as a child, it certainly has been, Mignon," Jacques said, emphasizing her name.

The glance they exchanged across the table made it clear that she and Jacques were not on friendly terms.

Her lips tightened. "To you I am still Madame Jourdan, young Sir."

Jacques curved his lips upward in the smirk I knew all too well, and he nodded. "Touché, Madame. However, that is still kinder than what some call you."

Although Jacques had spoken far too softly to be heard at the other end of the table, the marquis seemed aware something was amiss. He glared at Jacques, then pushed back his chair and stood. "Ladies, you may be excused."

Suppose we do not wish to be? I thought rebelliously, but I silently followed Madame Jourdan and the other two women into a small parlor while the men went to the drawing room for cigars and brandy.

"Now we may talk without being disturbed, eh?" Madame Jourdan said as we took our seats, but the other two ladies showed no evidence they cared to talk at all. The doctor's wife yawned discreetly, and a heavy sigh from the merchant's wife revealed a similar state of boredom.

"Only if you do the talking," the doctor's wife said. "I am much too weary to attempt to be interesting tonight."

Mignon smiled at the woman, showing dimples I had not previously noticed. "Heavens, Jeanette, you sound like an old woman. The evening is young."

"Perhaps," the merchant's wife agreed, "but I am not." She turned to the doctor's wife. "Shall we go home in my carriage? Victor can take Francis home."

"A perfect solution! We will not disturb

the men to say goodnight. Madame, do thank the Marquis for us. It was nice to meet you, Mademoiselle. Perhaps we shall see you again while you are in Paris."

"I hope so," I said politely. Although I couldn't honestly say I found anything very compelling about either woman, when they had departed and left me alone with Mignon, I wished for their company.

Who is this woman? I wondered.

"This is better, is it not?" she said, joining me on a small sofa. "Now we may talk freely. Tell me, Ellen, what are we going to do about poor Lucy?"

"I beg your pardon?" I understood the woman's words well enough, but could think of no decent reply.

Mignon leaned back and regarded me through slightly narrowed eyes. "Your French is not inadequate, although your accent leaves much to be desired. Surely you must know that Lucy needs settling."

Settling? "Is that not a matter for the Marquis to decide?"

"Arranging a young woman's life is no matter for a man. The Marquis has asked my opinion."

"What do you have in mind?"

Mignon's gesture took in the entire house. "The Marquis is not a pauper, you know. He can afford to give Lucy a fine dowry, which would attract a number of men needing capital. I believe it is time to begin to make some inquiries."

"You plan to marry Lucy off for her money?" I asked, horrified at the prospect.

Mignon looked at me as if I had lost my senses. "Well, of course, my dear. Why else would anyone want to marry the girl? I have not seen her lately, of course, but the fact that she is in that wheeled thing —"

"Lucy is too young to think about marriage, and certainly not to any man bought for her."

Mignon drew back, smiling faintly at my outrage. "Perhaps you Americans have other arrangements, but here a young girl makes her debut in society by the age of seventeen and usually marries within the year. Arranged matches are quite common. In fact, the Marquis was able to keep his land and add this house by marrying well. It is done all the time."

"Did you know the Marquise?" I asked.

Mignon frowned and shook her head. "No, she was a bit before my time, but I knew of her. She was from a *petit bourgeois* family in Orleans that had money and wanted a title. The Marquis' father had run the property into the ground with his inattention and wasteful ways, so the Rosiers' money was heaven-sent."

"What is your interest in this matter?" I asked, thinking that Mignon must arrange matches for a fee.

Mignon shrugged and shook her head. "Please do not sound so suspicious, Ellen. I merely want to help my friend."

The slight emphasis she put on the last word brought a blush to my face, as too late I realized what should have been obvious from the first. Mignon Jourdan must be the marquis' mistress. I suddenly felt a knot in my stomach that had nothing to do with what I had eaten that evening.

"That is very generous of you, Mignon, but from what he has told me, I do not think the Marquis really expects Lucy to marry."

Mignon raised her eyebrows. "Oh, really? Then what other choices does she have? Not even a convent will take in a cripple."

My hand itched to slap the false show of concern from Mignon's painted face, but I managed to restrain myself.

"I have another plan in mind," I heard myself say.

"Oh? What sort of plan, Mademoiselle?"

"I have yet to discuss it with the Marquis, so I would rather not say just yet. But believe me, Mignon, marriage is not Lucy's only hope."

"You must be one of those women who call themselves Feminists," Mignon said, as if that would explain my strange attitude.

"Hardly. But I believe a woman should do whatever she has the talent to do, even should she happen to be crippled."

Unexpectedly, Mignon leaned toward me and touched my cheek, and I pulled back as if I had been slapped.

"You really are different, *cherie*," she said. "Now I see why Jean-Paul has been singing your praises."

Ignoring Mignon's last remark, I stood. "I am very tired. If you will excuse me, I should like to retire now."

"Of course. I shall see you at breakfast."

Somehow I got out of the room and found the stairs, which were at the opposite end of the foyer from the elevator. At the second floor landing, I looked down the hallway and wondered which of the rooms belonged to the marquis.

Did he share his room with Mignon? It was absolutely none of my business, but the mere thought made me feel slightly ill.

Despite saying she would see me at breakfast, Mignon was not in the dining room when Lucy and I came down at mid-morning. I hadn't expected to see Jacques and I did not, but the marquis was sipping coffee when we entered. He came over to Lucy and kissed her cheek.

"I am sorry I was out when you arrived last evening," he told her. "I trust you slept well and are ready for the rigors of the day."

"Rigors? Just what have you planned for me this time?"

"Besides your horse, you mean?" he said, but his attempt to tease Lucy failed.

"My horse is not why you brought me here. You could have let Philip find one for me in Dampierre."

"Perhaps, but first we have to make certain it will not hurt you to commence riding again, after all these years. There is someone I want you to see, first."

Lucy's face darkened. "I knew it! Who is it this time?"

"Had you come to dinner last night, you would have met him and his wife. Victor Dubois has done a great deal of work with cases of paralysis."

"Not another quack doctor," Lucy muttered. "You know he will be just like the others, and seeing him will be another waste of time."

"Perhaps, but you need a good looking-over, anyway. And after that, if the Doctor agrees you are able, we shall ride in the *bois de Boulogne*."

Lucy looked more resigned than happy. "Very well. How soon can this doctor see me?"

I had no opportunity to speak privately with the marquis that morning, but I tucked my last warning note into my pocket in case I should have a chance to show it to him during the day. Mignon still had not come downstairs when we left around eleven o'clock. I wanted to ask the marquis about her status in his household, but could think of no tactful way to broach the subject.

Lucy allowed herself to be lifted and placed into the carriage, her wheeled chair riding as a passenger opposite her, with that seat removed. I sat beside Lucy and the marquis shared the driver's perch as we started off for Dr. Dubois' office.

"What a wide street!" I exclaimed as the carriage turned into a long boulevard.

"This is the Champs-Elysses. The Marquis does business with many of the merchants on this boulevard."

I tried not to gawk, but it was hard to pretend not to be impressed by the new sights on every block. Lucy gazed out of her window without any show of interest, expressing pleasure only when we arrived at Dr. Dubois' office and she saw that the carriage was entering a back alley where we would get out.

"The cats may look at me all they like," she said as the carriage scattered a yowling group of felines.

Several steps led to the doctor's back entrance, and after some discussion it was decided to leave Lucy's chair in the carriage and simply carry her in. The driver scooped her up easily and started up the stairs, the marquis and I following behind. Dr. Dubois stood awaiting us at the top of the stairs.

"Welcome, welcome, Marquis, Mademoiselles." Dr. Dubois rubbed his hands together as if he might have been planning a feast for us. I could see Lucy was not impressed.

"Shall I come in with you?" I asked her.

"No, Mademoiselle," Dr. Dubois said. "First I will want to see the patient alone. My nurse will assist me. Just put her in the examining room — on that table, yes."

The door closed behind them and the driver returned to the carriage, leaving the marquis and me to wait on a bench in the hallway.

"Sir, I need to speak with you about

something that has happened at the chateau," I said.

"I heard about the boar hunt, if that is what you mean. Jacques said you escaped injury, but it was foolish for you to go into the deep forest alone, especially during any sort of hunt. I hope you realize that."

"Yes, I do, and it will not happen again. But this appeared in my room, and I thought you should see it." I handed him the note. "It is the second such warning I have received. The first one came the day before you left for Paris, and I threw it away. I thought Madame Albert had written it. But now, I'm not so certain."

A small muscle twitched in the marquis' jaw as he read the note. "May I keep this?" he asked, and I nodded. "This has not made you afraid to remain at the chateau, has it?"

Once again the marquis had seemed to know my mind before I could speak it. His eyes probed my face, and even before I shook my head in denial, I felt he knew what I would say.

"No, but it's rather unsettling to know that someone has been in my room and gone through my things. I found my mother's sketches — the ones I showed you that later disappeared — in Madame Albert's room, torn in half. And my hunting

222

brooch is still missing."

The marquis sighed. "I am sorry about the pictures, but as for the brooch —" He reached into the pocket of his morning coat and withdrew a metal object. "Is this it?"

My mouth opened in surprise as he handed me the brooch. "Where did you find it?"

"It was in the carriage. Perhaps you lost it there?"

I shook my head. "I wore it my first night at the chateau. Jacques noticed it then. He asked me to wear it to dinner the night the boar hunters arrived, and that is when I missed it. The carriage was in Paris at that time."

"The brooch belonged to your mother," he said, making it a statement.

"Yes, but how do you know that?"

"I remembered it. As for the notes — I suspect Jacques had a hand in them. He has a twisted sense of humor, I admit. He enjoys playing games with people, but he means no harm."

Did he mean no harm when he attacked me? Somehow, I knew it would be a mistake to tell the marquis what I thought of Jacques. It was possible he might think I had encouraged Jacques' advances by my own behavior.

No, I would keep quiet for the time being. If Jacques bothered me again, the marquis would have to know about it. But, in the meantime, perhaps the threat to tell him would suffice to keep Jacques at a safe distance.

"I do not find it very amusing," I said instead.

He nodded. "Please let me know if any other such incidents occur."

"I will. And there's another matter," I began, but the marquis held up his hand.

"I should have given you some money before now," he said, once more eerily anticipating my thoughts. "Certainly you deserve a salary. This will be a start."

He reached into the breast pocket of his coat and pulled out a thick wad of franc notes, held together with a gold clip. Its design was the twin of the brooch I still held in my hand, and I put mine beside it.

"Yes, they are alike," he said. He handed me a modest stack of franc notes, then replaced the rest of the bills.

"You gave my mother this brooch," I guessed. *Why had she never told me?*

The marquis shrugged. "That was a long time ago — I had forgotten."

At that moment Dr. Dubois came out into the corridor where we waited, closing the door behind him. We both stood, eager for his verdict.

"As far as the matter we discussed earlier is concerned, you should have no fear, Jean-Paul. Lucy has a strong constitution and I suspect she will outlive us all many times over. I want to make further tests, but in the meantime, I see no reason for her not to ride if the proper precautions are taken."

"And what might those be?" the marquis asked.

"She must never ride alone, of course, or gallop or jump. But otherwise, I believe Mademoiselle Lucy can sit a horse quite well."

"Thank you, Victor. I know she will be delighted to hear it."

Dr. Dubois smiled ruefully. "On the contrary, Jean-Paul. It was she who told me that. The girl knows her own mind."

"This is welcome news, indeed," the marquis said. "You may find the driver, Ellen, and tell him we are ready to leave."

As I left, Dr. Dubois lowered his voice and spoke to the marquis. "Did you use the medicine I gave you last night?"

"Not yet. The pain is somewhat better," the marquis said; then his words faded as I started down the stairs.

As I went in search of the driver, my mind was not entirely on Lucy's problems. My brief conversation with the marquis had let me know he would probably be of little or no help to me when I returned to the Chateau d'Arc.

He is a sick man, I thought, and the knowledge chilled me. Without the marquis, my life would be far different.

I found it ironic that even as Lucy seemed to be showing some improvement, her father's worries might just be worsening.

Chapter Nine

I had presumed that renting a few horses for a short ride would be fairly simple, but I was mistaken. When Lucy and I came back downstairs after changing into our riding skirts, Madame Jourdan was waiting in the hall. She wore a russet morning gown that almost matched her hennaed hair.

"How lovely that we can have this little outing," she said.

"You are not dressed to ride, Madame," Lucy said, and, from the way the two eyed one another, I perceived there was no love lost between them.

"I shall stay in the carriage, of course, but one must see and be seen, Mademoiselle." Mignon turned to me with a conspiratorial wink. "More than one match has been made on the bridle path."

"I am interested in riding, not in making a match, Madame." Lucy's tone was even frostier than usual.

Mignon smiled engagingly. "Ah, but you should be, *cherie*. I had no idea you had

227

grown to be so lovely. A fresh, pretty face like yours could be the sensation of the Paris season."

Lucy flushed angrily. "Especially when the quadrille is called. No doubt all the men will fight to see who will push my chair."

The marquis entered the hall in time to hear Lucy's last remark and he frowned reprovingly. "There is no need to use that tone of voice, Lucy. Madame Jourdan will think you lack manners."

"In that, at least, she will be correct," Lucy said.

"It is all right, Jean-Paul." Mignon took the marquis' arm with a placating smile. "We just need to become reacquainted. It has been too long since I have seen dear Lucy."

"But not long enough to suit me," Lucy muttered, too low for them to hear.

"Shall we leave, then?" the marquis said. "The carriage is waiting."

"Is Jacques going with us?" I asked, hoping that he was not.

"As usual, he has other plans for the day," the marquis said. "It is just as well — there would not be room enough for us all."

"I wish she had other plans too," Lucy murmured as I held her chair while the driver lifted her from it.

So do I. Watching the marquis help Mignon into the carriage, as if she were a piece of fine porcelain which might break in his hands, I felt a surge of anger that such a woman could manipulate him.

When it comes to women, all men become fools. I had heard the saying and dismissed it as folklore. But now, seeing the marquis with Mignon, I was beginning to believe it might be true.

"What a beautiful place!" I exclaimed when the d'Arc carriage entered the *bois de Bologne.* I thought if the chateau's forest land had bridle trails and a wide boulevard through it, interspersed with smart shops and restaurants, it would look very much like the bois de Boulogne.

"Longchamps is over there," Mignon said, waving toward an area that seemed to be attracting a large number of elegant carriages.

"This is not racing season," the marquis said.

"No, but there are daily sales. Surely you remember when we bought Caliph?"

We. I didn't know how long the marquis had owned his horse, but I gathered it had been at least a few years. Mignon had apparently been in the marquis' life for some time, then.

The carriage stopped at the livery stable, but no one made a move to get out.

"Are we here to talk or to ride?" Lucy asked.

"To ride, of course, unless you have changed your mind," the marquis said.

"I would not be here if I had," she said shortly.

"Well, I do not propose to sit here and smell the stable while you are gone," Mignon declared. She held a lace handkerchief to her nose and looked up at the marquis, rapidly blinking her eyes.

"Is something in your eye, Madame?" Lucy asked, her voice sweetly solicitous.

Mignon glanced at Lucy as if she could throttle her, and I had to look away to keep from laughing out loud.

"How lovely of you to be concerned, *ma petite*. It feels better already." Mignon managed to direct a forced smile to Lucy.

"I will see to the horses," the marquis said. He seemed relieved to have an excuse to leave three bickering females.

"Perhaps I should go with him," I said, and moved as if to follow.

"No!" Lucy dug her fingernails into my arm with surprising strength. "He can certainly attend to it by himself."

"The Marquis is so pleased you are here,

my dear," Mignon told Lucy. "And of course, so am I. We must make sure you make the most of your visit."

"And just what does that mean?"

Mignon's generous mouth curved in a warm smile. "That would be telling, would it not? But plans are being made, my dear. I think you will be pleased."

"Who is making these plans for Lucy, you or the Marquis?" I asked.

Mignon looked pained. "Why, all of us, of course, including you, Mademoiselle. Lucy, has Ellen told you what she has in mind for your future?"

Lucy looked at me as if I had slapped her in the face, and I wanted with all my heart to thrust my fingers into Mignon's elaborately dressed red hair and pull it out by its dark roots.

"No, she has not," Lucy said.

"Our plans are of no concern to you, Mignon," I said, struggling to sound halfway civil.

"I think you will find otherwise," she said coolly.

"We have found some good mounts," the marquis said, arriving back at the carriage with the driver.

"Surely you do not intend to ride with them, Jean-Paul," Mignon protested.

"This is an important occasion and I must make certain it goes well. The driver can take you over to the sale if you like. We shall not ride long, in any case."

Mignon nodded. "Very well, then. It might be amusing to see who has come out to buy today."

"Be thankful Mignon does not ride," Lucy muttered to me as the driver and I helped her from the carriage. The marquis had found a docile, black gelding who seemed quite disinterested as Lucy was placed on his back.

I watched closely and saw Lucy's face pale, then gradually recover color as she grasped the reins and stretched her legs and eased her feet into the stirrups. If she had any fear at all, she did a good job of suppressing it. In fact, Lucy looked happier than I had ever seen her as we slowly rode out of the stable yard and into the *bois de Boulogne.*

"Are you all right?" the marquis inquired anxiously.

"Of course I am! A two-year old could ride this nag," Lucy said crossly, and the marquis and I exchanged relieved glances.

Assured that Lucy didn't need my attention, I studied some of the other riders along the path. Both men and women were stylishly dressed, the men in English-style jodhpurs, the women in voluminous riding skirts. Only a few of the women wore split skirts, but no one we met seemed to heed what Lucy and I wore or, in fact, to notice us at all.

"Good day, Sir, Mademoiselles," a young man called out as we passed him on the path. His glance lingered on Lucy and brought fleeting color to her cheeks.

"Who was that man?" she asked the marquis.

"I have no idea, but he seemed to want to know you. Many such men ride in the *bois de Boulogne* — that is why you must be escorted at all times."

"Does that mean the bridle paths aren't safe?" I asked.

"Not entirely. Two ladies riding together would not likely be bothered, but riding alone is considered to be an invitation for male companionship."

"That is when I would use my whip," Lucy said.

"Knowing you, you probably would," the marquis said glumly, and I laughed with Lucy.

We had been going along at a sedate walk for some time when, without warning, Lucy slapped the reins against her horse's withers, encouraging it to trot.

The marquis and I both called out a warning at the same time, but we were too late. Lucy hung on, jouncing along in disarray for a few yards. Then she managed to push her knees against the saddle with enough force to post to the trot. We caught up with her; each aware we'd have been powerless to help her if she had fallen.

"You will not do that again, young lady!" the marquis said with as much harshness as I had ever heard him use.

"No, Sir," Lucy replied solemnly. "Next time, I shall be far more graceful."

We had just returned the horses and were waiting for the marquis to come back with the carriage when I saw a couple alighting from a cabriolet. The man turned slightly, and I realized it was Jacques.

"I see the other plans that Jacques had for the day," I said.

Lucy and I watched her brother circle the lady's waist and set her on the ground.

"That must be Mathilde Lambert," Lucy said.

All I could tell from a distance was she seemed to be a bit taller than Jacques. She was stylishly attired, but her large hat concealed most of her features.

"Is Jacques courting her?" I asked.

"Comment?" Lucy asked.

"Are they a couple?"

Lucy shook her head. "I have no idea, but I hope so. I hear her father is rich. I wish Jacques would find someone with money to marry and leave us in peace."

"Madame Jourdan said something to me last night about making matches. Do you suppose she might arrange one for Jacques?"

Lucy's laugh was bitter. "The only marriage Mignon is really trying to arrange is her own to the Marquis. Jacques would never allow her to speak on his behalf."

I wasn't surprised by Lucy's evaluation of Mignon, but I thought the woman had more power than Lucy credited her with. "Has the Marquis known her for a long time?"

"Long enough. Thank heaven she hates the country. She came to the chateau once, and that was quite enough for all of us."

There was another question I had to ask, disagreeable though the answer might be. "Does Mignon always stay in the town-house?"

The closed look I hadn't recently seen returned to Lucy's face, shutting me out. "You must ask her that. I refuse to speculate about her living arrangements."

235

Immediately I realized I had asked a tactless question and tried to steer the conversation toward a safer channel. "She said arranged matches are common. Is that true?"

"I would not believe everything that woman says, but yes, some people make their living by matchmaking."

"How would you feel about taking part in such a marriage?" I asked, already suspecting I knew what her answer would be.

Lucy's eyes widened in horror. "I would kill myself first."

I nodded. "That's what I thought."

"Are you trying to tell me that Madame Jourdan has the notion she can marry me off?" Lucy asked, sitting up straight and narrowing her eyes.

"She mentioned something about it last night, but I am sure she did not mean it," I said, now sorry I had told Lucy.

"Oh, she meant it, all right! Madame Jourdan would love to be rid of both Jacques and me. I think the Marquis uses us as an excuse to keep from marrying her."

"You don't know that for a fact," I said. I was now quite alarmed at the hornet's nest I had stirred. Lucy could create considerable havoc when she wanted to, and I'd never seen her more agitated.

"I know more than they suspect I do," she said, "and I shall certainly tell them what I think of their matchmaking!"

I looked up to see the d'Arc carriage returning and knew I didn't have much time to persuade Lucy to remain silent. "That would not be wise," I said quickly, and she looked at me questioningly. "You would be making a mistake to confront Mignon and the Marquis while they are together. Say nothing until I can speak to the Marquis about the matter."

"You think your words have more influence than mine?" she asked disdainfully.

"About this, perhaps. I can lay a plan for your future before him, one that doesn't include an arranged marriage."

Lucy looked unconvinced. "And do you actually have such a plan, Ellen?"

I smiled and shook my head. "Not yet. But by the time I speak with the Marquis, I will."

"You will ruin me yet," Lucy said glumly.

The marquis and the driver were almost upon us, while from the carriage Mignon waved and smiled. I waved back. "Better me than Mignon, *n'est ce pas?*"

Lucy sighed. "That remains to be seen, I suppose."

And so it does, I thought. But almost any

future for Lucy would be better than being bartered by her own father. Surely the marquis could see that — unless Mignon had blinded him to his daughter's needs.

By the time we reached the townhouse, Lucy had managed to extract a promise from her father to write Philip immediately and authorize him to search for a horse.

"A mare or a gelding will do, as long as it is both gentle and spirited," she said.

"And where is he supposed to find a combination like that?" The marquis tried to sound cross, but I could tell her enthusiasm pleased him.

"Anywhere he can, and the sooner the better. In the meanwhile, I intend to ride in the *bois de Boulogne* every day."

Despite her show of energy, Lucy retired to bed as soon as we got back to the townhouse. The marquis, Mignon, and I gathered in the salon for tea, but Mignon soon asked to be excused, pleading a headache.

"Do forgive me, Jean-Paul, but I simply must apply a poultice before the pain gets worse. You know how horrible a headache can be, I am sure," she added in an aside to me. "I shall hope to see you both at dinner — if I recover by then."

The marquis stood and I nodded and

murmured something polite as Mignon left the room. A moment later the elevator door clanged shut and cables banged as it rose to the second floor.

"You do not care much for Madame Jourdan, do you?" the marquis asked, breaking the silence her departure had left behind.

"What makes you say that?"

"The evidence of your eyes, for one thing. I noticed the way you and Lucy both avoid looking directly at her. Mignon warned me you might resent her, and as usual she seems to be correct."

"As usual? Has Madame Jourdan been with you a long time, Marquis?"

His face reddened and his voice was chilly as he replied. "Your directness can be quite unsettling, Ellen. Mignon is not 'with me' in the sense you mean, although if she were, it would not be a matter of consequence to you. She is useful when I require a hostess, however."

I relaxed slightly. If she and the marquis were not romantically involved, I stood a much better chance to defeat her schemes for Lucy. But I knew I must be careful; the marquis obviously valued this woman's opinion.

"You are right, Sir. I should not have

spoken as I did. But she said something last night about Lucy's future that disturbed me a great deal, and I wondered what you thought about it."

"I cannot tell you that until I know what you are talking about," he said, the edge of annoyance still in his voice. "As I recall, we discussed Lucy's future not long after you came to the chateau."

"Yes, and at that time you were afraid someone might try to put her away. Now, Madame Jourdan seems to think you are ready to settle a dowry on Lucy if she marries."

The marquis looked surprised. "She told you that? We did discuss it, but I told Mignon I doubted Lucy would ever find a man who could please her."

"Then you would not force Lucy into marriage against her will?"

The marquis looked uncomfortable. "Of course not, but I do have to consider her future. What sort of life would she have, confined to the chateau and never seeing anyone? If someone came along who could take care of Lucy, it would be in her best interests to marry him."

"Even if they felt no love for one another?"

The marquis stood and began pacing

back and forth in front of the tea table; his hands plunged into his pockets. "Love is probably the poorest of all reasons for two people to marry, Ellen. Those who are swept up in it find they have nothing left when it dies. As a reason for marriage, love is greatly overrated."

"Do you speak from experience, then?" I dared to ask.

The marquis sighed and resumed his seat opposite me. "My wife brought a large dowry with her. In fact, it saved the Chateau d'Arc from total financial ruin. But —"

His voice caught, and the pain in his eyes made me long to put my arms around him and comfort him. I moved toward him slightly, and immediately he rose and shook his head as if to clear his thoughts. "That was a long time ago, and things are different now. A suitable marriage would solve the problem of Lucy's future."

"Not according to her. What about some kind of an alternative plan?"

"Is there one? Find it and we shall see. In the meantime, I hope you and Lucy will both try to be civil to Mignon. She means well."

That's what you said about Jacques, I thought, but he was another matter altogether.

I nodded and excused myself to dress for dinner. I was not unhappy with the way the interview had gone. Perhaps I had yet to win any battles, but I thought the first skirmish had gone fairly well.

After missing dinner the night before, Mignon seemed bright and cheerful at breakfast.

"Today Lucy and I shall visit the House of Worth," she announced, biting into a hard roll. "Being poorly dressed at the Chateau d'Arc might be acceptable, but in Paris it is practically a scandal. Lucy must have a more suitable riding suit, at least."

I didn't have to ask about the House of Worth. I knew it was the most exclusive fashion house in Paris, where a woman might spend thousands of francs for a single ensemble. I glanced at Lucy, who was calmly sipping her chocolate.

Mignon is clever, no doubt about it. Had she proposed any other kind of clothing for Lucy, Mignon might have been quite coldly received. But Lucy must have noticed what the other riders in the *bois* had been wearing, and that, coupled with her interest in design, would make her eager to see the fashion house even if the devil himself led the tour.

"There are many other, more reasonable shops," the marquis began, but Mignon wouldn't let him continue.

"Reasonable, indeed! There must be a thousand dressmakers plying their trade in Paris — and some of them very good, indeed. That new place on the Champs-Elysses is even selling gowns already made, if you can imagine such an abomination. If one wants merely to cover the body, they will undoubtedly suffice. But when one wants fashion — well, the House of Worth and Madame Paquin are the only designers in Paris worth a sou."

The marquis smiled faintly and threw up his hands in mock surrender. "Very well, Mignon, but Ellen should also have a riding dress, since she will be accompanying Lucy."

"She should have a dinner gown too," Lucy said. "You saw those hideous things she has been wearing. They are the best she has."

"Lucy!" I exclaimed, horrified at the all-too-accurate picture she had painted of my wardrobe. Turning to the marquis, I mumbled an apology. "Pay her no heed, Sir. In any case, I cannot accept a gown from the House of Worth."

"Then I shall make you one," Lucy announced. "While we are out today, we can look for suitable material."

"Good, then that is settled," Mignon said quickly, as if she feared the marquis would overrule us and insist I must have a Worth gown too.

The marquis frowned. "It is not fitting for Lucy to sew for her companion. I am certain Ellen can find something suitable while she is here and spare Lucy the trouble."

Lucy's chin squared. "It is no trouble. You know I like to sew, and it helps pass the time."

"We will discuss this later," the marquis said. "In the meantime, do not overtire yourself. You are not accustomed to going about so much. I fear you may become ill."

"And what about you, Marquis?" Lucy asked. "I notice you seem to be looking very tired these days, yourself. Worry about your own condition, and I shall take care of myself."

Although those who had not been around Lucy as long as I had might think she was being insensitive, I knew better. In her own way, she was concerned about him, and I realized she was right. The marquis had apparently acquired some new clothes that fit well, but still failed to disguise his weight loss. His pallor remained, enhanced by smudges under his eyes that perhaps bespoke of recent sleepless nights.

"Doctor Dubois takes good care of him, never fear," Mignon said, placing her hand on his for a moment in a gesture of intimacy that turned my stomach.

Why do I dislike this woman so much? I asked myself, but I had no good answer.

"And so do you, my dear," the marquis replied.

Lucy's convenient coughing fit gave me the opportunity to escape with her into the hall.

"I hate that woman," Lucy said when we were out of earshot.

"She means well." Lamely I echoed the marquis, but Lucy would hear none of it.

"She means herself well. I would not turn my back on her."

The House of Worth was located at *number 7 rue de la Paix,* on the left side of the street between the *place Vendome* and the *Opera,* in what appeared to be a private home. Only a small brass plate on the door identified it. The street was virtually empty as the driver carried Lucy inside, nor did we see anyone except a doorman as we entered. We were ushered into a salon furnished with

245

expensive-looking antiques from the Empire period, and I thought it quite likely the huge paintings on the walls were even more valuable.

"Monsieur Worth seems to have done rather well for himself," Lucy observed.

"He had help at the start from the Empress Eugenie," Mignon said. "When he came over from England, he sought her patronage. She was so pleased with his work that she sponsored him, and from that time on, he has dressed the cream of Parisian society."

"I have heard he is a terrible snob," Lucy said, and I wondered where she had gotten her information.

Mignon chuckled, a rich, earthy sound suggesting the laugh of a peasant woman. "He once said the bourgeois were made to take his orders. They love to be bullied by him, and even to pay dearly for the privilege."

"Good morning, ladies. How may we serve you today?"

A gnome-like woman dressed entirely in black stood in the doorway, and I wondered how much of our conversation she had overheard. Mignon didn't seem to be embarrassed, however. She rose and took the woman's hand as if they were the oldest and best of friends.

"Ah, Madame Rachel. How fortunate you are here today. May I present Lucy, daughter of Jean-Paul, Marquis d'Arc? The young lady is in need of a riding dress."

Madame Rachel's black-eyed gaze swept over Lucy's frame, then she glanced at me questioningly. "And you, Mademoiselle?"

"This is Ellen," Mignon began, then broke off, and I realized she had forgotten my last name.

"Mademoiselle Ellen Edmonds, from America," Lucy put in quickly. "She does not require your services."

Madame Rachel nodded. "I shall have Mademoiselle Barbara attend to you today. In the meantime, will you take some refreshment?"

Even as she spoke, a butler entered the room, carrying a huge, oval tray on which a silver tea service gleamed.

"Thank you, Madame," Mignon said, her tone considerably cooler. We remained silent as the butler set the tray on a table and poured each of us a cup of tea, but, as soon as he left, Mignon spoke again. "Mademoiselle Barbara is probably barely past being an apprentice. I should prefer for Madame Rachel to fit Lucy herself."

"It really is of no matter to me," Lucy

said. "Ellen, I brought my sketchbook. Perhaps you can look at some of the gowns while we are waiting — you might find one you like. Then we shall get the cloth to make it. The material depends on the design, you know."

I took Lucy's book and moved closer to the window, where lace curtains let in some light in the otherwise gloomy room. I'd seen many of the sketches before, including the one she had originally ascribed "for Ellen." The design was still there, but the words had been scratched through. At any rate, that gown was far too elaborate for everyday use, as were most of her designs.

"These are lovely, but they all have such low necklines," I said. "I have never worn such dresses."

Once more Mignon laughed. "*Cherie,* you are in Paris now, not out in the woods. Fashionable women are expected to show a little more décolletage."

"I have no need to be fashionable," I began to protest, but the entrance of Madame Barbara and her entourage stopped me.

I watched in fascination as one young woman measured Lucy, as she remained seated, while another offered a bundle of fabric swatches. Mademoiselle Barbara, who appeared to be little older than Lucy, handed her a booklet of riding dress designs.

"These are some of our recent models, Mademoiselle. Please look at them and find something you like."

Mademoiselle Barbara and her assistants left us, and I looked over Lucy's shoulder while she turned the pages.

"Your designs are better than these," I told her.

"And that material!" Lucy regarded the offending fabric samples with disdain.

Mignon took the swatches from Lucy. "These are expensive goods," she said stiffly. "I cannot believe that a mere child presumes to know more than a couturier of the House of Worth."

Lucy's cheeks flamed. "I am not a child, Madame, and I know good quality when I see it. If I have been given the best the House of Worth has to offer, then it certainly does not live up to its reputation."

Mignon's annoyance was evident. "Then perhaps we ought to leave before you shame us all."

"Is something the matter, Madame?" The girl who had taken Lucy's measurements rejoined us and looked from Mignon to Lucy in alarm.

"I want to see the best material you have," Lucy said calmly. "And if this is it, then I must bid you *adieu,* and the House of Worth will not have my custom."

Mignon groaned, and after a moment of shocked silence, the Worth employee blanched and curtsied. "Yes, Mademoiselle, right away."

She fled, only to return almost immediately with a small army of workers.

For the next few moments, the drawing room in which we sat became the center of a great deal of activity, culminating in the appearance of Charles Frederick Worth himself. He was a large man in his mid-fifties, with a high brow, penetrating dark eyes, and a flowing mustache. He wore a navy blue velvet smoking jacket, and his ivory silk cravat was tied in a huge bow.

Mignon gasped when she saw him. I was surprised she did not cross herself, so reverential was her gaze. From the reaction of the staff, I knew Worth must rarely condescend to visit inconsequential customers. Lucy also realized who he was, but didn't appear to be the least bit intimidated.

He addressed Lucy directly. "I understand there is some problem, Mademoiselle?"

"I am afraid so, Monsieur Worth. I am

disappointed to be offered such inferior materials and indifferent designs. I can do better work myself."

"Then perhaps you should, Mademoiselle."

"Wait, Sir," I said in English as he turned to leave.

"And who are you?"

"I am Mademoiselle d'Arc's companion. She really is a talented *artiste,* Sir. She knows a great deal about designing and making garments."

He did not look impressed. "The House of Worth has the world's greatest designers, Mademoiselle. Go out to the opera and the *bois de Boulogne* and you will see many ladies of quality wearing my suits. Examine the rich, dark fabrics I use, the white collars, and the silk linings with not one stitch visible. I give my ladies what they should have, not what they think they want. That is why the House of Worth is the best."

"Nevertheless, what I was shown today is not your best," Lucy said in English.

Worth made no effort to mask his irritation. "Oh? And what does Mademoiselle think she should have had from us?"

"Something like this, perhaps." Lucy opened her sketchbook and held it out to him.

"Where did you get this? Is it a Paquin design?"

"No, M'sieu. After riding in the *bois de Boulogne* yesterday, I sketched this design for a riding dress. With my sewing-machine, I could make it in a few days' time, including the handwork on the bodice, and no one would know it did not come from a couturier."

Worth looked at the sketch again, then examined the other pages, giving them his full attention. When he returned the book to Lucy with a slight bow, there was a new note of respect in his voice.

"You have talent, Mademoiselle, but you also have much to learn. And the first lesson is that you must never insult anyone who is able to teach you."

Lucy's face reddened and I held my breath in expectation of some sort of outburst. Instead, she inclined her head briefly in acknowledgment. "I shall remember that, M'sieu."

Worth turned to his nearest assistant and barked out a series of orders that sent them scurrying to do his bidding, and I gathered they were also being scolded. When he had finished, he turned back to Lucy.

"You may design your own riding-dress if you like, Mademoiselle. If it can be made from your design, Madame Rachel will select the material and have it ready to be fitted in one week. The cost, however, will be the same."

He named a figure even higher than I had expected, then turned on his heel and left, his staff scampering after him like puppies.

Mignon was the first to find her voice. "Well! I never saw such a display of temper in my life," she said to Lucy. "Your behavior will not please the Marquis."

"Why does he have to know about it?" I asked. "And as far as displaying temper is concerned, M'sieu Worth did that fairly well himself."

Mignon sighed heavily. "That is true, but Lucy certainly provoked him to it. It is a wonder he even consented to make the costume at all."

"I am glad he did," Lucy said. "It will allow me to see how their finishing details are applied."

"Well and good, but if there are any consequences to this little incident, I wash my hands of the whole matter."

"I certainly hope there are consequences," Lucy said brightly. "The House of Worth richly deserves them."

Chapter Ten

I expected Mignon to tell the marquis about Lucy's encounter with Monsieur Worth, but she apparently decided it would be in her best interest to say nothing. She allowed Lucy to purchase far more expensive material for my gown and riding dress than I would ever have chosen for myself and seemed resigned that it would be made, with or without her approval. As soon as we returned from our errands, Lucy and Mignon went to their rooms to rest, but I didn't feel tired.

Thinking Jacques and the marquis had gone out, I brought my needlework downstairs and had just settled myself in a chair by a window in the salon when I heard their voices in the hall. Apparently they were standing just inside the drawing room, unaware of my presence.

"I will not stand for it, do you hear?"

There was no mistaking the anger in the marquis' question and Jacques' reply.

"Stand for what, Sir? What crimes am I supposed to have committed?"

"You know better than anyone what you might have done, Jacques. It would not be the first time your antics have frightened people away. But I will not have Ellen treated that way."

Jacques' voice was filled with scorn. "Oh, so it is Ellen now, is it? Getting to know her rather well, are you?"

"Hold your tongue, Jacques! I will not allow you to change the subject. Apparently you have been up to your usual mischief. Now that you have been found out, what do you have to say for yourself?"

"I have no idea what you mean. I cannot be blamed for what your sweet Ellen might imagine."

I half-rose, ready to burst in on them and add my own accusations to those of the marquis. Then I realized how tenuous my position would be if I should do so, and reluctantly I stayed where I was.

"You know quite well what I mean. Let me put it to you as clearly as I can. You will not do anything — and I mean *anything* — to cause Ellen, or anyone else, to feel afraid. You are not to go into her room or take any of her things. Is that clear enough?"

There was a short silence, and for a moment I thought they had parted ways without saying anything further. But then Jacques laughed, a sound that set my hair on end.

"Mademoiselle Ellen has all but invited me into her bed more than once. If she keeps on such pursuit, you cannot blame me if I allow myself to be caught."

Liar! I wanted to scream out the word, and I stood. I had taken a few steps toward the hall when I realized how awkward it would be if I came forward then, having eavesdropped on the rest of their conversation, and once more I stopped.

Following another pause, the marquis spoke slowly, his tone now more sorrowful than angry. "The truth is not in you, Jacques."

"How can you say that? What do you really know about that American, anyway?"

"I know you, Jacques, and that is more than enough. Now get out of my sight while you still can. And remember, I shall be watching you very closely. If you lay a hand on that girl, you will answer to me."

I heard footsteps as someone left hurriedly — Jacques, I assumed. I held my breath and prayed the marquis would not come into the salon and discover me.

Then I heard the elevator door open, and a female voice called to the marquis.

"Jean-Paul, there you are! Do come upstairs and rest a bit. You look perfectly ghastly."

"I am quite all right," he replied, but apparently he joined her without any further protest, for the elevator cables clanged again, then all was silent.

I gathered my needlework, tiptoed up the two flights of stairs to my room, and closed and locked the door behind me.

I must remember to ask the marquis to put a lock on my door at the Chateau d'Arc, I thought.

However, I feared it might take more than a locked door to discourage Jacques.

The days melted into a week, and Lucy became increasingly impatient when we heard nothing from Philip. I, too, wondered if he had found her a horse, as the marquis had requested, and I hoped all was well with him and the Chateau d'Arc.

"You must write Philip again and remind him I am waiting," Lucy said, but the marquis brushed aside her concern.

"Finding the right horse can take a while, and besides, Mailley has an estate to run, you know. In the meantime, you have the use of a perfectly good mount."

"Too good," Lucy muttered under her

breath. "That nag could be dead for two days and no one would even notice."

So safe did the marquis think Lucy's rented horse that after the first few days he stopped riding with us and sent the carriage driver in his place. One afternoon Jacques arrived with Mathilde Lambert at the same time we did and was forced to introduce us to her. Seen up close, the girl was rather plain and had very little to say.

Jacques must want money terribly badly, I thought.

"Do you live in Paris, Mademoiselle Lambert?" I asked. My question caused her to blush and, when she replied, I noted a slight speech defect made her difficult to understand. "No. My home is in Compernay. I have been living in Paris with my Aunt Henriette for about a year."

"You must miss the country a great deal," Lucy said. "Perhaps Jacques will bring you to visit our chateau soon."

Jacques pulled at his cravat and tapped his palm with his riding whip. From the way he glared at Lucy, I knew he'd like to strike her with it.

"I know nothing about the Beauce region. My family lives in vineyard country."

Lucy's eyebrows raised. "Really? What wine do they produce?"

Mathilde's tone was apologetic. "We grow grapes for a *vin ordinaire* which is bottled under several labels, Mam'selle d'Arc. But the last few years have been quite difficult. My father lost most of his old vines to phylloxera."

"Phylloxera?" I repeated.

"It is a plant disease that destroys vineyards. Have you not heard of it?"

"We do not grow much wine in New York," I said. I hadn't intended my statement to be humorous, but Jacques laughed.

"No one grows wine, Mademoiselle Edmonds. Grapes are grown to make wine. And perhaps you did not grow them on your farm, but Americans do grow grapes."

Mathilde nodded and smiled at Jacques, as if he had just said something profound.

Poor child, I thought, even though she was scarcely younger than I. She seemed to hang on Jacques' every word.

"My father says the phylloxera came from infected American grapes."

Lucy glanced at me, then back to Mathilde. "All sorts of things seem to be coming from America these days. However, I assume your father is still in business, no?" Lucy's questions again brought fleeting color to Mathilde's cheeks.

I shot Lucy a warning look, which she ignored. Jacques didn't look at Lucy at all but flashed his most charming smile on Mathilde, who obligingly blushed again.

"You must excuse my sister's manners," he said smoothly. "When you visit the Chateau d'Arc, you will see she can be quite agreeable."

"Oh, really? And just when may we expect the pleasure of your company, Mademoiselle Lambert?" Lucy asked sweetly.

"That has not yet been decided," Jacques answered for her. "And now we must take our leave of you, ladies. Do enjoy your ride."

"He is such a scoundrel," Lucy said when Jacques and Mathilde had ridden out of earshot. "If I did not want him out of the house so badly, I would tell her so."

"Is she really an heiress? It sounds as if her family has been going through a bad time."

"All the wine growers have, but there was enough money to send her to Paris for the season last year. Her father probably told the girl not to come back until she had snared a husband."

"How terrible!"

Lucy cast me a sidewise glance. "You think she should not try to find a husband?"

"I do not know the customs in your country, Lucy, but in America, women who

260

seek out men are not considered to be . . ." I paused, seeking the right word.

"Genteel?" Lucy supplied.

"Yes, you could say that. But here, both men and women seem to be considered fair game."

"Only if they want to hunt."

Lucy's eyes contained a message I couldn't quite read. Was she thinking of her own situation, or implying I might have that sort of "hunting" in mind for myself?

"We came here to ride," I reminded her. "Let's be on our way."

Every evening I expected Mathilde Lambert to appear at dinner, but she never did, nor was Jacques often present, either. He went to the *Opera* and the *Comedie Francaise* and attended several soirees, activities Mignon constantly urged Lucy to join in, and which she steadfastly refused to consider.

Mignon sounded exasperated. "You will never meet any suitable men if you never go out."

"That will be soon enough for me," Lucy replied.

"You must understand that Lucy doesn't like to be stared at," I tried to tell Mignon one afternoon when Lucy was resting.

"My dear, girls come here from all over France for just that opportunity, and she is wasting her chance. Lucy will die bitter and unfulfilled because of her stubbornness."

I didn't report my conversation with Mignon to Lucy, but I tried to steer her away from their almost daily collisions as well as I could. Mignon knew how Parisian society worked, and she did manage to get Lucy out in the carriage a few times to leave her calling card at the homes of people she wanted Lucy to meet. During our own at-home hours, we prepared for visitors who sometimes arrived, but more often did not. I felt curiosity probably led some of them to come to see what Lucy was like, while a few others seemed to want to extend their business contacts with the marquis. However, while Lucy was as polite as I had known her to be with these visitors, she did nothing to impress them, and I was sure most left with the idea it was just as well that the marquis' eccentric daughter preferred to live in the country.

"Where do all these counts and dukes come from?" I asked Mignon one evening after Lucy had been unusually rude to a Sorbonne student with a title but little money. "I thought the Revolution was supposed to do away with the aristocracy."

"Yes, until some of the liberated citizens managed to get themselves titles to replace them. I daresay there are more titles now than there were before the Revolution. The more things change, the more they stay the same, you know."

That's what Philip said, I thought, and suddenly I wished I could see him. "How important is a title, anyway?"

Mignon looked at me through narrowed eyes. "Why do you ask?"

I felt irritation that I had allowed Mignon to make me feel uncomfortable. "It seems a strange system, where aristocrats look down on rich tradesmen but marry their children to them to finance the social demands of their titles."

"Perhaps, but it works because each has something the other wants. Many good marriages have been built on far less."

But I knew there was nothing Lucy wanted to acquire badly enough to marry a man she didn't love.

As if she understood my thoughts, Mignon leaned over and lightly touched my hand. "That is why a match needs to be made for Lucy, *ma cherie.* Think about it."

I withdrew my hand and stood. "I have, Mignon, and my opinion remains the same. I join Lucy in resisting any attempt to marry her off to the highest bidder."

Mignon's face became a study in anger. "You do not need to pretend to be so righteous. You do not fool me, Mademoiselle Edmonds. It is yourself you are thinking about, not your charge. I know what you have in mind, and you are mistaken if you believe you can achieve it. The Marquis is no fool."

My gaze never wavered. "And neither am I, Mignon."

We faced one another for a moment, then she shrugged. "That remains to be seen, does it not? Good day, Mademoiselle."

After Mignon left the salon, I considered our encounter. I understood Mignon's first words well enough; if Lucy were to marry, my services would no longer be required. But what did the marquis have to do with it?

Well, Ellen, you've managed to make another enemy, I told myself. I did not fear Mignon, but she had considerable influence with the marquis. She would bear watching closely.

By our second week in Paris, we had settled into a routine that included riding in the *bois* on days when the weather was fair. We always had the same horses, but on Wednesday, much to her displeasure, Lucy was presented with a different mount.

"I want the black gelding I have been riding. We are accustomed to one another, and you were not to let it to anyone else," she told the stabler.

"I believe you will like this one better," a voice behind us said. "At least it is your very own."

"Philip!"

Lucy held up her arms and my heart contracted as he scooped her from her chair and set her atop a little roan mare.

"Her name is Ginger," Philip said.

"Did you ride her all the way from Dampierre?" Lucy asked. "The poor beast must be worn out."

"No. As I suspected, the best horses were gone from Dampierre, so I came to the Longchamps sale. It took me the better part of two days, but I finally found what I wanted."

"You have already been in Paris for two days?" I asked.

Philip turned to me and nodded. "I decided to wait until I had the right horse and then surprise Mademoiselle Lucy."

"You know I do not care for surprises, Philip. You should have let me go to the sale with you."

"A horse sale is no place for a lady.

Anyway, this is the best of the lot, I assure you."

Lucy rubbed the horse's neck and inspected its ears, causing Ginger to shake her head. "Well, this horse may look all right, but how does it ride? I will not be jounced about."

"This is a special kind of American horse called a Morgan, Lucy. I think you'll find her way of going quite pleasant."

"This horse is not a jumper?" Lucy sounded disappointed as she looked down at the mare's short, powerful legs.

"You have no need of a jumper. But you will need riding boots — try these on."

Lucy looked dubious. "How do you know they will fit me?"

"If they do not, I can return them."

The boots fit perfectly and, after the driver handed his horse over to Philip, the three of us set out on the bridle path. More than one lady turned to stare at Philip, who wore his riding clothes as if they had been tailored to fit. As usual, he had unbuttoned his shirt to a degree fashion would probably find alarming. I also noticed something else that made him look even more handsome.

"You seem much tanner, M'sieu. You must have been out-of-doors a great deal of the time since we left," I observed.

"This time of the year calls for supervising the work in the fields."

"How long will you stay in Paris?" Lucy asked.

"I should return this afternoon, but the Marquis wants to see me, so it will probably be tomorrow before I leave."

"You must have dinner with us tonight. Jacques is dining with the Lamberts," Lucy added, as if she knew he would be reluctant to come if her brother were present.

"The Lamberts?"

"Jacques has been seeing Mathilde Lambert," Lucy said, her tone neutral. "You really must come to dinner," she again insisted.

"That is up to the Marquis."

"I shall see that he asks you. And now I am going to trot."

"You should let the horse do that," Philip said solemnly, and we were treated to Lucy's laugh, a sound made all the sweeter because of its rarity.

Philip and I exchanged a pleased glance, and I knew he too enjoyed seeing Lucy come alive, even if only briefly.

She really cares about Philip, I thought, and I wondered what Madame Jourdan would think of a match between them. She might be horrified, but it would be far better for Lucy than any marriage Mignon could arrange, if Philip were agreeable — and if the marquis had no objections.

Mailley would like to own the Chateau d'Arc, Jacques had told me. In that case, Jacques would never allow such a match for Lucy.

As I glanced over at Philip, I was shamed to admit I took comfort in the knowledge he wouldn't be considered an acceptable match for Lucy. Further than that, I didn't care to allow myself to speculate.

The marquis not only invited Philip to dinner that evening, he also loaned him a spare suit of evening clothes. Although Philip's shoulders were much broader than the marquis' and the material strained a bit around the biceps as well, Philip created quite a striking appearance. I was not at all surprised when Mignon seated herself beside him.

"It has been too long since you have come to Paris, M'sieu Mailley. The Marquis must have you here more often."

"He knows I have too much work to do to allow that, Madame."

"Then he must get some help for you."

Philip seemed unruffled by Mignon's endless chatter, but the marquis was not.

"M'sieu Mailley has hardly had a bite of his eels in *beurre blanc,*" he finally told her. "Let the man eat — you may talk after dinner."

I looked down at my plate, where something dark swam in a sauce made up of shallots, white wine and fresh butter. *Eels?* My stomach fluttered and I forced myself to swallow the mouthful I had so innocently taken only a moment before the marquis spoke. I'd learned it was sometimes better not to know what I was eating, but at times even the most innocent-looking dishes turned on me. Jacques always seemed to enjoy such occurrences.

"I see you are not a gastronome, Mademoiselle Edmonds," Philip said with amusement.

He never called me by my given name when the marquis was present, although when we were alone or with Lucy, Philip was far less formal.

"Americans do not have trained palates. They can no more enjoy fine food than crows can sing," Mignon said.

"And just what is your palate trained to do, Madame?" Lucy asked.

Unruffled, Mignon looked at Philip. "Alas, eating good food is my second favorite thing," she said.

If Philip dares to ask what her favorite thing is, I'll strangle him with my bare hands, I thought, but fortunately the marquis intervened at that point.

"Now that you have your own horse, Lucy, you should also have your new riding costume. Ought it not be ready by now?"

"I have the fitting tomorrow," she said. "I will be glad to get back to my sewing-machine and start working on some of the material we have bought."

"When will Lucy return to the chateau?" Philip asked the marquis.

"Doctor Dubois may wish to see her a few more times. I expect she may be here another two weeks."

"Two weeks! I shall die if I have to stay in Paris that long," Lucy said.

"Most young women would give their eye teeth for the opportunities you are scorning, my dear," said Mignon. "You have only a short while to be young and in Paris at the same time. It would be a pity to toss it away."

"But it is *my* pity."

"Lucy! Please remember yourself."

"Yes, Sir. Ask the waiter to give me some more wine, please. If I must stay in this wicked city, I might as well enjoy some of its vices."

★ ★ ★

I was somewhat surprised Philip and Mignon seemed to know one another so well, considering her name had never been mentioned by either Philip or the marquis. During dinner, Mignon continued to flirt outrageously with Philip, who responded with smiling politeness.

How would he behave if they were alone? The question made me wonder. Mignon was not unattractive, and I had seen her in action enough to know many men found her appealing. However, after dinner the marquis took Philip aside to discuss estate affairs, thus denying any of us the further pleasure of Philip's company.

He was to stay overnight in the townhouse and, as I brushed my hair and prepared for bed, I felt a faint thrill to know we would be sleeping under the same roof. My rational mind told me there was no reason I should have any fond feeling for Philip Mailley. The man had been rude to me more than once at the chateau, shouting out foolish warnings and trying to upset me. He had paid me absolutely no attention during dinner, and I knew it was unlikely I would even see him again before he left Paris. Yet I found myself hoping for a chance to speak to him alone. Perhaps it was anticipation of

271

that opportunity which caused me to awaken early the next morning.

Hearing his voice in the hall, I paused only long enough to throw a peignoir over my nightgown before I opened my door and looked out.

"I will be down presently," Philip said to the servant who stood in the hall.

"Yes, M'sieu Mailley. The carriage will be waiting."

Philip's room was diagonally across the hall from my own, and the door stood invitingly open. Feeling more than a little foolish, I crossed the hall and stood in the doorway until Philip saw my reflection in the mirror where he stood, adjusting his cravat.

"Sorry, but you missed the show this morning. As you can see, I am already fully dressed."

My cheeks flamed as I saw myself in the mirror. A wild-haired wanton looked back at me, reflecting more of my feelings than I wanted to admit.

"I did not come here for a show," I said.

Philip turned from the mirror to face me, his eyes steely blue in the early morning light, and I felt naked under his steady gaze.

"Then what is it?"

"I want to thank you for seeing to Lucy's

horse. I think being able to ride will help her a great deal."

He nodded briefly in acknowledgment, and I felt even more foolish when he continued to look me over as he had done the first time we met. "Your hair needs a good brushing, but otherwise, you do well for so early in the morning. Is there something else you had to say?"

I blurted out the words without thinking. "Why did you not tell me about Mignon?"

Philip laughed. "You mean why were you not warned, do you not? She must have come as quite a shock."

"She wants to marry Lucy off," I said quickly. "I think the Marquis is agreeable."

Philip's expression sobered. "And Lucy? What does she say about it?"

"You know her as well as I do. She said she would kill herself before she'd be bartered away to someone for her dowry."

"Our Lucy tends to exaggerate. I doubt any such plan will come to pass, and, even if it does, it could be the best thing for her."

My eyes widened in surprise at the indifference in Philip's voice. Either he was a good actor, or he really didn't care if Lucy married and left the Chateau d'Arc.

"Surely you don't mean that!"

"Never presume to know what I mean,

Miss Edmonds. I warned you not to meddle into things that don't concern you."

"Lucy's welfare does concern me. And by the way, your hints I might be in danger were quite groundless."

"Oh? What makes you say that?"

"I spoke with the Marquis about some . . . some incidents, and he assured me they would not be repeated."

"What incidents?"

His expression told me nothing about whether he had any knowledge of what had happened to me at the chateau.

"Never mind," I said. "A few things occurred which were worrisome at the time, but I don't expect they will be repeated."

"I would not be too sure of that if I were you. But I can give you some good advice."

"And what is that?"

I tilted my head back to look up at him and felt a sudden dizziness. Philip seemed too close, and I took a step backward, an action which brought a fleeting smile to his face.

"Now that you know about Mignon and have met Jacques' latest quarry, you should realize it is quite unlikely you will ever snare either of the d'Arc men. So while you and Lucy are in Paris, I advise you to start looking for a new post."

That again! I had hoped Philip might have changed his mind about my intentions, but it was evident he hadn't. I looked Philip squarely in the eye and made no attempt to mask my irritation.

"I told you I didn't come to France with marriage on my mind. And I have no intention of searching for a new position, either. The Marquis expects me to be Lucy's companion for at least a year, but I am willing to stay with her as long as I am needed."

"You should remember what I told you."

I lowered my voice, even though no one could hear us. "Do you still believe I am in danger?"

A tiny muscle worked in Philip's jaw. He opened his mouth as if to speak, then closed it again. "Perhaps. Nothing has changed."

"Will you tell me what to watch out for, at least?"

He shrugged. "I have no idea. But with the d'Arcs, things are not always as they may appear to be."

"I wish you wouldn't speak in riddles. If you know something, you should tell me."

Philip searched my face for a long moment, then put out a hand to touch my unruly hair.

"What I know cannot help you."

"Then what can?"

Philip withdrew his hand and his mouth tightened. "Leaving the Chateau d'Arc before you get caught up in something you have no power against."

I squared up my chin and he smiled. "You have been too long with Lucy already. That is just the way she looks when she defies us all."

"She usually gets her way. Perhaps it will work for me as well."

Philip took a step toward me and took my hands loosely in both of his. "That remains to be seen, Ellen. Just be very certain that what you think you want is worth it."

Once more I had the feeling Philip Mailley wanted to kiss me, and I knew I wouldn't try to stop him. Still holding both my hands, he pulled me to him and bent to touch his lips to my forehead so lightly I was scarcely sure he had done so.

"I must go now," he said. "Take care of Lucy."

I had been leaning toward him, and when Philip released me I almost fell backward. Seeing me grab at the dresser for support, he smiled and waved from the doorway. I heard him start down the stairs just as Nicole left the elevator, carrying water for my morning ablutions.

"Bonjour, Mademoiselle," the maid said.

I knew she was eyeing my state of undress and duly noting I had just emerged from Philip's room.

I mustered as much dignity as I could and wished her a good morning.

"I trust you slept well, Mademoiselle," Nicole said over her shoulder as she set down the water and busied herself with laying out my towel and soap. It was what she said every morning, but her expression suggested her speculation about why I might not have gotten much sleep the night before.

"Yes, thank you," I said. "This is a most comfortable bed."

Nicole glanced at the jumbled covers and the single indentation in my pillow, and I hoped she would take notice Philip's bed was in the same condition.

At any rate, servants were trained to be discreet, and no matter what a maid might observe, surely she would keep it to herself — at least I hoped so.

Chapter Eleven

I felt some uncertainty about our reception at the House of Worth when Lucy returned for the fitting of her riding dress, especially when Mignon refused to accompany us.

"She says she has a headache, but if you ask me, Madame Jourdan is afraid of Monsieur Worth," Lucy said, as we waited in the same room as before for someone to acknowledge our presence.

"Mignon afraid of anything? That is hard to imagine."

"This is different. I understand that the women he turns away lose their standing in society altogether. Monsieur Worth does not dress just *anyone*, you know."

Lucy's tone was mocking, and I thought it unfortunate Madame Rachel chose that moment to make her entrance. From the way she narrowed her eyes, it was obvious she'd overheard Lucy's remark and did not approve of her in the least.

"Ah, good morning, Mademoiselles," Madame Rachel said with professional brightness. "We have a lovely riding costume for you to see today."

She nodded toward the butler, who placed the tea tray on the same table as before, then withdrew. "Enjoy your refreshment, ladies. Someone will be with you in a moment."

It was quite some time before anyone arrived, however, and I was on the verge of going in search of Madame Rachel when she re-entered, followed by the same group who had attended her during our first visit. She carried the riding dress draped over her outstretched arms and presented it to Lucy as if she were offering rare jewels.

"Is this what you had in mind, Mademoiselle?"

Lucy fingered the fabric and frowned while she examined the garment with a critical eye. "Only if it fits," she said, which I took to be high praise.

"Then let us see." Madame Rachel turned to me. "Can she stand alone?"

"I am not deaf," Lucy said crossly. "I will stand as long as is required if I can support myself on a straight chair with a high back."

Madame Rachel looked flustered. "Certainly, Mademoiselle d'Arc. Will that chair by the desk do?"

Lucy nodded and the chair was brought.

While she said she would stand as long as they wanted her to, I watched Lucy closely for signs of fatigue as several apprentices helped her exchange her everyday dress for the riding habit.

"Watch out with those pins," Lucy said as they adjusted it to her figure.

"The House of Worth does not injure its patrons," Madame Rachel assured her.

"Ouch! Only the ones you want to be rid of, perhaps."

A flustered apprentice bit her lip and apologized. "I am so sorry, Mademoiselle. I was admiring the design when I should have been paying more attention."

"The design is quite smart," another apprentice said, and they all nodded agreement.

Lucy ignored their remarks to stare at her reflection in a large pier glass that had been brought into the room with great ceremony. There could be no doubt the costume was handsome, or that its bottle green shade nicely complimented Lucy's fair coloring. The lightweight Austrian wool fabric felt soft to the touch and formed itself into graceful, floor-length folds. The sleeves were full and graceful, and the tapering collar emphasized Lucy's heart-shaped face.

I wondered what Lucy thought when she saw herself standing upright. It took but a few seconds for her to scowl at her image.

"This *soutache* braid is at least two millimeters too large."

Madame Rachel nodded. "Yes, Mademoiselle, I see your point. It makes the proportions of the bodice wrong. That will be attended to. Does anything else trouble Mademoiselle?"

"This dress was made from my own design. I want my sketchbook returned to me today."

Madame Rachel nodded. "Of course, Mademoiselle. I am sure I can find it. I shall be back in a moment. Come along," she added, gesturing to the apprentices.

"Your riding dress is lovely," I said when we were alone once more.

"It will do, I suppose, but for what the Marquis is paying for it, I could make a dozen of the same quality."

"Could you now, Mademoiselle d'Arc?"

We both looked up, surprised to see Charles Frederick Worth himself had once more honored us with his presence.

Lucy lifted her chin and looked the great designer in the eye. "Yes, I could, although I would prefer not to make a dozen of anything."

Monsieur Worth nodded. "Exactly, Mademoiselle. We do not produce our garments *en masse,* nor will we ever do so."

"Your designs are a different matter, though." Lucy pointed to a book of fashion plates on a nearby table. "I do not care to see my dress all over Paris, even if it is from the House of Worth."

Worth shrugged. "We cannot prevent others from copying our work. Once you appear in public in your riding dress, any competent pattern maker can trace its lines. But without the Worth quality, those other dresses are pale imitations."

"You will not use my design again?"

"Not without your permission. A certain duchess who saw it on a mannequin is quite eager for us to have a similar one in maroon, however."

"A duchess?" Lucy repeated, and I knew she wished Mignon were there to be impressed. "I designed the riding dress for myself, M'sieu Worth. If you want to use the design, you may pay for the privilege."

"Indeed?"

I couldn't tell if Worth were amused or outraged; his expression was carefully neutral. When he said nothing more, Lucy spoke again.

"My companion needs a dinner gown. I

have the design and the material to make it, but my sewing-machine is not here in Paris. If you will allow me to use your facilities to make Miss Edmonds a dress, you may copy my riding dress design as much as you like."

Monsieur Worth's expression didn't change, but he shook his head. "No, Mademoiselle, that is quite out of the question. My sewing-machines are all in use and, in any case, no one is allowed into our workrooms."

"Perhaps you could make the dress for me, then," Lucy said.

Worth smiled faintly. "Your design is not that valuable."

"Neither are your dresses. Make Miss Edmonds' gown for half of what you charged for the riding dress, and you may use both my designs."

"I cannot agree to that without even seeing it. The gown could be quite impossible to make."

"As soon as you return my riding dress sketch, I will bring you my design for the dinner gown."

"Very well. I shall look at it, but I make no further promises."

Lucy nodded. "Neither do I, M'sieu Worth. We agree on that, at least."

At that moment Madame Rachel entered

with Lucy's sketches. "I finally found Mademoiselle's designs," she said breathlessly. "They were quite hidden under some material in the workroom."

"Was the material maroon-colored, by any chance, Madame Rachel?" Lucy asked, and the woman seemed bewildered when her employer chuckled.

"I — I did not notice."

"It is no matter," said Monsieur Worth. "I believe Mademoiselle d'Arc and I have reached an agreement."

"I'm certainly glad Mignon wasn't with us," I said when Lucy and I were once more in the carriage, on our way back to the townhouse. "Can you imagine what she would have done when you started bargaining with Charles Frederick Worth himself?"

Lucy's mouth curved upward in a sly smile. "She would be displeased with me, for certain." Then her smile faded. "Mignon has always been displeased with me, as a matter of fact."

"It is probably just her manner," I said. I wasn't eager to defend Mignon, but neither should I encourage Lucy to speak against her.

Lucy glanced at me and shook her head. "No, she really hates me, and she feels the same way about Jacques."

"Why do you say that?"

The closed look returned to Lucy's face and she shook her head. "It is something that happened a long time ago, and I do not want to talk about it. Just take my word for it. Mignon will do anything she can to get rid of us."

Between us, Lucy and I decided not to tell the marquis the whole story about her bargain with the House of Worth. We merely said she had made arrangements to have my dinner gown sewn. On the excuse that I needed some embroidery silk, I used the carriage again that afternoon. I handed Lucy's sketch and the material she had chosen for it to the House of Worth's doorman with strict instructions they be given only to M. Worth himself.

When I returned, I found Lucy and the marquis in the salon, engaged in what seemed to be a pleasant conversation. His color had improved, and I even imagined he had gained some weight since Lucy and I had arrived in Paris. Lucy turned to me and raised a questioning eyebrow.

"I accomplished my errand," I said. I held up the skein of thread I had purchased to keep myself from being a liar, and Lucy nodded.

"Good."

The marquis, who had stood when I entered the room, pulled the cord to summon a servant. "I am glad you returned so quickly. Doctor Dubois has sent for Lucy. If we are to get there at a decent hour, we must leave immediately."

Lucy made a face to show her displeasure at returning to the doctor's office, but her mood was better than usual on the short trip there.

"How many more times do you think Lucy must see the Doctor before she can leave Paris?" I asked the marquis when she had been taken into the examining room.

"He did not say, but I believe he could have some new treatment in mind for her."

"She really is eager to return to the chateau, you know."

The marquis compressed his lips and shook his head. "Yes. I wish my daughter cared more for social activities and Jacques cared less. He would stay in Paris most of the time if I let him, while Lucy would always stay at home."

"The other day Lucy and I met a young woman Jacques seemed to be courting. Perhaps she is the reason he wants to stay here."

The marquis laughed humorlessly. "Courting? That must be an American expression — I do not know it. But from what I heard today, I doubt Jacques will continue to call on the young Mademoiselle Lambert at all."

"Oh? Has something happened?"

"Her father lost a great deal of money because of some disease that ruined his vineyards. The word around my club is his creditors will soon foreclose on the property."

I thought of what I had been told about Mathilde Lambert's being sent to Paris to catch a husband and felt pity for her. A plain girl without money, she'd have a hard time finding any place in French society.

"That is unfortunate," I said, "but I fail to see what her father's problem has to do with whether Jacques continues seeing her."

The corners of the marquis' mouth twitched briefly. "You do not lie well, Ellen. You surely know Jacques is looking for a rich wife. He thought Mademoiselle Lambert was a good prospect, but he wanted to make certain she would bring a large dowry. If her father is financially ruined, I predict he will see her no more."

"Perhaps Mignon will arrange a marriage for him, then."

I had intended to speak lightly, but instead I merely sounded spiteful. The mar-

287

quis looked disappointed that I had maligned his friend.

"Even Mignon would be hard-pressed to find anyone who would have Jacques," he said.

The office door opened, and Dr. Dubois entered the hall. "Mademoiselle Edmonds, you may assist Mademoiselle Lucy to get dressed. Jean-Paul, a word, if you please."

Clad only in her chemise, Lucy sat on the examining table with her legs dangling from the side. A nurse knelt before her, taking some kind of measurements and entering figures in a notebook.

"She must think this is the House of Worth," Lucy said in English.

"What *haute couture* item is she designing for you, then?" I asked.

Lucy shrugged. "Another one of the wild schemes doctors are always trying on me, I suppose. He said he would tell the Marquis about it, but I fear the worst."

"What is that?"

Lucy gestured toward the far side of the room, where a number of leather and metal devices rested on shelves. "Doctor Dubois makes braces and crutches to order. I suspect he wants to outfit me with a set of leg irons."

"Perhaps you could walk with them," I

said, although I could tell that doing so could be extremely difficult.

"Have you ever seen convicts attempt to walk in irons? It should be quite a spectacle, to say the least."

"But you will try if the Doctor thinks it best, won't you?"

Lucy turned down the corners of her mouth. "Really, Ellen, sometimes you can be quite tiresome. Which would you prefer, sitting in a wheeled chair where you could look at least somewhat normal, or trying to hobble about with a medieval torture device strapped to your legs?"

"I think you overstate the case," I said mildly. "Let me help you get dressed. It is getting late."

The lighter mood which attended our ride to the doctor's had departed as we rode back through the crowded streets.

"All two and a half million Parisians must be in the streets this afternoon," Lucy observed glumly as our carriage barely moved in the crush of traffic. A light, misting rain had begun to fall, and I wondered idly if it were also raining at the Chateau d'Arc.

Philip should have arrived there several hours ago. All day I had tried without success to put my early morning interview with

Philip from my mind. For a while I managed it, but then I would see a man who reminded me of Philip, and once more I remembered the look in his dark blue eyes. I wondered if he had really wanted to kiss me as much as I had, at that moment, wanted to be kissed.

Don't be foolish, I chided myself to no avail. I had never known a man like Philip Mailley, who seemed as changeable as the weather and more difficult to predict. At times, I was certain he felt attracted to me, but it was a strange kind of interest.

"Ellen, are you all right?"

The marquis' words brought me from my reverie and I realized the carriage had stopped before the townhouse, and that I was expected to get out.

"I'm sorry. I must have been wool-gathering."

"Wool-gathering?" He looked so puzzled, even Lucy laughed.

"Daydreaming is more like it," Lucy said. "I wonder about whom?"

I blushed, of course, giving them both the opportunity to laugh at me again, but at least everyone was in a better frame of mind as we entered the townhouse.

After Lucy had gone to her room, assisted by Nicole, the marquis motioned me to follow him into the drawing room, then closed the doors behind him.

"We must discuss a matter. Sit down, Ellen."

Obediently I sank onto the somewhat stiff Empire-style sofa and folded my hands in my lap in an attitude of attention as the marquis sat down beside me.

"What is it?" I asked, certain it had to do with Lucy.

"Doctor Dubois tells me he is quite puzzled about Lucy's condition."

"She seems so much better, though, does she not?"

"Yes, in a way she has made a great deal of improvement recently. But Doctor Dubois' tests have confirmed the suspicion I have long entertained myself."

He paused, and with the same sort of uncanny knowledge the marquis had often shown for my thoughts, I spoke for him.

"Lucy ought to be able to walk. There is nothing physically wrong with her legs."

The marquis nodded. "Yes. Doctor Dubois calls her condition 'hysterical paralysis.' He claims he has done all that is medically possible."

"What about braces? The nurse seemed to be measuring Lucy's legs. We were both afraid he planned to make braces for her."

"No, he was merely checking to be sure her legs are not wasting away. Doctor Dubois says she has an amazing amount of useful muscle. Her legs are weaker than normal, of course, because she does not walk. But she has some use of her legs, as you know."

I thought of the sewing-machine treadle turning as Lucy pumped it and of the way she was able to stand with a minimum of help. And when she rode, Lucy pushed herself up from the stirrups. "Does 'hysterical paralysis' mean Lucy is willing herself to be crippled?"

"Not consciously, of course. He thinks it could have a connection to something that happened years ago, when she first had her accident."

"You told me Lucy was injured while on horseback, yet now she is riding again, apparently without fear. So something other than the fall itself must have been responsible."

The marquis nodded. "That is so. I have encouraged Lucy to talk about that day, but she refuses. Perhaps it would help if she could bring herself to discuss it."

"I have asked her about her accident myself and gotten the same response. But perhaps as Lucy learns to trust me more, she might become more willing to speak of it to me."

The marquis took one of my hands from my lap and lightly pressed his lips to it. "You have already done more for her than I could ever do."

"Not as much as I want to, if she would only let me."

"Perhaps, in time, she will. In the meantime, say nothing of this to Lucy. Doctor Dubois thinks it would be a mistake to tell her she ought to be able to walk."

"I disagree. Perhaps that's just what she needs to give her confidence to try to walk on her own."

"He said he wants to be certain there is no further physical deterioration before he tells her."

"And how long will that take?"

"A few more months at the most. Perhaps you can persuade Lucy to come back to Paris on some other grounds, and she can see the Doctor while she is here."

"I believe I can manage it."

"Good."

The marquis stood and helped me up, still holding my right hand. "Ellen, you can never know how glad I am you came to us. You have been a godsend."

I was too embarrassed to look into his

eyes, and Philip's warning rang in my ears.

The marquis will never marry you.

I still had no romantic notions about him, but as the marquis put his arms around me and I rested my head against his broad chest and heard the slow, steady beating of his heart, I felt great compassion for him.

He is a lonely, vulnerable man, and the right woman could wrap him around her little finger.

The right woman, but not Mignon. And not me.

I began to disengage myself from the marquis' loose embrace at the same moment the drawing room doors were thrown open.

"Jacques!" the marquis exclaimed. His son stood on unsteady legs, his eyes red-rimmed. Even from several feet away, I could detect a strong odor of alcohol. "Go to your room. You are in no condition to be seen."

Jacques looked from me to the marquis, an evil smile on his lips. "And what about you, Sir, caught in the act of making love to dear Lucy's companion. Tsk, tsk."

"I owe you no explanation, Jacques, but for the lady's sake I must tell you that you are badly mistaken."

As he spoke, the marquis rang for the butler. He stood behind the sofa as if he had to distance himself to keep from striking Jacques. Not wishing to pass Jacques on the way out, I stayed where I was until the butler and carriage driver, one on either side, took hold of him and carried him away.

The marquis' hand trembled as he passed it over his brow. "I am terribly sorry you had to witness that scene."

I attempted a reassuring smile. "Think nothing if it, Sir."

"Jacques should never drink — alcohol is poison to him. He can tolerate a moderate amount of wine with dinner, but hard spirits turn him into a raging monster."

He's not so tame when he's cold sober, either, I thought, but kept it to myself. "Will he be all right?" I asked instead.

The marquis nodded. "He will sleep for several hours. When he awakens he will feel wretched, but otherwise he will be back to normal — whatever that means."

We exchanged small smiles, acknowledging that we two, at least, knew about Jacques. The small moment of intimacy made me feel close to the marquis, but it was totally devoid of the kind of romantic interest Jacques had accused his father of having in me.

As I left the drawing room, I was glad

Philip hadn't been there to witness the scene. Only recently I had vowed not to give anyone cause to think I had any romantic interest in the d'Arcs.

I will have to do a better job, I decided.

Jacques made himself scarce about the townhouse for the next few days, for which I was quite grateful. Lucy was so relieved Dr. Dubois hadn't ordered her to wear leg braces, she didn't even bother to ask what else he had said.

The couturiere Mignon had found to make my riding dress finished it the same day Lucy picked up her riding costume from the House of Worth. It was a serviceable brown serge, a color I wore well, and I felt quite elegant the first time Lucy and I rode in the *bois de Boulogne* in our new outfits. Our hair, styled by Nicole, was topped by fashionable hats. Mine boasted a feather that curled under my chin and tickled when I moved my head, and Lucy's golden plume made a halo around her head.

"The only one I am ever likely to have," she said when I pointed out the effect.

The young man who had greeted us on the first day we rode in the *bois* seemed to know when we were going to be there, and one day he managed to find a mutual acquaintance to introduce him to Lucy.

"Antoine Boucher, at your service, Mademoiselle," he said.

"I do not believe I require any services today," Lucy replied with her usual acerbity. Still, I thought she must be secretly pleased that this handsome young man with curly, black hair and a face which could have been painted by Botticelli had sought her out.

Discreet inquiries revealed that the Bouchers were in the interior designer trade and therefore not aristocrats. However, they had made a small fortune by winning the custom of many *nouveau riche*. It was said *Boucher et Fils* had the good taste to refuse a commission if the customer's desired effect would be too gaudy.

I said nothing to Mignon about the boy, however, aware she would either frighten him away or make Lucy distance herself from him, or both. He seemed a bit shy, a trait not especially desirable for anyone dealing with Lucy, but I thought he might at least make her a good first suitor.

That no one had sought me out didn't bother me in the least. When I told Philip I hadn't come to France in search of a husband, it was the truth. Someday I might feel differently, but at least for the time being, I was content to stay with Lucy, preferably in the Chateau d'Arc.

I was informed the marquis would hold a dinner party the day after my dinner gown was finished; then we would all return to the Chateau d'Arc the following day.

"Including Mignon?" I asked when the marquis told us.

He drew his brows together and his mouth made a straight line. "No. Madame Jourdan will remain in Paris."

"She doesn't like the chateau, I hear."

The marquis consulted his pocket watch. "You must excuse me now, Ellen. I am late for an important appointment."

Why does the marquis refuse to speak to me of Mignon? I thought I knew at least one possible answer. Whatever the nature of their relationship in the past, the marquis seemed to want to distance himself from her now. More than likely, I told myself, it was because of the way she had treated Lucy. It certainly had nothing to do with me.

On the day I returned to the House of Worth for my dinner gown, Lucy declined to accompany me. Therefore, I spoke to Monsieur Worth alone when Madame Rachel directed me to his office. It was opulently furnished, with wall hangings and thick carpets worthy of a Turkish harem.

Worth rose from his cluttered desk to kiss my hand.

"I hope your gown pleases you, Miss Edmonds."

"I haven't seen it yet. Madame Rachel said you wanted to speak to me?"

"Actually it was Mademoiselle d'Arc I wanted to see, but you are far easier to talk with. At least you do not insult me as she does."

I smiled at his rueful tone. "She does not mean to give offense."

"I am not at all sure about that. In fact, I rather admire that quality in her. It reminds me of myself when I came to Paris at the age of twenty without a *centime*. Mademoiselle d'Arc has a great talent for dress design. I would be interested in purchasing her work on a regular basis."

I swallowed hard and tried to understand what he had said. "Her designs, you mean, or the finished garments?"

"Designs, of course," he said somewhat impatiently, as if I should know better. "I took the liberty of preparing this contract. The Marquis will probably want his attorney to examine it, but I can assure you the terms are eminently fair."

I took the stiff pages from him, having no idea what the fancy French phrases and penmanship flourishes meant, but aware it was an important document.

Worth mistook my silence and spoke again. "It is unheard of for a fashion house to buy designs from anyone other than its own workers, Miss Edmonds. A clause in the contract states Mademoiselle d'Arc will not show anyone else her work, including any designs I do not choose to purchase."

"And Lucy may do this work anywhere she likes?"

He nodded. "I understand Mademoiselle d'Arc is not fond of Paris. While I cannot imagine anyone with the slightest interest in fashion wanting to live anywhere else, I have no objection to receiving her work by post, if that is her wish."

"I'm sorry Lucy did not get to talk with you today. She will be delighted."

Worth smiled again. "I am not too sure that young lady is delighted by very much, Miss Edmonds. Perhaps that is one reason I am doing this."

"That, and because you know she does good work," I said.

He smiled slightly. "Now, Miss Edmonds, do try on your gown. I am eager to see it on a live model."

When I stood in front of the pier mirror a few minutes later and looked at myself, I felt

I had truly been transformed from a Cinderella of the ashes into a princess. The drape of the dress was as flattering, as Lucy had known it would be, and the color and texture of the material she had chosen set off her design perfectly.

Worth nodded, unsmiling. "It will do."

"It is cut a bit too low for my taste." I tugged at the bodice, trying to raise the level of its décolletage.

"Oh, no, Mademoiselle!" Madame Rachel's face reflected her horror. "For a formal ball, it should be cut even lower and perhaps have a train. For the theatre, opera, or a dinner party, however, this costume is perfect."

Changing back into my sensible serge dress, I knew at least one thing about my new dress was less than perfect.

Philip Mailley would not be present to see me wear it.

Chapter Twelve

I wanted to tell Lucy the good news immediately, but when I returned from the House of Worth she was not in her room, nor did I find her in the drawing room.

"If you are looking for Lucy, she is riding," Mignon said when I came into the salon.

"I thought she would have waited for me," I said, then was struck by another thought. "I was out with the carriage. How did she manage to get to the *bois de Boulogne?*"

Mignon smiled in a self-satisfied manner. "A young gentleman called for her in his carriage."

I was immediately suspicious. "She said nothing to me about such plans. Where did this 'gentleman' come from so suddenly?"

"You need not think Lucy tells you everything, Ellen. The young man invited her out several days ago, I believe."

Was she lying? I doubted Lucy would willingly agree to go out with anyone and suspected Mignon had arranged the outing behind both our backs. "Who is this young man?"

"You would not know him, of course, but his name is Raymond Boucher."

"Oh, yes, the decorator." I spoke in a properly disdainful tone and enjoyed the surprise on Mignon's face.

"The wealthy decorator," she corrected. "And handsome, as well."

"He is a tradesman, however. The Marquis will not care for that."

"You have not known the Marquis as long as I have. He can be quite surprising."

"Perhaps. At any rate, I'm glad Lucy will have her outing today, since I was unable to accompany her. Good day, Mignon."

Although I had tried to put a good face on it, I worried about what might happen to Lucy, alone with a strange man. Knowing Lucy, I thought perhaps I should worry about him instead. But the situation made me uneasy, and I tried to keep busy as I waited for Lucy's return.

I took the linen covering from my new gown and hung it in the clothespress and put away the elbow-length white gloves which must be worn with it. I barely resisted the impulse to try on the dress again. I did don the new shoes M. Worth had insisted I must have and took a few turns up and down the carpet. With their unaccustomed high heels and tapering toes, the shoes would take some getting used to before I could walk in them gracefully.

"You must have stockings with designs," Worth had also decreed and, at a snap of his fingers, his assistants produced a froth of silky film quite unlike anything I had ever seen. When I protested, he laughed.

"The Marquis will not question my bill. He knows a lady's costume must always include the proper accessories."

As I regarded my new finery, I felt vaguely worried I had spent so much of the marquis' money on myself. I had been brought up with the admonition that a lady should never accept an expensive gift from a gentleman unless they were engaged to be married. Yet here in Paris, it did not seem at all unusual for men to lavish money on women they had no intention of marrying, and no one seemed to think anything about it.

This is different, I told myself. Improving my wardrobe had been Lucy's idea, not her father's. Surely no one could fault me for allowing her to have her way, when everyone else had been doing so for years.

I shook my head at my own deceit. *People can talk themselves into believing almost anything.* Maybe one day Lucy might even talk herself into walking. The thought made me feel a bit less guilty. At last I heard the elevator door opening. The butler pushed Lucy's chair into her room, then left us alone.

She had taken off her riding hat and now tossed it in the direction of her dresser, where it landed briefly before diving to the floor. "Well, at least that is over. Did you get your gown?"

I retrieved Lucy's hat and replaced it in its box before I spoke. "Did you not enjoy your ride? Mignon told me about it."

Lucy's eyes blazed angrily "That woman! She knows how I feel about her matchmaking, yet she continues to try to interest these poor men in me. I can hardly wait to get back to the chateau, out of her clutches."

"She said you were out with Raymond Boucher. Is he the young man we met on the bridal path?"

"The same, and that meeting was no accident. The witch! She put him up to asking me to ride!"

"But you do not know that, do you?"

"He admitted he asked Madame Jourdan to help him meet me."

"That could mean he admires you. I

thought he seemed to be a rather pleasant young man."

"Then you can ride out with him next time. Maybe he will marry you and take you away from me and my misery. Now, am I going to see your gown or not?"

I had not heard such bitterness in Lucy's voice in a long while, and I welcomed the change of subject. "Of course you will. But I have something else from the House of Worth that you might like even better."

"I doubt it," Lucy said sourly.

"You should see the look on your face. I've seen people biting into lemons with more pleasant expressions."

"And I would prefer eating lemons to this tedious talk. Let me see if your gown does justice to my design."

I brought the dress into Lucy's room and held it up for her inspection.

"I hope it is a decent fit," was her only comment.

"I think it is too low-cut, but Monsieur Worth and Madame Rachel both assured me otherwise."

"You saw Worth again?"

"Yes. He asked about you, and then he gave me this."

I handed the contract to Lucy and watched her expression as she began to read.

"This does not make any sense," she said after skimming the first page. "What is it supposed to mean?"

"Monsieur Worth really is impressed with your designs, Lucy. He will pay you for them."

It was one of the few times I'd seen Lucy at a loss for words. "Pay me? After the way he insulted me?"

I felt a faint prickle of alarm that Lucy's pride might prevent her from accepting the designer's offer. "He told me you are very talented, and he understands you have no wish to live in Paris. He is willing for you to work wherever you like and mail in your designs."

Lucy looked back at the paper and shook her head. "The man must be mad."

"If so, take advantage of his insanity. The Marquis' lawyer must look it over first, of course, but I think you should agree to it before Mr. Worth changes his mind."

Lucy looked up at me, a faint smile stirring the corners of her mouth. "Madame Jourdan will hate this, you know."

I smiled back. "Yes. Won't that be terrible?"

"The Marquis must be in a good mood when we tell him about it," Lucy said, and I agreed.

"But do not spring it on him at the dinner party. You two should be alone when he hears about it."

"No, I want you there. The Marquis seems to trust your decisions. He will not yell at me so much with you around."

"Yell?"

"You have seen his good side, Ellen. Since he cannot raise his hand to me, he raises his voice instead, often quite loudly."

"All right, I'll go with you, but I don't see why Worth's offer would displease him."

"You will see I am right. Now call Nicole. I must bathe before dinner."

Despite my show of confidence with Lucy, I didn't feel at all certain of the marquis' reaction to the prospect of having Lucy work in a trade, even a glamorous one. Aristocrats were expected to dabble lightly in the arts, but not to accept money for the work of their hands. While the marquis didn't seem to care about such conventions, Mignon did. Apart from that, Mignon was likely to frown on anything that Lucy favored.

We decided that just after dinner that evening would be the best time to approach the marquis. No guests were expected, and it was unlikely that Jacques, even if he were present, would join us in the salon. To my relief, the butler said Jacques felt indisposed and was taking dinner in his room.

However, Mignon was present and seemed in rare form. She could hardly wait for the salad course to arrive before she began to tell the marquis about Lucy's riding engagement.

"I am sorry you were not here to meet the young man, Jean-Paul. I believe you would find Raymond Boucher quite suitable."

The marquis glanced at Lucy, who sat with her lips compressed as if trying to keep from speaking, then back at Mignon. "The Bouchers are in trade, are they not?"

Mignon nodded. "Yes, but such taste they have! Why, the Comte de Vincennes has just given the firm a huge commission, and you know what that means!"

"It means they will have even more money to spend," Lucy said. "That does not, however, make them a whit more interesting."

Mignon flushed. "Interesting or not, young Boucher is a highly eligible bachelor. He does not have to look for a woman with a dowry, I can assure you."

"If you know so much about him, Madame Jourdan, then you no doubt also know he wants a titled wife with her own money and a large country house he can visit while he pretends to be a gentleman."

Seized by a paroxysm of coughing, Mignon hid her face in her napkin as the marquis looked at Lucy, his expression sober.

"Why do you say such things, Lucy? You are too old to make up stories."

Lucy returned his look. "I am making up nothing. You may recall M'sieu Boucher spoke to us the first time we all rode in the *bois de Boulogne*. Lucy and I saw him almost every time we rode; then a few days ago he had the Rachelars introduce us to him. He knew Ellen would be out today." Lucy glanced at Mignon, who seemed to be studying her plate with great interest, then resumed talking. "And he came by to ask me to ride with him. At Madame Jourdan's urging, I went. While we rode, I asked him why he was interested in me, and he was honest enough to tell me."

"That is no way to conduct yourself with a gentleman!" Mignon declared, having recovered enough to speak again.

"And it is no way for a gentleman to conduct himself, either, Madame. I will not be bait for any man who wants to fish for an aristocrat!"

"Enough!" the marquis cried. "Lucy, I

will see you in the salon after dinner. In the meantime, I intend to finish this meal in peace. Anyone who finds that too difficult to manage may leave the table at once."

No one moved, and the rest of the meal passed in tense silence. Lucy looked sullen as I wheeled her chair into the salon.

"So much for finding the Marquis in a good mood," she said. "Thanks to Madame Jourdan, this evening is ruined."

"Maybe not. Try to look penitent and I shall fetch the contract. That ought to give him something new to think about."

"To be angry about, you mean."

The elevator whirred and the doors opened as I walked into the hall. Nicole emerged, carrying a cloth-covered tray and stood aside as I passed. I noticed her hair was uncombed and the long apron she wore over her black dress was askew.

Jacques, I thought. "Are you all right, Nicole?"

She nodded without meeting my eyes. "Yes, Mademoiselle."

"You should not let the Marquis see you in such a state. He is not in the best of moods tonight."

At that Nicole raised her head and gave me a strange look I could not read, then nodded and went on her way.

I hurried up the stairs, hoping Jacques would stay in his room. I didn't think he would likely initiate another confrontation, knowing the marquis was in the townhouse, but I knew if he were, indeed, drinking heavily, he just might. The elevator was in use, and I wondered if Jacques might be on the way down. But when I reached the second floor landing, Mignon stepped from the elevator.

She regarded me with a strange look, almost as if she were very pleased about something I didn't know about, but neither of us spoke.

At least Lucy and I can now talk to the marquis in peace, I thought, retrieving the contracts from my room.

At the salon door I paused, then rapped lightly.

"Come in," the marquis called.

He stood with his back to me, looking down on Lucy. Her expression gave no hint she was upset, but I knew that did not necessarily mean she was not.

"The Marquis agrees with me about Raymond Boucher," she said.

"Oh?" I glanced at Lucy's father, who seemed to have gotten over the worst of his anger.

"Mignon should not have interfered, but

at least Lucy now knows that being in a gentleman's company is not necessarily fatal."

"Not instantly fatal, but definitely dreary," Lucy said. "In any case, I have something to show you."

At Lucy's nod, I handed the contract to the marquis and watched his dark eyes move over its fine lines.

"What have you done, Lucy?" he asked after a moment.

Lucy tried hard to sound unconcerned. "The House of Worth wants to use my designs. They will pay me for them, as you can see."

The marquis sat down hard on the sofa as if his surprise had made his legs suddenly weak. He read through the entire document while Lucy and I watched and awaited his reaction.

"This says you do not have to be in Paris to do the work," he said.

Lucy nodded. "That was one of my conditions."

"You gave Worth conditions?"

"Of course. I enjoy designing, but I will not be tied down to living in Paris."

The marquis turned to me. "Why was I not told about this?"

"Neither Lucy nor I knew Worth would make this offer, Sir. It is unheard of for him to hire outside designers. We had no reason to believe he would break that tradition. I was completely surprised when Monsieur Worth handed me the contract today."

The marquis looked at Lucy. "How do you feel about this?"

"Even though I know it violates the silly rules about what ladies are supposed to do, I very much want to do it."

The marquis sighed. "Probably for that reason," he said. "You will not actually be sewing the designs, I hope?"

"No. I will probably make up some of them up in muslin to be certain they work, but Worth wants only detailed drawings, not the garments themselves."

"It is all spelled out in the contract," I said.

"Very well. I will have Betancourt look this over after dinner tomorrow evening. If everything seems to be in order, I suppose I must sign it."

"You, Sir? Why not Lucy?"

The marquis looked at me as if I were not quite bright. "Lucy is a minor and a female. No contract bearing her name alone would be legal."

"Suppose she chose not to do this and you signed it anyway?"

"Then I could be sued by the House of Worth for breach of contract. That is why I must make sure you intend to follow through on this," he said to Lucy. "I will not be made the laughingstock of Paris."

"No, Sir, and neither will I. Call off Mignon and her matchmaking and let me return to the chateau and start to work."

The marquis and Lucy stared at one another for a long moment. Lucy's hands were clasped tightly in her lap, and a small muscle in the marquis' cheek twitched.

I felt almost as much suspense as Lucy as we awaited his verdict, but when the marquis sighed and his shoulders slumped slightly, I knew Lucy had won.

"You drive a hard bargain, Lucy. For the time being, at least, you will have your way. Off to bed with you now. Tomorrow will be a busy day."

"Off to bed with me, indeed," Lucy said as I pushed her chair into the elevator. "The greatest fashion designer in the entire world asks me to do something no one else has ever done, and yet I am addressed as a mere child."

"You are still young in years," I reminded her. "How does this elevator contraption work?"

"You should have learned that by now. Push that lever all the way to the right and hold it down."

With a loud hum and the thumping of many cables, the elevator made an uncertain, jerky ascent.

"You will kill us both with your clumsiness," Lucy predicted when the door opened to reveal a huge gap between where the elevator had stopped and the third floor, and it took several jolting attempts before I finally put it in its proper place.

"Next time you can drive it yourself," I told her.

"Or perhaps I shall just walk up," Lucy said.

She thinks she speaks in jest, but Lucy might do just that someday, I thought. If sheer stubbornness could make her walk again, then Lucy was already well on her way, whether she knew it or not.

The next day the townhouse came alive with the stir of preparations for the gala dinner party that evening. A steady stream of deliveries brought a variety of food and drink into the kitchen, and many fresh flower bouquets arrived to be arranged for all the public rooms.

Lucy was delegated to make the place cards, and at Mignon's direction I arranged them on the table.

"The Comte and Comtesse will have the

places of honor, of course, being the highest-ranking nobility, and M'sieu Betancourt must sit above Doctor Dubois," Mignon decreed. "But what shall I do with the Marquis' business associates, all equally important?"

"Seat them in alphabetical order." My suggestion was facetious, and Mignon did not appreciate it.

"You Americans have no feeling for social nuances. In France, such things are very important."

To some people, I thought, but I would not argue with her. We would soon be back at the Chateau d'Arc, where the kind of conventions which so concerned Mignon would be but a memory.

Like Lucy, I could scarcely wait.

I hadn't particularly looked forward to the marquis' gala dinner party, but when Nicole helped me into my new gown, careful not to disturb the curls she had just arranged, I felt a pleasant edge of anticipation.

"Your gown is lovely, Mademoiselle." There was an almost wistful note in her voice, and as I looked at my reflection, I found it hard to believe I was, like Cinderella, going to the ball after all — or at least, to a formal dinner party.

"Thank you, Nicole. Mademoiselle Lucy designed it, you know."

"She should be very proud. What jewels will you wear, Mademoiselle?"

"None. I have no jewels."

The girl seemed embarrassed. "The dress really does not require them, anyway."

"Thank you for saying so. Now you may attend Mademoiselle Lucy."

Nicole opened the door and started out, almost colliding with the marquis. Holding a velvet-covered box, he stood in the hall.

"Good evening, Ellen."

"I shall see to Mademoiselle Lucy," Nicole murmured.

Just before the marquis stepped into my room and closed the door behind him, the maid looked back over her shoulder, and once again I realized Nicole could easily misinterpret what she saw.

"You look elegant," I said. I had never seen the marquis wear the diagonal ribbon from which hung an honorary gold medallion.

His tone was almost apologetic. "One is expected to display medals from time to time. When I took it from the safe, I came across this and thought of you."

He handed me the black velvet box, its

covering worn with age.

"Open it," he prompted, helping me when I could not find the catch.

"Oh!" I gasped.

The case opened to reveal a single strand of gleaming pearls. I knew they were genuine and expensive and I couldn't accept them, but I allowed the marquis to open the clasp and place them around my neck. The strand felt cool on my bare skin, and I shivered slightly.

"There," he said, taking a step backward to admire the effect. "That was just what your new gown needed to make it complete."

I moved to the dresser and looked at my reflection. The dress was a rich rose color, and the pearls seemed to glow with a paler hue of the same shade.

The marquis moved to stand behind me, and as I looked at him in the mirror, my heart caught at the expression I saw in his eyes.

"Sara," he whispered, so softly that I wondered if I'd imagined it. "You look so much like your mother," he said more loudly, and suddenly I realized what I should have known all along.

I turned to face the marquis. "You were in love with my mother, weren't you?"

The marquis paled and looked away. "She was a beautiful and vital young woman, but I was already married. If things had been different . . ."

I fingered the pearls and turned to regard my reflection.

"People always say we should forget the past, but it isn't easy, is it?"

"No, Ellen. But we must try to do the best we can in the present. That is why I want you to have these pearls."

"If they belonged to her mother, Lucy should have them."

The marquis drew his brows together and spoke sharply. "Do you think I would offer you anything of Madeline's? I bought these for Sa— for your mother, but she never wore them."

"Then perhaps I shouldn't, either." I reached my hands to my neck, intending to unclasp them, but the marquis seized my wrists.

"It would be foolish for you not to accept them, Ellen. Do not misunderstand me. I expect nothing in return. You may consider the necklace as a reward for putting up with us all."

I nodded, and the marquis released my wrists. "Very well," I said. "Thank you for the pearls, and the gown as well. I will always do my best for Lucy."

"I know, and I thank you for it." He stepped back, and when he spoke again, his tone was impersonal. "You and Lucy may go downstairs when you are ready. She always wants to be seated before the guests arrive."

The marquis left, and I returned to the mirror.

You look like your mother, the marquis had said. He admitted he had loved her.

Had she returned his love? The marquis would have been handsome then, I knew. But he was also married and a father at the time. I couldn't imagine my mother ever allowing herself to fall in love with a married man.

And where was Madeline d'Arc then? Surely she would know if something was amiss with her husband.

He probably only thought he loved my mother, and now he has some sentimental notion about the past.

With a final glance at the pearls glowing against my skin, I left the room.

Whatever might have happened when my mother was young had nothing to do with me, and since the Marquis d'Arc obviously wanted me to have the pearls, I would accept them.

Lucy approached the dinner party with all the enthusiasm of a condemned man being served his last meal.

"Thank heaven this is the last time I shall have to endure these dull people for a long while," she declared.

"Surely you'll want to come back when the next Worth collection comes out with your designs."

"That might be interesting, but it is many months away. And in the meantime, I shall have a great deal of work to do."

The dinner guests began filing in and the necessary introductions were made as efficiently as possible. The marquis wasn't the only man who wore decorations, and most of the women were laden with fine jewels.

"A tiara — how vulgar," Lucy whispered when the countess entered.

"Is it real?" I asked, noting it contained dozens of brilliant diamonds.

"Of course. A lady who cannot afford genuine jewels never wears imitations."

Seated near us, Mignon frowned and put a warning finger to her lips. "Watch yourselves, Mademoiselles. You must not insult the Marquis' guests."

My dinner partner, chosen with special care by Mignon, no doubt, was a very old man so hard of hearing I soon gave up any attempt at conversation, merely nodding brightly whenever he said anything.

Lucy had been paired with the young son of the count and countess, who seemed to be so miserable at his first dinner party even Lucy took pity on him and pulled in her claws for the evening.

Jacques was seated next to a rather large woman who giggled at his infrequent remarks, and I knew he would rather be almost anywhere else at that moment.

As the meal proceeded through several courses, I noticed the countess and another woman had placed their gloves over their wine glasses, and discreetly I questioned Lucy about the practice.

"That means they do not want to be served any more wine. It is not considered good manners to drink every wine offered."

"But you always do," I said, a fact that had surprised me, given Lucy's young age.

"Yes, but I lack good manners. Besides, they water the wine they give us. Have you never noticed how weak it is?"

"No, I cannot say I have. I never drank wine in America."

"Such an uncivilized country," Mignon murmured.

I noticed she had been eyeing my bodice

all evening, and when the wine had loosened her tongue enough, she leaned toward me and pointed her finger at the pearls. "Do I notice something new besides the gown, *cherie?*"

"My earrings, perhaps?" I fingered the delicate silver-filigreed loops Lucy had loaned me. "They do not belong to me."

"And the pearls?"

"The pearls are mine, Madame."

"Are you certain? I believe they belong to the Marquis."

"Not any more."

"Here is a wine you must sample, ladies," Jacques said at my elbow.

"I have had enough," Lucy said, but I allowed Jacques to fill my sherry glass.

I had drunk more wine than was my custom, but I felt quite alert and in control at the moment, an advantage I didn't want to lose. I sipped the wine Jacques had offered and wondered at its bitterness. I refused a refill; with Mignon around, I needed to have all my wits about me.

At the head of the table, the marquis stood and raised his wine glass. "Attention, ladies and gentlemen! As you know, my family and I shall soon return to the Chateau d'Arc, so this is something of a farewell to Paris. But it is also fitting that we recognize a great honor which has just come to my daughter Lucy."

"Oh, no!" Lucy groaned. "Why does he have to do this to me?"

"Because he is proud of you. Now sit up and smile."

Mignon looked at Lucy with such malevolence, I knew the marquis must have told her about Lucy's contract with the House of Worth. The knowledge he had confided in the woman irritated me far more than it should have.

While the marquis told his guests Lucy had been chosen to design for the House of Worth, Jacques' face was a study in incredulity, and the others seemed equally puzzled that Lucy would even consider doing such a *bourgeois* action.

"So I propose a toast to Lucy d'Arc, the next great fashion designer of the House of Worth," the marquis concluded.

"Hear, hear!" A few of the men exclaimed, and all stood with their wineglasses raised to Lucy.

Her face reddened with embarrassment, but she didn't let the unexpected attention keep her from responding.

"Help me stand," she whispered, and an alert waiter helped her rise from her chair.

Calmly Lucy picked up her own wine

glass. "To Monsieur Worth, who has found value where no one else has."

There was a momentary pause, then a scattering of applause.

Lucy sank back into her chair as Mignon rose from hers and turned to face me, her cheeks reddened by more than her makeup.

"You wretched creature! This is all your doing!"

Her hand shot out to my cheek before her words had registered. I tried to stand, and the room spun alarmingly.

What on earth is the matter with me? I thought, just before my head struck something hard and sharp, and I fell senseless to the floor.

Chapter Thirteen

I had never fainted before, and when I came to my senses and realized I had become the center of a great deal of unwelcome attention, I wished I could repeat the performance.

Instead, I lay very still with my eyes shut and concentrated on the voices eddying around me. From the confused babble, I picked out Mignon and the marquis, who seemed to be engaged in a shouting match somewhere nearby.

"She must not stay in this house another night!" Mignon shrieked.

"You have had too much wine, Madame. You should retire before you say something you will regret."

"Ha! There is nothing I could say about your precious Ellen I would ever regret. Do you know what she has been doing under your roof?"

"Yes, I do. And it is all fine with me."

"Oh, really? You will sing a different tune when you hear what Nicole has to say.

Where did that girl go? Nicole, come here this instant!"

I opened my eyes enough to see I lay on the sofa in the grand salon, the room nearest to the dining room. The marquis and Mignon stood facing one another at the end of the sofa, and from the corner of my eye I saw Nicole coming toward me, bearing a damp towel. I had to close my eyes when she placed it on my forehead, and although I couldn't see her expression, I detected the dread in her voice.

"Did you want something, Madame?"

"Yes. Tell the Marquis what you told me about Mademoiselle Edmonds — all of it."

"But Madame —"

"Do not be afraid, Nicole. Nothing will happen to you," Mignon assured her, lowering the volume of her voice.

I held my breath and waited to hear what the girl would say. If I were going to be asked to leave, I wanted to know why.

"What have you to say about Lucy's companion, Nicole?" the marquis asked.

Nicole spoke so softly I could barely hear her. "I saw her in M'sieu Mailley's room, Sir."

"Is that all? I hardly think that is scandalous."

"Tell the Marquis what she was wearing

at the time," Mignon prompted.

"Mademoiselle was dressed in a night-gown and peignoir, Sir."

"And Mailley? Was he in night clothes as well?"

"No, Sir. He was about to leave."

"So he was fully dressed?"

"Yes, Sir."

"And did you observe them in any sort of intimacy?"

Nicole's "no" was almost whispered, and I had to force myself to lie there and listen quietly.

"Very well, Nicole. You may go now and prepare Mademoiselle Lucy for her bed. Then come back here."

I was considering letting them know I was awake when Mignon spoke again. "I thought you should know how your precious Ellen has been betraying you under your very nose. She would never tell you."

"Betraying me?" The marquis sounded very tired. "Mignon, you are in no condition to discuss anything tonight. If you still remember any of this tomorrow, tell me then."

"You will not get rid of me so easily, Jean-Paul. Nicole also told me of the times she has seen you with Ellen when she was in a state of undress. You see, I know everything."

Mignon's triumphant declaration went unchallenged for a long moment; then I heard the marquis groan as if in great pain.

"You know nothing, Mignon, and you never have. Go to bed and sleep off your wine. Tomorrow, you will pack your things and leave my house."

"You cannot mean that!" Mignon's triumph swiftly turned to panic. "After all these years, after all I have done for you —"

"And all you have done against me, as well. Lucy was right. I should have rid myself of you a long time ago."

Mignon began to sob, the sound receding as she apparently left the room. Assuming the marquis had also left, I removed the towel from my forehead and opened my eyes to see him standing beside me. He looked years older than he had only a few hours before, and I felt guilty I had caused the marquis such pain.

"How do you feel?" he asked quietly.

I put a tentative hand to my forehead and winced. "My head hurts."

"Yes, I should think it would. You struck the arm of Lucy's chair when you fainted. Doctor Dubois said you probably suffered a slight concussion."

"What does that mean?" I tried to focus my eyes, but on seeing two of everything, I wearily closed them again.

"You will have a knot on your head and you must be careful for a few days, but no real damage was done."

"Except to your dinner party." I opened my eyes again and tried to sit up, but sank down again when a wave of nausea swept over me.

He chuckled. "That is the least of my worries, Ellen. I was quite glad to get rid of them so early. Some of the guests never know when it is time to leave."

Deceit had never been one of my strong points, and as uncomfortable as the admission was, I must admit I'd heard Mignon's accusations. I forced myself to meet the marquis' steady gaze.

"Madame Jourdan seems to be quite upset. I heard some of the things she said about me."

The marquis compressed his lips and his eyes darkened. "That is unfortunate. She was not at her best tonight."

"She disliked me from the first," I said, then regretted the self-serving statement.

"I know. But do not concern yourself about this, Ellen. She cannot hurt us."

Us. What did he mean? I wished my head didn't ache so badly, and that I didn't see two of everything. I felt some great truth waited to be discovered, but I was too weak to search it out.

"Mademoiselle Lucy is ready for bed now, Sir," Nicole said from the doorway.

"Very well. Doctor Dubois does not want Mademoiselle Ellen to be moved tonight. Bring her a blanket, then wait for me in the drawing room."

"Yes, Sir."

"Try to sit up, Ellen," the marquis ordered. In one hand he held a small vial, while with the other he supported my neck and brought the bottle to my lips. "Doctor Dubois said to administer this when you regained consciousness. It will help you rest tonight."

The liquid was bitter and burned my throat, but obediently I drank it all down. "I am sorry to be so much trouble," I murmured.

"You are no trouble, my dear. Go to sleep now."

Dimly I was aware of being covered by a blanket and kissed lightly on the cheek. My last conscious thought was that my new dinner gown would surely be ruined if I slept in it, but I was too tired to remove it myself.

I awoke on the sofa with the morning sun

streaming in through the lace curtain and a brackish taste in my mouth. I had never drunk enough spirits to have a hangover, but the way my head pounded and the queasiness in my stomach made me feel I must have come close. My double vision was gone, however, and although I felt lightheaded, I believed I would feel better after I ate breakfast.

"So you finally woke up," I heard Lucy say. The butler pushed her chair to the couch and she handed me a cup of tea. "This is what you are supposed to have first. When you have drunk it all, you may have a croissant."

"Thank you, nurse," I said dryly. "I'm so very glad you are here to take care of me."

Lucy's sober expression did not change. "How do you feel? You look terrible."

I struggled to a sitting position and looked down at my dress. "So does my beautiful new gown. Someone should have removed it."

"You were in no condition to be undressed."

"I have never fainted before. I cannot imagine what happened."

"Perhaps it was the combination of rich food and wine and Madame Jourdan's unfortunate remarks. At any rate, you certainly gave everyone a fright. I have never seen the Marquis turn so pale."

"Where is Mignon this morning?" I was beginning to recall her accusations, and I wanted to confront her and refute them.

"She and Nicole are gone."

"Gone? You mean for good?"

Lucy's lips lifted in a rueful smile. "For good, definitely. And also — what is the English word? Permanent?"

"Permanently," I supplied, but my mind was not on Lucy's problems with English adverbs. "Why did they leave?"

"There was a big fuss, and Mignon said she knew when she was not welcome and would not stay another moment. Actually, she stayed most of the night, but the carriage driver was awakened at dawn to take them away."

"Where do you suppose they went?" I asked, uneasily imagining we might find them camped out at the chateau when we arrived there.

"Madame Jourdan has her own apartment on the Left Bank. She would have gone to it as soon as we left, anyway. But this will make a much better story."

"So we're part of a *scandale*?"

Lucy shook her head. "Not we, Mademoiselle, you. The Marquis is furious."

"With me?"

"With Mignon, for telling tales about you. She had Nicole say you had entertained Philip and the Marquis in your bedroom, dressed only in your chemise or your nightgown. No doubt Mignon bribed her to say those things."

Lucy's words made me feel distinctly uncomfortable. Should I try to explain that Nicole had misunderstood the situations she had witnessed, or should I simply let my silence confirm Lucy's belief in me and thereby tacitly lie?

Before I could decide the issue, the marquis entered the room. When I saw how relieved he seemed to be that I had revived, I decided to leave well enough alone and remain silent. Except where Lucy or Philip or the marquis were concerned, I didn't care a fig for my reputation. And I had often heard that sleeping dogs should be left to lie.

If sleeping dogs can lie, then so shall I.

We didn't get back to the Chateau d'Arc as soon as planned. Dr. Dubois said I should stay in Paris for a few more days to make sure I'd suffered no ill effects from my fall, and the marquis wanted to ascertain Lucy's contract with the House of Worth was in good order. He took it to his lawyer,

335

Edouard Betancourt, who'd had no chance to see it when the dinner party had broken up so suddenly. Finally the marquis signed and conveyed it to Charles Frederick Worth, relieving Lucy's suspense.

Then after we were packed and ready to leave, the marquis said another matter had arisen that would delay his departure from Paris for several more days.

"I do not care, as long as we can return to the chateau ourselves," Lucy said when she heard the news. "Some way must be found to get Ginger back safely, as well."

"I will ride your horse to the chateau," Jacques offered. "With that huge chair of yours in the carriage, there's no room for me, anyway."

Lucy frowned at his suggestion. "I said I want my horse to get back safely. I will not have her run into the ground like you do poor Boxer."

"I do not mistreat him. Anyway, I intend to have a leisurely ride, since I have no reason to hurry back to the chateau." Jacques looked directly at me and added, "There will be quite enough time."

Jacques had been unusually subdued since the evening of the dinner party, but I hadn't imagined there had been any permanent change in him, and I didn't like the challenge I read in his eyes. I thought of mentioning it to the marquis, then dismissed the thought. I would make Jacques keep his distance, and should that fail . . .

Philip could always help me.

"Jacques cannot stay in Paris, you know," Lucy told me later. "There has been too much talk about the way he dropped poor Mathilde Lambert when he heard her father was in financial trouble. For form's sake, he should have kept seeing her for a while longer, then picked a quarrel and exited with grace. No young lady is likely to allow him the opportunity to be treated the same way."

"Somehow I have a hard time feeling sorry for Jacques."

"Then feel sorry for me — and for yourself. We will have to put up with him at the chateau."

The next morning the marquis helped Lucy and me into the carriage, and I was quite sincere when I said I hoped he could join us soon.

"So do I, Ellen. It will be good to be back home again. Have a safe journey."

The marquis waved to us until the carriage turned the corner, and I was struck by how lonely he looked. I hoped the scene I'd caused at the dinner party wouldn't make his life more difficult. No further mention had been made of anything that had transpired after that evening, nor had I asked him about its aftermath. What he had said to Nicole or Madame Jourdan after they left the salon, I had no idea.

Of one thing, however, I was certain. In whatever way my relationship to the marquis might have changed while I was in Paris, it had made Jacques even more dangerous.

At Lucy's request, we returned to the Chateau d'Arc in the marquis' carriage rather than by train. It was a longer and, to me, more tiring journey that way, but I knew Lucy disliked the stares she received in the train stations. She seemed preoccupied and uninterested in the passing scenery, and my questions seemed to annoy her. "I am not a very good tour guide and I want to rest," she finally said.

She closed her eyes and soon fell asleep. I hadn't felt tired, but the rocking of the carriage and the syncopation of the horses' hooves lulled me into a light slumber from which I did not awaken until we stopped at the chateau gates.

When the gateman did not immediately

come into view, the driver sprang down from his box and shouted. Still holding his noontime bread in one hand, the man finally appeared and swung the great iron gates open to admit us.

Once more I viewed the Chateau d'Arc from the long sweep of the drive. It was a sight that never failed to stir me, but as we covered the last few hundred yards, I had no sense of homecoming. The chateau's towers cast long shadows onto the lawn, and I wondered what secrets it still concealed.

In the distance I could hear the hounds barking, but apparently they were kenneled and did not come out to greet us as they had when I first arrived. Neither did the estate manager, although I had hoped to see him.

"Where is M'sieu Philip?" Lucy asked Marc when it was evident he would not appear in time to help her from the carriage.

"In the summer meadow, I believe, Mademoiselle Lucy."

"Help the driver remove my chair from the carriage and be quick about it," Lucy ordered.

"You must get out before we can reach the chair, Mademoiselle," the driver said. "I shall carry you into the house."

He proceeded to do so without waiting for her to protest, and as Marc opened the door to the family salon for them to enter, I realized why she expected Philip to be there.

Philip has carried her about for years. To him, Lucy was probably still his employer's spoiled child. However, I doubted Lucy felt like a child around him.

"Welcome back, Mademoiselle Lucy," Sophie said. "We did not know when to expect you, so your bed has not been prepared."

"Fortunately, I slept in the carriage and do not require rest now, but you should have known we were coming. I know the Marquis sent word."

Sophie did not seem cowed by Lucy's displeasure. "We thought the Marquis would be with you, Mademoiselle."

"It is a good thing he is still in Paris. He would not like knowing that you have been idle while we were gone."

"He will be here in a few days, Sophie," I said. "Has everything been all right in our absence?"

She hesitated. "Yes, but Madame Albert is getting worse, Mademoiselle. She wanders all over the chateau at night, and none of us can do anything with her."

"Where does she go and what does she do?" Lucy asked.

"Once I found her in your room, Mademoiselle, and another time she spent the night on Mademoiselle Edmonds' bed. We always take her back to her room when we find her, of course."

Lucy looked annoyed. "The Marquis must make other arrangements for the poor old thing, if she cannot behave herself. Has anything else happened in our absence?"

"No, Mademoiselle. Will you have your luncheon now? I believe Henri is ready to serve you."

After we had eaten, I went to my room to unpack and to check to see if Madame Albert had taken anything else. Some of my belongings had been disturbed, but nothing seemed to be missing. I felt uneasy. The old woman had continued to violate my privacy and I realized she would probably continue to do so as long as we both remained at the Chateau d'Arc.

When I finished my room inspection, I entered Lucy's room and found her going through the drawer in which she kept her sewing supplies. She looked annoyed. "My dressmaker's shears are missing, as well as my silk pins and pincushion."

"Are you certain? Perhaps they have been misplaced."

"There is nowhere else they could be. I suppose Madame Albert must have taken them, unless Sophie stole them herself and made up the story about Madame to protect herself."

I shook my head. "In the first place, Sophie does not strike me as being a thief, and we know Madame Albert has taken things before."

"Go to Madame's room and get them back, then. She could hurt herself with those shears."

Herself — or someone else.

As I rapped lightly on Madame Albert's door, I wondered how much of our last meeting the old woman would recall. Disturbed as she was, I knew I must be careful not to make her angry.

"Madame Albert? May I come in?"

I opened the door and looked into the room. Madame Albert lay on her bed, fully dressed, her arms folded across her chest. Her faint snores told me she was sound asleep, as might be expected in someone who stayed up all night. Trying to move quietly so as not to waken her, I began to look for Lucy's missing items.

Her room was as cluttered as it had been on my previous visit, and the drawn drapes made it hard to see. I found bits of bread and other food she had apparently brought from the kitchen, some odd buttons, a vase I'd seen in the family salon, and finally, Lucy's pincushion. But what had she done with the shears?

I opened a drawer and cringed at the noise it made, but Madame Albert didn't seem to hear it. *She's deaf,* I recalled with gratitude. She was also sleeping soundly, so I wasn't likely to disturb her. With more confidence I went through her other drawers, finding a handkerchief I thought I had lost, but no shears. I looked in her clothespress with the same result. If Madame had taken the shears — and I was positive she had — she'd hidden them well. Perhaps she had even put them under her pillow. Could I get by with searching under it?

Cautiously I crept to the bed and placed my hand under the bolster. The heavy, crocheted edge of the pillow covering scratched the top of my hand, but my palm encountered nothing more than the rough counterpane underneath. I went around to the other side of the bed and repeated the process, but felt nothing. Finally, I knelt and looked under the bed, but found nothing but dust. The room would have to be searched when Madame Albert was somewhere else, I concluded.

When I straightened, Madame Albert's eyes were open, watching me calmly.

"He will never marry you, you know," she said almost conversationally.

"What, Madame?"

"He will never leave Madeline. I have seen to that."

She closed her eyes again. I knew I should go, but my curiosity overruled me.

"What have you done, Madame?"

She opened her eyes again and her mouth curved in a sly smile. "He will never read your letters. Never."

Madame Albert's eyes closed again, and this time she seemed to be in an even deeper sleep. Knowing I would learn no more from her, I took Lucy's pincushion and left the room, trying to make sense of what I had heard.

He will never marry you, Madame Albert said. "He" was the marquis, of course, but who was the "you"? From her mention of Madeline, I knew she wasn't talking about me. In some of our previous encounters, Madame Albert had confused me with my mother. Had Sara Littleton wanted to marry the marquis? He had loved her, he said.

Tears came to my eyes, and I stopped beside the hunting scene Jacques had called grisly. *Poor Mama, to fall in love with a man she could never marry.* It wasn't the Chateau d'Arc she had longed for all those years, but the marquis himself.

He will never read your letters, Madame Albert had said. I guessed at the heartache my mother must have felt if she had repeatedly written the marquis after returning to America but never received a reply. Madame Albert was so fiercely loyal to Madeline she would do almost anything to protect her. She must have destroyed my mother's letters, until Mama gave up and married another man.

And the marquis, never hearing from Sara Littleton, had tried to forget her too — until I wrote to tell him she was dead.

He has also suffered. The realization turned in my heart like a knife.

But Philip was right. Sad as it might be, what had happened in the past was done and should be left alone. That was best for all concerned.

Jacques had told us he was going to sleep late and start back to the chateau in the early afternoon, but when he hadn't arrived by the time dinner was announced,

Lucy began to fret.

"I'm sure Jacques is all right," I told her. "He probably had a late start."

"I am not worried about him," she corrected sharply. "I just hope he has done nothing to injure my horse."

"Daylight will last for a few more hours yet. I predict Jacques will be here before we have finished eating."

"Yes, that would be just like him to interrupt our dinner. And where is Philip? I told Marc to send him to me the moment he came in."

"I'm sure Marc will do that. In the meantime, Henri tells me the cook has prepared your favorite dishes. It would be a pity for the food to go to waste."

Lucy sighed and picked up her spoon, as if the aromatic soup being ladled into her bowl contained medicine about to be forced upon her. "Dining alone does not improve my appetite," she said.

"Then may I join you?"

We both looked to the doorway, where Philip stood with his arms folded across his chest. He smiled faintly in reply to Lucy's accusing scowl.

"Where have you been?"

"Did not Marc tell you I had to see to the sheep in the summer meadows?"

"Henri, set a place for M'sieu Mailley," I said, and Philip sat down beside Lucy.

"How has Ginger been? Have you been able to ride often?"

"Until today, I exercised her almost daily, and she was fine. But with Jacques riding her back from Paris, there is no telling whether I shall ever see her again."

Philip said nothing, but I noted that his lips tightened at the mention of Jacques. "What about the Marquis? Marc said he did not return with you."

"No, as usual he had 'pressing business' to attend to. He should be along in a few days."

Philip nodded, unsurprised. "Several papers need his signature. If he stays much longer, someone will have to go to Paris."

"Someone?" I asked.

"Not us!" Lucy said sharply. "I have seen enough of that place to last me quite a while, thank you."

We heard the sound of a door closing rather forcefully, then footsteps in the hall, as Jacques ordered Henri to set a place for him.

"Thank you for waiting dinner," he said, glaring at me as if I had been to blame for his late arrival. "I see that you have managed to find a dinner partner, anyway."

"You are very late," Lucy said. "Is Ginger all right?"

"What about me? I should think you would be more interested in my welfare than that of a dumb brute."

"You are more a brute than my horse."

Jacques laughed. "Only because I will not take your bit, little sister. I am relieved to see you looking so fit after your journey."

Philip addressed Jacques. "I see your stay in Paris has left you in equally fine form. Will you be returning soon?"

Henri entered with two place settings, putting Philip's in front of him and placing Jacques' at the head of the table.

"That remains to be seen. But at least the other servants know where I belong."

For a moment I feared an ugly scene, but Philip refused to take the bait. "I am sure we all do, Sir."

Lucy looked at Philip. "We know where M'sieu Mailley belongs, as well. What has happened on the estate since we have been away?"

Philip spoke of various matters, and I was encouraged to see that Jacques seemed to be taking some interest in his report.

If he has to stay here, perhaps he will learn to like it better. It was unlikely, but I knew how much it would mean to the marquis to believe his son would be ready to take his place. Then another thought came to me. *Jacques would fire Philip immediately if he had control.*

Glancing at the rapt attention Lucy was paying to Philip's rather dull explanation of his plans for some of the fields, I knew a monumental quarrel would take place if that should occur.

Don't borrow trouble, I told myself. After all, the marquis was still firmly in control and there was no point in worrying about what might happen in some vague future.

After dinner, we adjourned to the family salon. I knew Lucy wanted to tell Philip about her success at the House of Worth when they were alone, but Jacques brought it up immediately. He sat opposite Philip on the sofa and seemed to relish telling him Lucy was going to design clothes for the best fashion house in Paris. "You should know that Mademoiselle Lucy will likely be quite famous soon. I doubt she will have anything to do with any of us when that happens."

"You should be so fortunate, my dear brother." Lucy's cheeks glowed with anger, making Jacques' smile even broader.

"Will you have to go to Paris often?"

Philip asked Lucy.

"Not unless I want to — that is part of the contract. Of course, there is also a clause saying they do not have to pay me for work they do not use, so, contrary to what Jacques says, I doubt designing will make me rich."

Philip nodded his approval. "I know nothing about fashion, but I am glad you made good use of your time in Paris."

"Oh, we all made good use of our time, did we not?" Jacques looked at me with the peculiar smile that usually preceded some unwelcome remark. "Mademoiselle Edmonds managed to acquire a new wardrobe and make herself an object of gossip."

Lucy glared at her brother. "And shall we also tell M'sieu Mailley what you managed to accomplish and that you left Paris a social outcast?"

Philip ignored Jacques and stood to address Lucy. "The hour grows late and I must take my leave. If you and Miss Edmonds wish to ride tomorrow, let me know. Perhaps I can spare Marc to accompany you."

Lucy looked disappointed. "Spare yourself instead. I am not sure my tack is correct. You ought to be there to check it."

"Yes, Mailley, go with her by all means."

Jacques' tone was mocking. "We certainly do not need another riding accident."

"I wish he had stayed in Paris," Lucy muttered when Jacques left the room soon after Philip's departure.

So do I, I thought, but the admission wouldn't help Lucy.

"Jacques is unhappy and he doesn't want to see anyone else enjoying themselves. The best thing you can do is simply pay him no attention."

"And you, Ellen? Can you do that as well?"

"I intend to try. But Philip was right — it's getting late, and a good night's sleep will put us all in a better frame of mind."

"Except for Jacques. You do not know him as well as I do. Sometimes I think he —" Lucy broke off and shook her head as if unwilling to finish the thought.

I laid a reassuring hand on her shoulder. "I know him well enough, Lucy, and so does the Marquis. He may try to irritate us by what he says, but that is as far as it will go."

She pulled away, as if refusing my words along with my touch. "I would not be so sure of that if I were you, Ellen. That is probably what my first companion thought too."

I had asked the question before, but this

time Lucy's tone made me believe that she would answer. "What happened to her?"

Lucy looked up at me, her expression more than usually bitter. "My first companion was Marthé. She left the chateau in the middle of the night, during a terrible storm."

"Why?"

Lucy looked away and shook her head. She waited a moment, and when she spoke again, her voice was almost a whisper. "She had been assaulted."

"Assaulted?" I repeated, unsure of the French word I sought.

"In English, I believe it is called rape."

Even though I should have anticipated Lucy's words, a wave of shock washed over me. I had to force myself to speak again. "Who did it?"

Lucy shrugged. "He never admitted it, of course, but it had to be Jacques."

"He was never brought to justice?"

Her mouth curved in a sardonic smile. "By whom, Ellen? Poor Marthé left a note begging us to forgive her and refused to return or to name anyone."

"And the Marquis? What did he do?"

Lucy looked back at me, her eyes cold. "He did what he always does when Jacques causes problems. He gave her some money and she went away. It was said she was mentally unstable and had a breakdown."

"How terrible for her," I said, but at that moment I was thinking more about my future than the unfortunate Marthé's past. The words I'd overheard the marquis say to Jacques came to mind, and I felt a cold chill.

I will be watching you, and if anything happens to her, you will regret it.

But the marquis was in Paris and powerless to keep his word.

"They say Marthé is not the only woman he has taken by force."

"Well, don't worry about me. I can handle Jacques. But I want a lock put on my door, anyway."

Lucy nodded. "Get one for me too, Ellen."

Chapter Fourteen

The next morning I awoke to a steady rain and leaden skies that gave no promise of clearing during the day.

"If the rain keeps up like this, many people are going to be disappointed," Sophie said as she served our breakfast.

"Why?" I asked.

"Tonight is Midsummer's Eve and tomorrow is St. John's Day, Mademoiselle. There is always a bonfire at the crossroad and flowers to be gathered for it."

"Perhaps the rain will stop by then."

"It will be very bad luck if it does not," Sophie said.

"Peasants and their superstitions!" Lucy said scornfully, but at least she waited until Sophie had left the room.

"It sounds like fun. I would like to see a Midsummer Eve's celebration."

"You do not have them in America?"

"Not where I lived. We know it as the longest day of the year, but there is nothing to celebrate about days getting shorter."

"The Druids made much of it. Sometimes I think half the peasants still keep the Old Ways, although of course they do not admit it."

"If it clears off, let's go. You can tell me what is happening."

The closed look Lucy wore less frequently returned, and she shook her head. "I have not been to a bonfire since . . . for many years. Go if you like, but I shall stay inside tonight."

"You stay inside every night, dear sister," Jacques said as he joined us. "Where is it that Mademoiselle Ellen wishes to go? Perhaps I can escort her."

I made the effort to speak politely. "No, thank you. In any case, the rain will probably prevent the bonfire."

"Bonfire? Oh, yes, I had quite forgotten the date. Well, I never miss it myself. If you change your mind, let me know."

Sophie came back into the dining room with a carafe of coffee for Jacques, and they exchanged a look that spoke volumes. "Good morning, Sir," she said.

"And the same to you, Mademoiselle." He touched her hand when she set down his cup, and Sophie smiled at him for a moment, then seemed to remember where she was and pulled away.

"May I get you anything else?" she asked us.

"No, we will leave you alone," Lucy said, taking no pains to mask her disgust.

Jacques grinned. "How considerate you have become lately, Lucy. We all owe Miss Edmonds a debt of gratitude, I suppose."

"You owe me nothing," I said.

I had never felt comfortable in Jacques' presence, and now that I knew what he had done to my predecessor, I could hardly stand to be in the same room with him.

In the hallway, I half-apologized to Lucy for my behavior. "I told you to ignore him, and yet I did not. I will be more careful in the future."

"Speaking of being careful, you should see to getting a door lock right away. Ask Henri if there is one you can use."

"I will. Where do you plan to work today?"

"The southern windows in the grand salon have the best light. I shall go there first."

"You need some sort of board to rest your sketchbook on," I said when she had found a place to her liking. "I'll ask Henri to see what he can find."

Lucy sounded annoyed. "I will not be fussed over, Ellen. I have been making these sketches for months and nobody ever worried about how I was doing them before. Just leave me alone and let me work."

"Gladly." I hoped Lucy's enthusiasm for design wouldn't turn out to be a passing fancy which would leave her more embittered than ever, but I was proud of what she had accomplished so far.

I found Henri and asked him about the lock and a lap desk for Lucy, neither of which he had on hand.

"Ask M'sieu Mailley about it, Mademoiselle. He may have just what you seek."

How convenient, I thought, pleased to have an excuse to see Philip. I wanted him to hear what had happened in Paris from me before secondhand gossip reached him, with a distorted view of my role in Madame Jourdan's departure.

I took an ancient black umbrella from a brass stand by the side door and walked rapidly to the stable. The rain fell steadily but gently, the kind my uncle always welcomed to nourish the crops without damaging them. As I reached the stable, I briefly put the umbrella aside and turned my face to the refreshing drops.

"Come in where it is dry, Mademoiselle," Marc said, obviously puzzled that I lacked the sense to use my umbrella.

I stepped into the overhang of the stable eaves and shook the excess moisture from the umbrella before closing it. "The rain feels warm. Where is M'sieu Mailley?"

"I believe he is with the dogs, Mademoiselle." The boy added something else that I caught only snatches of, and once again I was struck by the difference between the language used by the people in the village and the marquis and his family. It was almost a different tongue, and even though I had gained facility in understanding Lucy and Jacques and the marquis, I still had trouble with Marc's patois.

"I can find him, thank you," I said, or hoped I said; sometimes the way I was regarded after making what I thought to be a perfectly sensible statement made me realize my own command of French was sometimes lacking.

The hounds began to bark as I approached, and Philip turned to see the cause. His head was bare and his shirt was wet through, but he didn't seem at all embarrassed by his appearance. He held three wriggling puppies in his arms while their mother prowled anxiously about his feet.

"Well, Miss Ellen, what brings you out on such a rainy day? I should think you would stay inside and not risk exposing your new

Paris fashions to the elements."

"As usual, Jacques exaggerated. I returned from Paris with a new riding dress and a dinner gown, hardly a whole wardrobe."

His head-to-toe glance took in the everyday dress he'd seen many times before. "Too bad. But I must not keep you standing in the rain like this. Do go into the office — I believe you know the way — and I shall join you presently."

I stayed where I was. "What are you doing?"

"Bridget whelped last night. To keep her puppies warm and dry, I was about to bring them inside."

"Can I help?"

Philip had a good grip on three of the tiny dogs, but a fourth still lay on the ground, squeaking faintly as it frantically sought its mother.

"No, you would get mud on your dress," he warned, but even as he spoke I had bent to pick up the puppy. Suddenly its mother growled and showed her teeth, and only Philip's restraining hand on her collar kept her from lunging at me.

"Why did she do that?" I asked, backing away from the hound and her sharp teeth.

"She knows I will not harm her puppies.

You are a stranger and she suspects your intentions."

"Tell her I will not hurt her baby."

"She will get that idea when you put it down. I have a bed prepared in the office. Take the puppy there — I cannot hold Bridget back forever."

I did as I was told and found a flannel-lined willow basket beside the fireplace. I gently placed the puppy in it, then stood well back as Philip brought the others in, with Bridget circling his feet and crying mournfully.

"She sounds so pitiful."

"You ought to be around during a full moon when all the hounds start howling like that. The sound can raise goose flesh, all right."

Philip put the last puppy into the basket and their mother joined them, licking each in turn with such vigor we both laughed.

"If they can stand that, I doubt a little rain will hurt them," I said.

"Nevertheless, they are valuable animals and the Marquis has been waiting for this litter. I would not want anything to happen to them. Sit down," he added, holding out a Windsor chair for me while he continued to stand.

The mere mention of the marquis seemed to place a constraint between us, and I spoke quickly. "Some things have changed at the townhouse since you were there." Briefly I sketched the events which occurred at the dinner party and immediately afterward. "Nicole saw me leaving your room, and Madame Jourdan made it sound as if there had been some sort of —" I faltered, searching for a word.

"Impropriety?" Philip raised one eyebrow, but otherwise his expression didn't change.

"Yes, or worse. But then she went on to accuse me of the same thing with the Marquis, and that charge made him so angry he told Madame Jourdan to leave."

Philip looked amused. "Really? I congratulate you, Miss Edmonds. You got rid of your chief rival, after all."

"You are impossible!" I exclaimed, exasperated. "Madame Jourdan was my rival only in the sense that she wanted to get rid of Lucy by marrying her off."

Philip looked impassive. "If you say so. What else should I know about?"

Deciding it wasn't prudent to discuss the marquis, I told him how Jacques' courtship of Mathilde Lambert had ended.

"So that is what Lucy meant last night

when she said he had left Paris in disgrace," Philip said.

I noticed that he didn't seem to have any more sympathy for Jacques than I did.

"Yes, and now he's in a terrible mood. Lucy and I need your help, especially until the Marquis comes home."

"My help? What do you expect me to do? You know how well Jacques listens to me."

"Lucy and I want locks put on our doors, and Henri said you could take care of it."

Philip walked over to the willow basket where the puppies were happily nursing. When he turned to face me, I read genuine concern in his expression. "Has he gone so far, then? The Marquis would kill Jacques if he knew of that."

My face colored as I realized Philip might have read more into my request than was warranted. "Nothing has happened yet, and we'd like to keep it that way. And it's not just Jacques. Madame Albert has made a habit of entering my room at will, and I don't care to have her going through and taking my things."

Philip sighed and shrugged in a gesture of acquiescence. "All right, but when the Marquis wants to know who has been ruining his doors, I do not intend to take the blame."

"Thank you." I rose from the chair and started for the door, then turned back. "Oh, I almost forgot. Lucy needs some kind of lapboard to steady her sketchbook. Could you make one for her?"

He nodded. "It may be tomorrow before I can find time to see to it. I assume you want the locks first."

"Yes, please."

Philip followed me to the door and handed me the umbrella. "I think Jacques will be all right, but if there is any trouble, you know where to find me."

Philip's words were reassuring but impersonal, and at this parting, it was evident he didn't have even the slightest thought of kissing me.

On the way back to the chateau, I wondered why Philip Mailley seemed to be so different each time we were alone. Part of the time he seemed to believe me when I said I had no interest in marrying into the d'Arc family, but there was still something about me he did not trust, and I had no idea what it could be. On the other hand, there were things about him I didn't quite trust, either.

I looked over at the grand salon windows and picked out the one where Lucy sat sketching.

Lucy would make a good match for a man who needs her dowry, Mignon had said.

She would also be a good catch for a man who wanted land of his own. *No wonder Philip has no interest in me.* I could play the role of spoiler to his plans.

My reason told me I was a blind fool to care for Philip, but my heart refused to listen.

Lucy was a little dispirited at luncheon because she hadn't made the progress she had expected on her first new sketches. She had brought home a book of fashion plates from the House of Worth and complained that everything she tried to start was too much like a style he had already produced.

"Throw that book away and do what you like, as before. You have a very good instinct for the way your designs will actually look on a woman. I think that's what M'sieu Worth wants."

"I am not sure even he knows what he wants. Anyway, all I have to show for the morning's work is an aching back and many ruined pages."

"It will go better, and Philip promised to make a lap board of some kind to hold your sketchbook. That ought to take the strain off your back."

"You saw Philip this morning?" she asked, and I explained that Henri had sent me to him for door locks.

"What do you intend to lock up?" Jacques asked, strolling into the room just as we were finishing our meal.

"Ourselves," Lucy replied. "Madame Albert has been roaming again. She took several things from my room while we were in Paris, including my sharpest scissors. She is a danger to herself, as well as to us all."

"I suppose I could pay her a little visit and recover the loot."

"Sophie keeps an eye out when she cleans Madame's room, but she has not yet found my dressmaker's shears. I want to make sure she does not take anything else of mine."

"But locks on every door? The Marquis will not like that."

"Why would he object?" I asked.

Lucy answered me. "Because he wants to keep the chateau as it was in its glory, with nothing altered."

Jacques scowled. "There has been no glory in this place for two hundred years or more. Maybe one day he will realize that and get rid of this pile of bricks."

"Sell the chateau?" Lucy shook her head. "The Marquis would never agree to do that."

"When it is mine, that is exactly what I intend to do."

"I know you want to sell some of the land, but surely you would want to keep the Chateau d'Arc," I said.

Jacques turned to me, his eyes hard and accusing. "Who told you that? No, do not bother to answer — I already know. What else did Mailley tell you about me?"

"Nothing," I replied, truthfully enough.

"I wonder," he muttered. "The man is so eager to get the chateau for himself, he would do almost anything." Jacques glanced over at Lucy, his meaning perfectly clear.

"I will not listen to any more of your foolish talk," she snapped, but Jacques merely leaned back in his chair and smiled.

"What can you do about it, Lucy? Run from me?"

"I wish I were a man." She beat her clenched fists against the arms of her chair and glared at her brother. "I swear I would fight you, even from this chair."

"You would never win." Jacques' smile was far more infuriating than his anger had been, and I knew exactly how Lucy felt. A man could fight another man with his fists and settle a dispute fair and square. But a woman had to find other ways to settle her scores.

"Come, Ellen, it is time I got back to work," Lucy said calmly, and I was gratified to see the disappointment in Jacques' face.

"You would leave me to dine all alone? How cruel."

"I hope you choke," Lucy said pleasantly.

By the time Philip had returned from Dreux with the door locks, the rain had all but stopped and a ragged rainbow arched over the garden, promising a fair evening.

"It's good the rain won't interfere with the bonfire tonight," I said.

Philip looked up from the auger he was using on my doorframe. "Who told you about that?"

"Sophie. She said it was a big event hereabouts."

"Yes, and a rather strange one. They say it honors St. John, but it is more an observance of the ancient Druids' Midsummer's Eve ritual."

"It sounds interesting. Would it be all right if I watched it?"

Philip resumed turning the auger and didn't immediately reply. "Not alone. However, I expect Jacques would be happy to take you."

"I would not go to see the Pope with him," I said, naming the most unlikely place

Jacques would be invited.

"Then I suppose that leaves me."

"You don't sound very enthusiastic. Is that an invitation or not?"

"Somewhat. I will also ask Lucy, of course."

"I hope you can persuade her to go along, but from the way she talked this morning, I doubt she will."

"Hold this bracket for me so I can see where to put the striker — this is a job for four hands."

As soon as my lock was installed, Philip handed me the oddly shaped key to unlock it and invited me to try it.

"It turns to the left," he said when my first efforts failed.

"Like this?" I asked, still without result. Only when Philip put his hand over mine and guided it did I succeed.

A shock jolted through my body at the contact of his hand on mine, and I wondered if he had felt it too.

"Try it again," he said, removing his hand. Clumsily I scraped the key in the lock, and this time the door yielded.

"You should put the key on a chain and wear it around your neck," he advised. "If you lose it, you may find yourself locked out of your own room."

Philip picked up his wooden tool carrier and we started toward Lucy's room.

"What about Lucy's key? Should I carry them both?"

"Lucy is old enough to care for her own key, I hope. But you should have a duplicate in case of an emergency."

"What kind of emergency?" Lucy asked from her doorway. "What do you expect to happen?"

Philip spoke to her as if lecturing a child. "No one ever expects emergencies, Lucy — that is what makes them emergencies in the first place. But if there should be a fire, for example, and no one could unlock your door, you might never awaken."

"What a cheerful thought!" Lucy exclaimed. "Do not share it with Jacques. It might give him ideas."

"He has enough ideas of his own without mine. Now if you ladies will kindly move out of the way, I will finish this work."

I excused myself as soon as my bracket-holding duties were completed, knowing Lucy was more likely to do something Philip suggested if the same idea came from him. However, he reported a few minutes later that Lucy had no intention of going with us.

"The bonfire is lighted at nightfall and everyone must stay until the fire burns to ashes. Come to the stable after dinner and we will walk over."

"Will you come for dinner?" I asked, although I was almost certain he would refuse, since Jacques was in the house.

"Not until the Marquis comes back, and then only if he invites me. You are not yet in a position to speak for him, you know."

My face flushed and my mouth twisted in annoyance. "I wish you wouldn't keep presuming I want to take over the Chateau d'Arc. I have the authority to speak for Lucy as well as myself in the Marquis' absence, and I know Lucy would like you to come to dinner."

Philip's lips compressed. "All the more reason I should not. And one other thing. Bring a scarf or a shawl to cover your head tonight."

"I have never been to a pagan ritual," I told Philip as we walked the few hundred yards from the stable to the crossroad where the Dampierre road forked to the left.

He laughed. "You had better not let these people hear you say that. They certainly do not consider themselves pagans."

"Then we shall just talk in English. You are the only one around here who can understand me."

"Well, most of the time I do, although that American accent of yours is really quite barbaric."

"Barbaric! Just because I don't swallow half my words and broaden all my A's?"

Philip smiled. "Did you know that your hair always starts flying when you are angry?"

I took my scarf from around my neck and tied it under my chin, covering my hair as well as I could.

"You still do not resemble a peasant," he said.

"And you certainly bear no resemblance to a gentleman!"

Philip's laughter was with me, not against me, and it was contagious. By the time we reached the bonfire site, we were both smiling, yet neither could have said why.

Such a large crowd had already gathered that I thought the whole village must have turned out for the occasion. An old man with a white beard, apparently the village elder, held a flaming brand. He stood quietly, his bright eyes scanning the gathering crowd, until a younger man who had climbed to the rooftop of a west-facing house shouted something in a language I had never heard, and the crowd cheered.

"What did he say?" I asked, but even before Philip could reply, I understood, for the old man stepped forward and threw the flaming brand into a nest of hay and twigs in the middle of a towering stack of wood. There was a bright flare as the hay caught, then a satisfied murmur from the crowd as the twigs flamed and lighted the wood around it.

The old man raised both his arms and looked up to the heavens. Again he shouted something I could not understand, and this time the others shouted it back.

"That does not sound like French," I said.

"No. It is Breton, an old dialect that has all but faded out."

The crowd had hushed, and all seemed to be watching the growing flames with an almost hypnotic intensity. "What happens next?" I whispered.

"Watch, then be ready to join in. Spectators are not allowed at this bonfire."

Slowly, almost imperceptibly, the people nearest the fire began to sway back and forth. Behind them, the next group swayed in the opposite direction, until all were weaving in time to a guttural chant someone had begun. The swaying lines began to circle slowly around the bonfire, so slowly that at first I felt no sensation of movement. Philip took my elbow and nudged me to start walking.

He took up the same strange cry of the others, and soon my throat made the eerie sound. From time to time someone would leave the circle and slowly toss flowers into the fire — roses and lilies and vervain. As in a dream, I saw Sophie drift to the fire and add her offering.

Next, several women came forward and held their babies toward the fire. Although they were close enough to the fire to feel its heat, none of the infants cried. By the time twilight had faded into dusk and dusk into darkness, every stick of wood in the elaborate structure had ignited. Idly I wondered where so much dry wood had been found on such a wet day, when most of the land around the village consisted of treeless fields.

The deep woods, of course. There would be enough fallen wood in two or three acres of the deep woods to build several bonfires. The oak forests, sacred to the Druids, would be a source of the wood, but a bonfire so large could never be held there for fear of burning the entire forest.

"This bonfire is always made at a crossroad," Philip said when the celebrants slowed to a stop and wiped their perspiring brows.

"Why?"

He pointed to the old man who had lit the fire and who now reached into and withdrew a flaming stick. I winced, sure he must have burned himself, but he held the brand aloft and cried out four times, turning as he did so to face all four directions. When he came back to where he had started, the crowd let out a tremendous cheer, and he threw the stick back into the fire.

"That is almost all," Philip said. We had backed away from the heat as the last wood charred to ashes, but many still stood next to it, holding out their hands as if seeking enough strength from its warmth to last them another year.

The old man backed away, and someone brought a stool for him to sit on and handed him a jug.

"Calvados," Philip told me. "It is made nearby and always drunk at the bonfire."

I watched the jug make its rounds and hoped it would run dry before it got to me, but when it did, another immediately replaced it. When Philip's turn came, he tilted the jug and drank, then wiped the top with his sleeve and held it for me.

"Not too much, now," he warned. I tried

to take a small sip, but someone standing behind me jostled my arm, and I gasped and choked at the flaming substance that seared my throat and took away my breath.

"Good, is it not?" someone said, and through eyes that watered I turned to see Jacques.

Philip's eyes narrowed in anger. "You could have hurt her."

"But I did not, did I, Mademoiselle? That first drink of Calvados is always the best."

I was aware the villagers were staring at us. "I want to go now."

"No, we cannot leave yet," Philip said.

"He is as superstitious as the other peasants," Jacques said, "but I have had my fill of the festivities. Good night to you both."

"That is not all he has his fill of," Philip said as Jacques staggered off into the shadows.

"The Marquis says Jacques gets wild when he drinks," I said. The knowledge I could lock my door against him warmed me — or was it the brandy?

"This is almost the end," Philip said when Father Campeau walked to the bonfire and began to sprinkle it with Holy Water, muttering in Latin as he did so. The villagers crossed themselves, and although I had no idea what it all meant, I followed

Philips' lead and crossed myself too.

The old man returned to his post and raised his hands to the heavens in a lengthy incantation. The people stood silent as he took an unburned stick and stirred the ashes with it. After a long moment, he held the stick up, showing it had not ignited.

"That is an evil omen," Philip whispered.

Many of the villagers fell to their knees with a sort of low keening, unlike anything I had ever heard.

"What do they think will happen?"

"They will expect bad times from now until the next bonfire."

Despite the heat generated by the bonfire's ashes, I shivered. I felt the despair of the people at that moment, a premonition that something awful was, indeed, about to happen.

"Can we leave now?"

"Wait. One more thing remains to be done."

One by one, the villagers approached the bonfire site. Using a variety of implements brought for the purpose, they each scooped up a handful of ashes and silently bore them away.

Philip joined them, filling what appeared to be a portion of an old stirrup with gray ash.

"Now we can go," he said.

"What will you do with the ashes?"

"Hold out your hand. You will not be burned," he added when I hesitated.

Philip poured a spoonful of warm ashes into my palm and closed my fist with his hand. "Sprinkle these on the hearth, and the chateau will be safe from lightning for another year."

Through the gap made by the village gate, the ramparts of the chateau brooded against the night sky. In the distance an owl called, and I felt a nameless dread.

Something bad is about to happen here.

I knew it as well as I had ever known anything, yet I was powerless to act against it.

"I hope partaking in the local customs was not too much for you," Philip said when we reached the chateau.

I am afraid — hold me, Philip.

"Not at all. Thank you for taking me," I murmured. I watched him walk away, unable to find the courage to call him back or the words to say if I had.

At least I can lock my door now. The knowledge reassured me, but it was cold comfort in the face of my fear and dread.

Chapter Fifteen

After a restless night of troubled dreams, I opened my drapes to a world enveloped in dense, gray fog. No landmarks could be seen from any window in the chateau, creating an eerie effect that reinforced my vague feelings of impending doom.

Even Nature knows something is wrong. But what?

Lucy complained she felt unwell and planned to stay in bed all morning, since the lack of sunlight would make sketching difficult anyway. Knowing his state the night before, I expected Jacques to sleep until noon, giving me the opportunity to revisit the tower room for another look at Madeline d'Arc's portrait.

Recalling the darkness of the stairway, I lighted my lantern and took it with me. It cast flickering shadows against the stone walls as I climbed to the third floor where the marquis and Madame Albert had their rooms.

Even though my kid slippers made no

sound against the strip of carpet in the hallway, I tiptoed past Jacques' room. The tower door seemed stuck, and I had to put down the lantern and pull on it with both hands before it opened, its hinges protesting loudly. I winced when the door slammed shut behind me and hoped Jacques wasn't a light sleeper.

I felt revulsion as I brushed against several spider webs, but I kept going until I had gained the tower itself. I set down my lantern and walked over to the window. The fog still lay thick around the ground, but the sun had already begun to burn through it. The stable's roof was vaguely distinguishable in the mist, but I could see nothing else.

Philip is probably already hard at work somewhere out there, I thought. If it weren't for the fog, I might be able to see him. A little ashamed I wanted to spy on him, I turned away from the window.

Taking the lantern, I went to the portrait I had come to view. The first time I'd seen it, when Jacques brought me to the room, all I could tell was its subject was a blond woman in a green dress. Carefully I lifted the canvas cover that half-concealed it, raising a cloud of dust. Although the portrait had evidently been stored for many years, its colors were still vivid. I raised my lantern to bring the subject's facial features out of the shadows.

It could be Lucy herself. From her imperial expression and delicate features to her heart-shaped face, Lucy was Madeline d'Arc made over. There were differences, though; if the painter had done justice to Madeline d'Arc, her eyes were a different shade from Lucy's, and her neck was longer and more slender. But there was no question this portrait was of the marquise, even before I dusted off the engraved plate at the bottom of the frame and read the inscription: *Madeline Rosier, Marquise d'Arc, 1854.*

Knowing Jacques was now twenty-five, I calculated the portrait must have been painted shortly after Madeline's marriage. Her dress was dark green, probably taffeta, with a sweetheart neckline and huge, puffed sleeves. She held a folded fan in one hand, while the other was half-hidden in the folds of her full skirt. In the background the artist had painted the left side of the Chateau d'Arc, where a close inspection revealed the figure of a man on horseback, surrounded by hounds. Madeline d'Arc's expression suggested that, as far as she was concerned, hunting would always be in the background.

What had Madeline d'Arc really been like? Her eyes seemed to be gazing directly into mine, but they told me nothing. Perhaps she was a woman who hid her true feelings.

"I wish you could speak," I said. My voice echoed hollowly in the tower room, and I shivered.

It is time to leave this place, I told myself.

I covered the portrait and wondered why the marquis had hidden it in a place where his daughter could never see her late mother's likeness.

I had just picked up my lantern when I heard the hinges squeak as the tower door opened, followed by footsteps ascending the stairs. Hastily I put out the lantern's flame and stepped into the shadows. I didn't want to be found in the tower room alone, especially if those footsteps were Jacques'.

The steps grew ever louder; then a lantern cast its glow into the gloom and Jacques emerged. From my hiding place I watched him walk over to an old round-top trunk, remove the small rug that covered it, and open the lid. I was too far away to see his every movement, but he seemed to be searching for something and not finding it. He paused every few moments to sneeze, cursing each time.

The dust tickled my nose too, but I dared not sneeze. I had no idea what Jacques was after, but I was sure he didn't want an audience.

It seemed an eternity before he finally slammed down the lid of the trunk. I had hoped he would leave then, but instead he walked around the tower room, pausing from time to time to investigate the few objects placed there. Finally, after sneezing several times in a row, Jacques uttered another oath before he kicked the trunk and started toward the stairs.

My heart nearly stopped when he paused before his mother's portrait. *Could he have seen me?*

"Poor *Maman*. You never liked dust, either," he murmured. He removed, then rearranged the canvas to cover the entire portrait. He sneezed again, then started back down the stairs.

Hearing the tower door slam behind him, I let out my breath in a long sigh of relief. I stayed where I was for several minutes before emerging from my hiding place, in case he might decide to return.

What was Jacques looking for in the trunk?

Curious, I raised the lid. The contents

were jumbled in disarray, probably from his search, and there was no doubt it held a lady's belongings.

When I set aside a top tray containing a tangle of ribbons, the scent of lavender filled the dusty air. I found several brightly-colored silk petticoats, then a delicate lace shawl that must have belonged to Madeline. Apparently, she had many garments of velvet, satin, and lace, and fans of sandal-wood and ivory.

Lucy should have these things of her mother's, I mused, and I wondered why no one had ever thought to give them to her. It was a matter I would take up with the marquis on his return.

I replaced the tray and sighed as I closed the trunk. Seeing a portrait of the marquise was one thing, but actually handling her most intimate possessions was another. I felt like a trespasser, and at that moment all I wanted was to get out of the tower room without being seen.

I picked up my lantern, useless since I had no matches to relight it, and started down the stairs. After the first turn of the steps, I was in almost total darkness, and panic threatened to overtake me. But I crept down the stairs, bracing my right hand on the wall and cautiously feeling for the next step.

Something furry brushed against my arm and I stifled a scream. A rat, perhaps, or a huge spider. There were probably poisonous spiders in France, but I had never bothered to inquire about them. I knew about Black Widow spiders; my uncle had shown me a nest once, the shiny red hourglasses gleaming on their undersides.

"Why are they called Black Widows?" I had asked, and when he told me, I accused him of making it up. What female would kill her husband? I thought he was teasing me.

I kept going, relieved that the turns were getting wider, proof I neared the bottom. At last I could see light under the door, and my foot encountered a flat surface.

I had made it down the stairs in the darkness; now I would have to return to my room without running into Jacques. I stood against the door and listened for a long moment but heard nothing but my own labored breathing. After a while, I reached for the door latch and pushed down on it.

Nothing happened. I put down the lantern and used both hands, but the latch refused to give. I tried again, this time pushing against the door with all my strength, but it still refused to budge.

If I didn't know better, I'd think it was locked, I told myself. The door hadn't been locked when Jacques showed me the tower room, nor had it been this morning. I gathered my strength and pushed hard, still with no effect. I probed the area around the handle with my fingertips to make sure there wasn't a keyhole I had somehow overlooked. Feeling nothing, I tried to open the door again, but again it resisted my best efforts.

Tired and perspiring, I began to feel an edge of panic. I'd never liked close, dark places, and the notion I might run out of air and never be found made me bold enough to bang on the door and cry out for help. If Jacques heard me and opened the door, I could make up some excuse. At the moment, dealing with Jacques seemed preferable to smothering only inches away from the hallway.

No one came to my aid, however, and after a while I was too hoarse to yell anymore. I sat on the bottom step and considered my plight. Jacques might or might not return to his room before nightfall. The other occupants of the third floor, the servants, probably wouldn't come back up until after dinner. By that time, I would have been missed and a search started. Would anyone think to look for me in the tower room? I rather doubted it. I had to find some way to attract attention to my plight, but I could not do it from where I was.

Leaving the useless lantern behind, I forced myself to climb back up the steep steps. Once I stumbled and almost fell backward, causing me to go much more slowly, until the welcome light of the tower room guided me up the last few steps.

I crossed to the window and looked out. All but a few wisps of fog had disappeared, and I could see the stable yard quite clearly. I saw no one, and even if I had, they would not be likely to look up at the tower window unless something attracted their attention.

I would have to break the glass. But what could I use? From the few objects scattered around the tower room, I chose an empty picture frame from which nearly all the gilt had flaked away. I hurled it against the window with all my might, with no more effect than if I had rapped the glass with my bare knuckles. Dropping the frame, I looked around again, but found nothing substantial enough to break window glass.

Back at the window, I saw Marc grooming Lucy's horse. If only he would look up and see me! I tried tapping on the glass with both hands and hitting it with my shoe, but although the din I made hurt my own ears, the sound never traveled past the stubborn glass. I had to break the window or wait to be found, one or the other.

The one thing in the room large enough to impact glass was Madeline d'Arc's trunk. Even empty, it would be far too heavy for me to pick up, but I might be able to use the lift-out tray. Quickly, I dumped its contents on the floor. The tray was wooden and heavier than I expected, but by turning it sideways, I could swing it with some force. Heaving it to shoulder-level, I struck the glass once, then twice, but nothing happened. The third time, I applied every last ounce of strength I had and was rewarded by the sound of breaking glass.

I had no time to congratulate myself, however, for I almost tumbled out of the window when it gave way, and a shard of glass scraped my right forearm, producing an alarming jet of blood.

I will not faint, I vowed as the tower room spun sickeningly.

Marc must have been too far away to hear the breaking glass, for he hadn't looked around. I still had to get his attention.

I put down the remnants of the tray, which had splintered along with the glass, and struggled back to the gaping hole it had created. Leaning out as far as I dared, I screamed.

"Help!" I called first, and then realizing Marc spoke no English, added, *"Au secour!"*

When he still did not seem to hear me, I cried out again.

Soon another figure emerged from the stable and looked in the direction of the chateau's lower floor.

"Philip! I'm up here!"

He shaded his eyes against the glare of the morning sun shining on the remaining mist and finally saw me. Still, he stayed where he was as if he didn't understand I needed him.

I cupped my hands to my mouth, leaned as far out as I dared and screamed loudly enough for everyone in the village to hear. "Help me!"

This time Philip began to run toward the chateau, and I sank weakly to the floor. My arm was bleeding badly, and, with a murmured apology to Madeline d'Arc, I used one of her silk petticoats to stem the flow of blood. As I wrapped the wound, I noticed what appeared to be a slender bundle of letters lying near the remains of the trunk tray. I hadn't seen it when I had looked into the trunk earlier — and I was fairly certain Jacques hadn't either. Could that be what he had sought?

I reached out for it, then heard someone coming up the stairs in a hurry. I knew a moment of panic when I realized that it might not be Philip, after all. I hadn't thought he could reach the tower room so quickly. Without inspecting it, I thrust the bundle deep into my pocket. A moment later Philip emerged from the stairs, and I smiled my relief.

He looked down at me in disbelief. "You just cannot stay out of trouble, can you?"

"You might be a little more concerned for my welfare," I said stiffly. I had not anticipated his reaction, and more than just my arm hurt.

"Not until you are more concerned with your welfare yourself. Whatever possessed you to come up here in the first place?"

"Nothing."

Philip laughed unexpectedly. "You look like a child caught with her hand in the cookie jar."

"Not my hand, my arm."

I had been holding the remnants of Madeline d'Arc's petticoat over my wound, but now I let it drop, revealing the blood-soaked sleeve.

Philip's eyes widened and he knelt beside me to inspect my arm.

His voice held an edge of anger. "You

could have bled to death up here, you know."

"I still might," I said, aware that blood was once more seeping through the material.

"Can you walk?"

I was aware of Philip's arm around my waist, pulling me to a standing position. My arm throbbed painfully, and a roaring filled my ears as the tower room began to revolve.

I believe I might faint, I tried to say.

It was my last conscious thought for some time.

"Mademoiselle, can you hear me? Wake up."

Someone was speaking to me from a long distance. I tried to open my eyes, but the effort was too great.

"The sedative should have worn off by now. Is there nothing you can do to bring her out of it?"

I recognized Philip's voice and wondered why he sounded almost angry.

"She will be all right, M'sieu Mailley. She is weak from the loss of blood, but that will take care of itself. Let her rest."

I know that voice, I thought, but my mind found no name to put to it.

"Thank you, Doctor Dubois. It is lucky

for Mademoiselle Edmonds you arrived at the exact moment she needed a doctor."

Dr. Dubois — of course. He was also present the first time I fainted. I wanted to mention that fact, but I couldn't make my mouth work.

"The young lady seems to make a habit of injuring herself," the doctor said. "The Marquis is quite concerned about her."

"And I am concerned about him, Sir," Philip said.

His voice faded and a door closed, leaving me alone.

Is something wrong with the marquis? I would ask Philip when he came back, but first I would rest a little while longer . . .

Philip and I were riding in the deep forest when he stopped and lifted me from my horse. He held me in his arms, murmuring how much he had loved me from the first moment he saw me. He covered my face with kisses, and I wept tears of happiness. But someone else was there, watching us. I knew we must leave, but I didn't want to go . . .

"Come, Sleeping Beauty. You really must wake up now."

Philip's voice was real, as was his light kiss

on my lips. Still under the influence of my dream, I kept my eyes shut and kissed him back. Immediately, he pulled away and I opened my eyes.

I saw I had been placed in a second-floor guest chamber, ironically the same one in which Jacques had made his unwelcome advances. A lantern glowed on the bedside table, the only spot of light in the darkness.

"Is it night?" I asked.

Philip nodded. "I thought you would never wake up. How does your arm feel?"

I tried to move it and winced. "It hurts a bit."

"I should think so, after what you did to it." He sounded cross again.

"Who bandaged it?"

"Doctor Dubois. He says you will be all right if you can manage to stay away from places where you have no business going."

"You made that up." Then I remembered what I'd heard earlier. "Has the Marquis returned from Paris?"

Philip folded his arms across his chest and nodded. "Yes. Doctor Dubois came with him."

"Why? Is he ill?"

"You know the Marquis is not a well man." Philip made it a statement.

I nodded. "I thought he was getting better."

"Perhaps, but yesterday he suffered some kind of collapse. When he insisted on returning to the chateau, Doctor Dubois came with him."

"What is wrong? How bad is it?"

Philip shrugged. "The Marquis is sleeping now. The Doctor will know more about his condition tomorrow."

"I must apologize to him for breaking the window."

"He knows nothing about it, and you should not tell him."

"Where did he think I was, not to be here when he arrived?"

"Lucy told him you were out riding."

"What about Jacques?" I spoke his name with reluctance. "Does he know I was in the tower?"

"Yes. But that is enough talk for tonight. You can see the Marquis tomorrow."

Don't go, I longed to say.

Philip turned the lantern down, but did not extinguish it. "Sophie will look in on you tonight."

"Is Lucy all right?" I asked, ashamed I hadn't asked about her earlier.

Philip smiled. "Lucy is still Lucy. She is even more angry with you than I was."

"Tell her I'm sorry."

"She knows it. Good night."

Although I had much to think about, eventually I fell asleep again. I awoke with a start some time in the night when I heard my door open.

"Sophie? Is that you?"

I struggled to sit up and peered into the shadows beyond the small circle of lantern light. I could see nothing, but even though no one had spoken, I felt a presence in the room.

Swinging my legs to the side of the bed, I sat up. I felt momentarily faint, then recovered. For a moment I thought my imagination had been playing tricks. Then I heard a low chuckle.

A witch, I thought shakily, but such creatures do not exist.

"Go away," I said aloud with as much force as I could, speaking French without even taking time to think about it.

"You did not heed my warning. You should not be here, Sara."

Madame Albert again. There was nothing supernatural about her.

My brief moment of relief was short-lived when she stepped into the lantern's glow and I saw the glint of light against the metal object she held aloft.

Lucy's shears — and she intended to use them on me.

As Madame Albert lunged toward me, I rolled to the other side of the bed and slid to the floor. Crouching, I ran to the door and closed it behind me, aware that Madame Albert would follow.

She is old and can scarcely walk, I told myself, but I wasn't in very good condition at that moment. I felt dizzy and leaned against the door to steady myself, but she banged on the other side, and since I couldn't lock her in, I forced myself to move away. I couldn't get very far, but I hoped I could outlast her.

I walked past the second-floor chambers and started down the steps, feeling almost as if I were floating. I made it to Lucy's room and kept going until at last I stood before my own door. Now I would be safe.

The latch refused to yield, and for a moment I couldn't think why. Then I remembered — Philip had put a lock on it. I had locked it before I visited the tower room, but where was the key? He had advised me to wear it around my neck, but I hadn't taken time to do so.

I thought it must be in my pocket. My right arm hurt, but I forced it into the pocket, where it encountered the bundle of letters from the tower room. Digging deeper, I finally felt the blessed cool metal of the key. My hand trembled as I fitted it into the lock and turned it.

"Sara!"

From the corner of my eye I saw that Madame Albert was already down the stairs and moving slowly but steadily toward me. The lock refused to budge. Remembering Philip's hand on mine, I jabbed the key to the left and almost fell into the room when the door swung open.

Madame Albert reached my door just as I managed to slam it in her face. I turned the key in the lock and leaned against the door, panting and enveloped in a cold sweat. On the other side, Madame Albert moaned and shrieked in frustration.

Surely someone will hear and take her away, I thought.

It seemed a very long time before I heard Henri's voice in the hall, but from its sound I knew he was keeping his distance. No doubt he had seen the shears and feared to come near her.

Madame Albert began to pound steadily at my door, calling over and over for Sara.

This is all a horrible nightmare, and any minute now I shall wake up and laugh at my imagination, I tried to tell myself. But the steady pain in my arm was real, and so was the danger. Someone was going to have to control Madame Albert.

I looked to my window and wished I had the strength to open it and go to Philip. But I was scarcely able to stand; even if the window were open, I could never walk to the stable.

Suddenly the noise ceased, and I hoped Madame Albert had given up and left. But then I heard Lucy calling to her and knew she must still be at my door.

"Madame Albert! Come here, I need you."

There was a moment of silence, and then Lucy repeated her request, her voice sounding closer this time.

How did she get into the hallway? Lucy would have been in bed for several hours by now, and she needed help to get into her chair. Perhaps Sophie had heard the commotion and come to help her. In any case, it wasn't safe for Lucy to confront Madame Albert, and I hoped Henri would take advantage of the madwoman's temporary distraction to take the shears away from her.

"Your mother will be upset, Mademoiselle Lucy," Madame Albert scolded. "It is late, and you should be in the nursery."

"Then come and help me back, Madame."

The old woman's voice was shrill. "The Marquis said that is no longer my work. You have others to help you now."

"No, Madame, only you. For my mother's sake, please help me."

What was going on? All was quiet, and I sensed Madame Albert had left her post outside my door. Hastily unlocking the door, I peered into the shadowy hallway and gasped in shock.

Madame Albert stood with her back to me, the shears hanging from her right hand. Henri was cautiously coming up behind her. Facing Madame Albert was Lucy, a ghostly wraith whose white nightgown and pale face glowed in the surrounding gloom. She leaned against the wall halfway between her room and mine and spoke again.

"You must assist me, Madame. I am growing weak."

Madame Albert stood motionless for a moment, then started toward Lucy just as Henri seized the shears.

I could scarcely believe my eyes. Not only was Lucy standing alone in the hall, but there was only one way she could have gotten there. The realization all but overwhelmed me, and I sank to the floor to keep from falling.

Lucy had heard Madame Albert and walked from her room into the hall to help me, unaided.

Dr. Dubois was right — Lucy d'Arc could walk, after all.

Chapter Sixteen

So many things now occurred at the same time that I couldn't sort them out immediately.

After taking the shears from Madame Albert, Henri rushed past her and reached Lucy just as she collapsed. At the same instant, Jacques came running down the stairs, tying the sash on his dressing gown. Sizing up the situation, he spoke quietly to Madame Albert while Henri picked up Lucy and carried her back to her room.

Whatever storm had triggered Madame Albert's outburst had subsided, and once more she was merely a frail old lady who allowed Jacques to lead her back to her room.

Having followed Jacques down the stairs, Sophie helped me to my feet and started toward my room.

"I must see Lucy," I told her.

"Mademoiselle must go to bed immediately," someone said, and I turned to see Dr. Dubois.

"Lucy just walked, Doctor!"

"You actually saw her taking steps on her own?"

"No, but she must have."

Dr. Dubois placed his hand under my left elbow and guided me into my room. "You have been under the influence of strong sedatives. You must not excite yourself." The doctor turned to Sophie. "See that Mam'selle rests now."

"But —"

"You will see Mademoiselle Lucy tomorrow."

Dr. Dubois left, closing the door behind him, and Sophie turned back my bed and began to unbutton my dress.

"What happened, Mademoiselle?"

"Madame Albert came after me with Lucy's dressmaker's shears and followed me back to my room. Lucy must have heard her and left her bed to help me."

Sophie looked skeptical. "Without her chair, Mademoiselle?"

"Apparently. I wish the Doctor would let me talk to her."

"You do not look well, Mademoiselle. I believe the Doctor is right."

I felt almost too weak to move, and meekly I allowed Sophie to help me into my nightgown and tuck me into bed. I was almost asleep when I became aware of voices in the hallway; then the door opened and Sophie returned.

"The Doctor wants you to have this, Mam'selle," she said.

I allowed Sophie to lift my head and pour the contents of a small vial down my throat. It was a thick, bitter liquid I had difficulty swallowing. I wanted to ask what it was, but before I could form the words, she was gone.

The draught made me feel queasy, and I managed to stagger over to the basin just in time. Cursing the doctor and his vile concoction, I crept back to bed and fell instantly asleep.

I awakened to a roll of thunder reverberating through the chateau, punctuated by flashes of lightning. But more than the noise of the storm, I was aware of something else — the faint creak of door hinges and slow footsteps coming into my room.

Sophie has returned to check on me, I thought groggily. I opened my eyes, intending to tell her I was all right. Then I realized my visitor was a man.

Dr. Dubois? But why does he not have a lantern? And why does he seem to be looking for something?

Although my heart pounded furiously, I

402

lay still and forced myself to breathe naturally. Through almost-closed eyes I saw the man move toward my dresser, and when he put his candleholder down, I saw his features reflected in the mirror.

Jacques.

My first impulse was to jump out of bed and run. But my legs refused to move, and I realized what was left of the drought Sophie had given me must have taken effect.

I now believed it hadn't come from the doctor at all. Jacques seemed to have Sophie under his spell. He must have asked her to give me the concoction. Had I kept it all down, I never would have known he had entered my room.

What is he looking for?

Whatever it was, Jacques wasn't finding it, and he cursed under his breath as he closed the door to my wardrobe. I shut my eyes tightly and clenched my fists as I heard him open the drawer to my bedside table, then close it again. I sensed he was bending over me and barely stifled the urge to scream when I felt my pillow move as his hand searched beneath it. Only yesterday — although it seemed much longer — I'd seen Jacques search through Madeline d'Arc's effects in much the same way, looking for something he hadn't found. He must think that I had —

The letters. He must be looking for the letters I had found but hadn't had the chance to read.

Boldly, Jacques threw back the covers and brought the candle so close I could feel the warmth of its flame.

If he touches me, I will scream, I decided. I was too weak to offer any other resistance.

I knew a moment of suspense before Jacques replaced the covers, and for a moment the only sound was the steady drumming of rain.

I didn't dare open my eyes, even when I heard Sophie enter the room and whisper to Jacques. "Hurry. The Doctor is asking for you."

The door closed behind them and I lay still for another moment before attempting to get out of bed. I wanted to lock my door, but my arms felt weighted down, and my legs refused to do my bidding.

I will lie here a moment longer and rest, then I can get up.

Outside, the thunder had subsided to an intermittent mutter, and soon the rain lulled me into a deep sleep that lasted until morning.

"Your coffee, Mademoiselle."

I opened my eyes when Sophie opened the draperies. I blinked at the brilliant sunlight streaming into the room. From the angle of the sun, I knew the day was already far advanced. I attempted to sit up, only to fall back on the pillow.

"Let me help you, Mademoiselle."

Sophie propped me against the pillow bolster and poured my coffee. Her dark-shadowed eyes hinted of a recent lack of sleep, and suddenly I recalled the nightmarish events of the previous evening. Had they actually happened, or had I dreamed it all?

"What was in that draught you gave me last night?"

Sophie avoided looking at me. "I do not know. I hope you slept well."

"Did we have a storm? I thought I heard thunder."

Sophie eyed me warily. "Yes, Mam'selle. What else did you hear?"

"I was not even sure I heard that. Did something else occur I should know about?"

"No, Mam'selle. All was calm."

"What about Madame Albert?"

"She is sleeping like a babe, but no one knows what will happen when she awakens."

"At least she does not have the shears.

How is the Marquis?"

Sophie lowered her eyes and shook her head. "I hear he is very ill."

"And Lucy?"

"She was still asleep the last time I looked in on her. The Doctor told me to let her rest. He also said you must stay in bed today."

"I do feel quite tired," I said, honestly enough. "Thank you, Sophie. You may go now."

As soon as she left, I set the coffee on my table and got out of bed. My head hurt and my arm ached, but I had no intention of lying idle a moment longer. The first thing I wanted to do was find and read the letters I'd brought down from the tower room. I remembered they were in my dress pocket, but the dress wasn't hanging in my wardrobe or lying on the chair. I dimly recalled Sophie helped me remove it the night before.

With difficulty I removed my nightgown and put on my blue dress. I hoped Sophie had taken the clothes I'd worn the day before to the laundry. I knew I must retrieve my dress before my pocket's contents were lost forever.

Hastily, I brushed back my hair and stuffed it into a chignon, all I could accomplish with my right arm so sore. My face looked pale, but at least it was unmarked. I shuddered to think of what might have resulted if Madame Albert had reached me with the dagger-like dressmaker's shears.

I hurried to the work area of the chateau, where the linens were washed in huge copper tubs and put through a mangle before being hand-pressed by a laundress from the village.

Like Marc, the woman's village patois made communication difficult, but with a look of disapproval stamped on her craggy features, she allowed me to pick through the clothing she was preparing to wash. The stack was high, and I had begun to think Sophie had done something else with my things when I saw the torn and bloody petticoat I'd used to bandage my arm, then the dress I'd put on only the day before.

The laundress looked alarmed when she saw its stained right sleeve, and she pointed from it to my bandage with what I took to be sympathy. I nodded and probed the pocket for the papers. I breathed a sigh of relief when I found the bundle, badly crumpled but otherwise none the worse for wear.

I left the laundress shaking her head at my odd behavior. Tucking my prize into the pocket of my blue dress, hoping to read the letters in privacy, I started back to my room.

But when I turned the corner into the main hall and saw Dr. Dubois emerge from Lucy's room, I hastened to intercept him.

He seemed surprised to see me. "You should be in bed, Mademoiselle! Do you not feel weak?"

"A bit, but I had to know about Lucy and the Marquis."

Dr. Dubois indicated we should go into the family salon, where he bade me sit down.

"Mademoiselle Lucy is in quite a state," he said. "She claims she has no idea how she got into the hallway last night. She said she heard Madame Albert and thought she was dreaming. Then she awoke and found herself standing in the hall."

"Do you agree that she must have walked there under her own power, Doctor?"

"Yes. But that only means that Lucy can walk, not that she will continue to do so."

"I don't understand —"

"Neither do I, Mademoiselle Edmonds, but it is as I told the Marquis in Paris. There is no physical reason for the girl not to walk. When she decides she wants to and with the proper treatment, Mademoiselle Lucy should be able to walk quite well. But she is not my main concern at the moment."

Dr. Dubois paused, and I read from his

eyes what he seemed reluctant to say aloud.

"The Marquis?"

"His heart is failing, Mademoiselle, but he is conscious and asking to see you all. Jacques is with him now."

Knowing the doctor would think I was impertinent, I spoke my mind. "I hope Jacques will behave himself and not upset his father."

Dr. Dubois almost smiled. "If Jacques behaves, it will be the first time. See that Lucy comes to the Marquis' room in fifteen minutes. That will give him time to rest a bit after Jacques leaves."

"Yes, Doctor. And thank you for taking care of my arm. Oh, the draught you gave me last night — what was in it?"

Dr. Dubois looked puzzled. "You must be mistaken, Mam'selle. I prescribed nothing else for you last evening. You had already taken all the sedatives I thought it safe to administer."

"You didn't ask Sophie to give me a bitter-tasting liquid in the middle of the night?"

"I did not. Perhaps the strain you have been under —"

"It is of no consequence. I shall go to Lucy now."

But it was of great consequence to me. If

409

the draught hadn't come from the doctor, that could only mean one thing —

I shivered as I rapped on Lucy's door, then entered her room.

"I was beginning to wonder where you were." She spoke tartly, as if the events of the previous day and night had never happened. "Sophie told me you were out of bed and wandering all over the chateau again."

"I feel much better, thank you," I said, as if she had asked. "The Marquis wants to see you. Henri will take you to him in a few minutes."

A shadow crossed Lucy's face and she drew her brows together. "Henri carries me like a sack of potatoes. I would prefer to have Philip."

"I can try to find him, but there is not much time."

There is not much time. The words echoed in my ears as I walked to the stable on trembling legs. It was clear the doctor thought the marquis might not have long to live.

What will happen to us all without him? I didn't have the strength to think about that now.

Philip looked annoyed when he saw me. "What are you doing out here? You should be resting."

"Do I look that bad?"

"Frankly, yes. Has something happened to the Marquis?"

"Doctor Dubois says he has asked to see us. Jacques is with him now. Lucy is next, and she wants you to carry her up the stairs."

Philip compressed his lips. "I suppose that is the least I can do."

He took my left arm and we began to walk back to the chateau. "I heard you had some excitement after I left last night."

"Excitement? Terror is more like it."

"At least no one was hurt. I was told that Lucy actually walked from her bed into the hall. Is it so?"

"No one saw her, but she must have. She claims she does not know how she reached the hall."

"I always said she could do just about anything she wanted to. She must care for you a great deal, Ellen."

Philip's words surprised me. I had not thought Lucy capable of having deep feelings for anyone other than herself. But Philip knew Lucy as well as anyone, and perhaps he was right.

"I care for her, too. I wish I knew what was going to happen to us all."

Philip opened the door to the family salon

411

and smiled faintly. "First you worried about
the past, now you are worrying about the
future. But you must live in the present."

Philip's words served to remind me of the
unread letters in my pocket. Leaving Philip
and Henri to see to Lucy, I entered my room
and locked the door behind me. Then I sat
down on the bed to read the letters.

Three in all, addressed to the marquis
with no return address. However, the
stamps were American and the handwriting
was definitely Mama's.

I shouldn't be doing this, I told myself,
but I had to know what was in these letters,
what would cause Jacques to be so eager to
have them. My hands trembled when I un-
folded the first letter.

To my surprise, Mama had written it in
French, and the first sentences told me why.
"I wish you knew my language, my love. I
fear that my French will not allow me to say
all I wish," I translated.

So the marquis must have learned English
later, perhaps to surprise Mama. My eyes
misted and a lump formed in my throat. I
tried to imagine what they had been like in
those days and could not.

The second letter was written a month
after the first and was different in tone.
Mama had not heard from the marquis,

whom she called Jean-Paul, and she was beginning to be concerned. "If your vows of love meant anything at all, please write to me. My situation here is —"

At that point, something had been scratched out, and the letter ended with rather conventional phrases.

I brushed away the tears that filled, then spilled from my eyes, and opened the third and final letter. With no salutation or signature, it was simple and to the point, a few lines which would forever change my life.

To the Marquis d'Arc,
   This is to inform you that your daughter was born August 1, 1861. She will be called Ellen Littleton Edmonds.

Sara.

I was still clutching the letters when a knock at my door jolted me back to the present.

Hastily, I refolded the letters and thrust them into my pocket before unlocking the door.

"The Marquis is asking for you," Philip said.

I wanted to throw myself into his arms and weep until I had no more tears, but the look on his face warned me not to touch him. My eyes again filled with tears. "Oh, Philip, I cannot stand to lose him."

"The Marquis was never yours to lose," he said.

"You don't understand —"

"He is growing weaker. You must hurry."

Philip turned and walked away, leaving me to mount the stairs alone, every step bringing me closer to a father I had never known.

I knew Philip could do nothing to help me, but having him by my side would have meant a great deal at that moment.

The marquis' room was dark and strangely cool. The drapes were closed and a candle on the bedside table had all but burnt out. Dr. Dubois stood by the bed, holding the marquis' left wrist as he counted his pulse.

Jean-Paul d'Arc lay propped on several pillows, his eyes half-shut. On my approach, he opened his eyes and reached his right hand out to me. I took it in both of mine, noting that his skin felt unnaturally cool.

"Leave us," he said to Dr. Dubois.

The doctor looked appraisingly at me. "Do not excite him, Mademoiselle. You may stay only a moment."

I nodded, but my eyes remained on the

marquis' ashen face.

He regarded me with the same intensity, and I realized he knew, had always known, exactly who I was. Tears ran down my cheeks and splashed unchecked on our joined hands.

"Ellen," he whispered. "There is no time for tears now."

I wiped my eyes against my left sleeve and nodded. "You should know that my mother never stopped loving you. She wrote to you several times. I found these letters from her in the tower room yesterday."

It was too dim for the marquis to see the words, but I placed the letters in his hands.

"I suspected Madeline had taken letters meant for me."

"You knew my mother had written to you?"

"Not then, not until . . ." He paused and closed his eyes as if against a memory too painful to recall.

"Maybe you shouldn't try to talk," I said, but he shook his head and spoke earnestly.

"You must know — the day Lucy had her accident, I told Madeline I meant to divorce her. She said she would counter-sue, because she had proof I had fathered a child out of wedlock."

"You did not know of it before?"

"No, God help me, I had no idea. I wanted Sara to stay in Paris until I could divorce Madeline, but she refused to let me support her until we could be married. When I never heard from her again, I assumed she never really loved me."

"Madeline must have intercepted Mama's letters."

"She, or Madame Albert. I tried to find Sara, but too many years had passed. I had no name or address until you wrote to me. By then it was too late."

"Why did you not tell me who you were? You must have known I was your daughter."

He smiled faintly. "Yes, Ellen, I knew. Looking into your eyes was like seeing your mother all over again, and it nearly broke my heart. But I feared you would either hate me for the way I treated her — or perhaps try to profit from it."

"I don't blame you, and I want nothing from you. I have no claim to the Chateau d'Arc."

He frowned and shook his head. "But you do. As soon as I knew I had another child, I made arrangements. All the proof needed is the letter you found . . ." The marquis winced in pain and moaned.

His pallor alarmed me, and I feared the emotional toll my visit must be taking was also shortening his life. "Please, you must be quiet now."

"Give the letters to Betancourt," he said in an urgent whisper. "He knows what to do."

I had scarcely replaced them in my pocket when Dr. Dubois came in and said I must leave. I bent to kiss the marquis' sunken cheek and heard him sob.

"Lucy has been my punishment, but I did my best for her. Take care of her."

"I will," I whispered back, then Dr. Dubois took my arm and guided me into the hallway.

I was only dimly aware of the others who were now gathered outside the marquis' room. I saw the servants and some of the villagers and Father Campeau, who pushed his way past me and entered the room just behind Philip.

I groped my way down the stairs to the click of rosary beads and murmured prayers. The marquis' deathwatch had begun, but my own mourning would be done in private.

Locking my door behind me, I threw myself on my bed and gave myself up to the racking sobs that I had suppressed for so long. Later I would try to comfort Lucy, but for the present, my own grief was too great.

I cried myself to sleep and awoke with my arm throbbing from having lain on it. Still feeling heavy and clumsy, I tucked my loose hair back into my chignon, smoothed my dress as well as I could, and walked out into the hall.

The clock had chimed twice when I rapped on Lucy's door. I heard her weeping and someone speaking to her in a low voice. Opening the door, I saw Philip kneeling beside her chair, holding her hand. Lucy's face was blotched and swollen from crying, and she seemed to be paying Philip no heed.

"I'm sorry, Lucy. I should have been with you. I must have fallen asleep," I said apologetically.

"It would not have made any difference," Lucy said bitterly.

From Philip's expression, I guessed he hadn't been able to calm Lucy's hysterics, and I felt pity for him. "I'm sure other matters require your attention — I'll stay with Lucy," I offered.

He stood and nodded. "Yes, many arrangements must be made. Doctor Dubois will look in on you both in a while."

"Arrangements?"

"The Marquis died about one o'clock," Lucy said flatly.

"I am told the end was very peaceful," Philip added.

Although the news shouldn't have surprised me, I swayed slightly and took hold of Lucy's bedpost to steady myself.

"Are you all right?" Philip asked.

"Yes, of course."

"Then I shall be going." He touched my shoulder as he walked past.

As soon as Philip had closed the door behind him, Lucy pounded her fists against the arms of her chair. "Peaceful!" she said. "Why does everyone say that death is peaceful?"

"I know you must be very upset," I began, but Lucy broke into a storm of hysterical weeping and would not be comforted.

"Upset! You have no idea how I feel, Ellen. Nobody knows what I went through with that man — nobody!"

"Lucy! How can you say that about your father?" I was genuinely surprised at her apparently unfeeling reaction, but her next words shocked me even more.

"My father? The Marquis drove my mother away from us, but he never loved her. And he is not my father, either."

The room swam around me. I sat down on the bed and stared at Lucy. "How can you say that? He loved you very much. The last words he said to me were 'Take care of Lucy.' Surely you are upset and imagining things."

"I imagine nothing! With my own ears I heard Mama tell the Marquis he was not the only one who could take a lover. She told him my real father was a man who truly loved her."

"Oh, Lucy," was all I could think of to say. "People say things when they are angry they don't mean. No matter the circumstances, you must know that the Marquis cared for you a great deal."

Lucy's mouth twisted. "Yes, he had to, did he not? Guilt can make people do almost as much as love, I have heard."

"Guilt?"

Lucy's eyes glittered. "You have always been curious about my accident, Ellen, so I shall tell you how it happened. The chateau was filled with hunters and I was going to be allowed to go out with them. I wanted Mama to see me in my new riding habit and I went up to their room. They were having a fight, which was nothing unusual, and I sat down outside the door to wait until it was over. I had never heard them shout at each other so much, and when I heard Mama tell the Marquis another man was my real father, I ran out of the house with my hands over my ears. I was crying so hard I could scarcely see when I went to the stable. I rode toward the deep forest as fast as my horse would carry me."

"And there you had the accident," I finished for her.

Lucy twisted her hands. "It was not an accident. I wanted to die that day, and I have wished a hundred thousand times since that I had."

I had thought I had no more tears, but they began anew when I knelt beside Lucy's chair and embraced her. "The past is behind us now, Lucy. We have to go on."

Her arms tightened around my neck for a moment and her voice was no more than a whisper. "Stay with me, Ellen. I am so afraid."

I drew back and looked at her. "So am I, Lucy. But together, we shall be all right."

She drew her mouth down in the familiar expression, then made an effort to smile. "I have heard the blind can sometimes lead each other."

"Perhaps that will work for us," I said.

At least it would be a start.

That afternoon I entered the formal salon with the other members of the household before the chateau doors would open to other mourners. According to custom, the marquis lay in state on a bier in the center of the room. His body was covered by a white sheet and his bare face was illuminated by twin *torchiers,* so even the slightest sign of life would be noticed immediately. A crucifix and a sanctified sprig of holly rested on his chest.

Until the funeral Mass, the marquis would be guarded only by the family and household servants. Prayers would be continually offered, sometimes as the rosary was recited in unison, at other times by individuals.

I had dreaded seeing the marquis in death, but pushing Lucy's chair helped steady me. For his sake, as well as hers, I had to be strong.

Jacques led the small procession of mourners, his face ashen and sober. I wondered if he regretted the way he'd treated his father, but he shed no tears.

The time for tears is past, the marquis had said, but when it was my turn to pray for him, mine were tears of regret, for I had scarcely known the man who had been the love of my mother's life.

At last the front doors were opened to admit a steady stream of mourners. From that time until the funeral Mass ended the next day, the Chateau d'Arc was filled with visitors, and I did what I could to see that they were offered hospitality.

Edouard Betancourt arrived from Paris and told Jacques and Lucy there would be a reading of the marquis' will the day after the funeral. The marquis had asked me to show him the letter announcing my birth, but fearing how Jacques and Lucy would react, I was reluctant to do so. My arm no longer pained me, but speculation about the past and uncertainty about the future kept me awake much of the night.

Jacques was a puzzlement to me. If he had been trying to frighten me away because he knew who I was, then how could he have tried to make love to me, knowing we shared the same blood? And if I decided to press my claim, would Jacques again react violently?

Yet, if I failed to come forward, no one else would be likely to look after Lucy's interests.

I'll ask Philip what I should do, I thought drowsily.

Falling asleep at last, I dreamed I lay safe in his arms in the sunlight, far from the menacing shadows of the Chateau d'Arc.

Chapter Seventeen

Until the marquis' burial, I had never ventured into the graveyard adjoining the chapel. Surrounded by a high brick wall, it could be reached only by going through the rear doors of the chapel. When we followed the casket to the crypt where the marquis would be laid to rest, I was surprised to see how many burial vaults and tombstones the plot already contained.

"The Chateau d'Arc has been continuously occupied for a third of a millennium," Lucy had said, and apparently most of its previous occupants were buried here.

"But not always by d'Arcs," Jacques had added. From where I stood to the left of the marquis' vault, I saw a large crypt and several tombstones, all bearing the same name: MAILLEY.

What a coincidence! was my first thought, then I recalled what Philip had said about himself and Jacques had said about him.

My mother was English, but I am a

French citizen, Philip had told me.

He would like to own it all, Jacques had said of Philip.

And the name of the village — I had never stopped to think about it before, but the road sign at the crossroads pointed to Maillebois.

Maillebois — French for Mailley's wood.

I looked over at Philip. He stood by Lucy's chair, his head bowed while Father Campeau recited a seemingly endless prayer, and I wondered about his true feelings for the marquis. Had he resented him because his family had taken what Philip's family had built, or had he accepted the fact and come back to be near the land he could never have?

Suddenly I felt closer to Philip than ever before. We shared a common bond of loss, and I longed for the service to end so I could seek him out and tell him so.

There were yet more prayers; then at length the marquis was placed into the crypt. Birds sang overhead and a warm breeze fanned our faces while we waited in silence for the tomb to be sealed. The marble grated as two burly villagers strained against it, and for a moment I feared it might even break under the pressure. But then the lid slid in place, Father Campeau offered a final blessing, and the service was over.

I had to return to the chateau to see to the light luncheon for the many who had traveled from Paris, but as soon as I could politely do so, I excused myself and went to look for Philip.

I found him in the office, copying figures into a ledger. He still wore his best clothes, although he had loosened his cravat. Intent on his task, he didn't notice my presence until I called his name.

"Philip, I need to speak with you."

He glanced up, then gestured toward the ledgers. "I hope it will be brief. Monsieur Betancourt has requested certain information concerning the estate and he wants it now."

"What I have to say concerns the estate, as well. I need your advice."

Philip raised his eyebrows. "Oh?"

"This is really a legal matter, I suppose. You see, the Marquis intended me to make a claim on his estate, and —"

"What?" Philip put down his pen and strode over to where I stood. "The man is barely in his grave and you are already scheming to cheat his children? You know, Ellen, you almost had me fooled."

Unable to bear the look of contempt I saw

426

in Philip's eyes, I thrust the letters at him. "It was his wish I have some portion, not mine. He told me to give these to Betancourt, but I won't do so if you think it could hurt Lucy."

"What kind of hoax is this?" he asked, after reading a few lines of the first letter.

"I wish you would just listen, instead of always being so ready to blame me for some imagined crime. Those letters are genuine. My mother wrote them more than twenty years ago, but the Marquis never got them because the Marquise or Madame Albert saw them first and kept them from him. The Marquis only found out they existed the day of Lucy's accident, when the Marquise told him she would use my mother's letters to prevent the Marquis from divorcing her."

Philip's eyes looked from the letters to mine and back again as he rapidly skimmed the first two. When he came to the last, the color drained from his face and he looked at me as if he'd never really seen me before.

"Of course," he said hoarsely.

"Believe me, I knew none of this when I came to the Chateau d'Arc."

He nodded, then looked back to the letters as if he could scarcely believe the evidence before his eyes. "Now I understand so many things. Oh, Ellen . . ."

Philip held out his arms and pulled me to his chest with a groan. I fitted into his embrace as if I belonged there and circled my arms around his neck.

This time when I lifted my face to be kissed, I was not denied. Again and again I tasted the sweetness of Philip's lips on mine, felt the warmth of his breath moving against my cheek, and relaxed in the security of his arms.

Finally he pulled away and looked down at me, puzzled.

"Why did you not tell me this before? When I was saying all those things about you. There were rumors about what happened in Paris, too."

"I couldn't tell you what I didn't know myself. Just before the Marquis died, he told me he had tried to find my mother, but he didn't know where she was until I wrote him of her death at my mother's bidding. The Marquis said he knew I was his daughter the moment he saw me, but my mother's letter is my only proof."

Philip returned my letters. "What will you do about it?"

"I don't know. I came here for your advice."

"It was the Marquis' wish for you to give the letters to Betancourt?"

428

"Yes. He said his lawyer would know what to do."

"Then you must give them to him, of course. But make sure you are not observed. Jacques will not welcome this news."

"I know."

Briefly, I told Philip of how Jacques had invaded my room, probably in search of the letters. "Although I still don't understand how he knew about them."

"Jacques was almost grown when Lucy had her accident, old enough for his mother to have confided in him. Or perhaps he got the information from Madame Albert. You say he was looking for them just before you broke the window in the tower room?"

I nodded. "He seemed to be searching for something and seemed quite angry when he did not find it."

"By then the Marquis had come back and Jacques saw how ill he was. Madame Albert had reminded him about your mother by calling you by her name, and perhaps she even mentioned the letters to him."

"Yes, she did. I overheard part of their conversation, but it meant nothing to me at the time."

Philip's lips tightened. "Jacques does not deserve to control the estate. He will run into the ground what took his father years to build up."

"Is there any other way to stop him?"

Philip shook his head and reached out to touch my cheek. "You have to come forward with your claim, Ellen. It is Lucy's only chance, as well as yours."

He cradled my face in his hands and kissed me again, this time quite tenderly. "You must be careful, though. Jacques is not a man to be crossed."

After a moment, I forced myself to break away. "And what do you expect to get from the estate, Philip?"

He looked puzzled. "What do you mean?"

"I know who you are, too."

He laughed. "I am who I have always been — that has never changed. I am Philip Mailley, the d'Arc estate manager. If Jacques and Lucy and Ellen do not want me to stay when the Chateau d'Arc is theirs, then I shall move on."

"Could you really leave this place your ancestors built?"

He returned my level look and his lips parted in a smile. "And they say that dead men tell no tales," he said lightly.

"You deliberately kept your secret, while I didn't even know I had one. I think the score is even."

"No, Ellen, I kept no secrets. Everyone at the chateau knew I was descended from the Mailley family who built it."

"I am surprised the Marquis would hire you, in that case."

"On the contrary. Who would better look after his land than someone whose ancestors loved it?"

"You must stay here." I allowed myself to be kissed again. "I refuse to let you go."

"As I must keep reminding you, Mam'selle, you do not yet own the Chateau d'Arc."

Philip's tone was light, but I felt the undercurrent of tension. He was right.

"Go back to your ledgers while I attempt to get Betancourt alone."

Philip pulled me to him and kissed me once more. "Did I mention I love you?"

I looked up into his eyes and smiled. Never had I felt more alive or happier than at that instant. "No, but you may tell me now."

Instead, Philip kissed me again, longer and more urgently than before, and I knew he stopped kissing me only with extreme reluctance. "Later, my dearest one. First, we both have work to do."

Edouard Betancourt was nowhere to be

found when I returned to the chateau, and Henri told me that he was with Jacques and Lucy in the grand salon.

"I believe he is reading the Marquis' will, Mam'selle. Is there something I can do for you?"

"No, thank you, Henri. I will wait in the family salon until they have finished."

After Henri left the room, I walked to the door between the two rooms and put my ear against it, but the wood was so thick I could hear only a faint drone, like bees circling a distant hive.

I sat back down and replaced the letters in my pocket. Still glowing from my encounter with Philip, I wasn't thinking about my claim; there would still be time to set the legal wheels in motion. In the meanwhile, I would stay on at the chateau, near Philip —

My pleasant reverie about the future was interrupted when the door to the grand salon was thrust open and Jacques emerged scowling.

Without speaking, he rushed through the family salon and ran toward the stable.

I hope he isn't going after Philip was my first thought, immediately dismissed as illogical.

Betancourt pushed Lucy's chair into the

family salon, and I saw that both looked shaken.

"Jacques seems upset," I said.

Lucy nodded. "He has just been told that he cannot touch the estate for at least a year. It was not welcome news."

"Why is that?"

Betancourt pushed Lucy's chair beside mine. He sat on the sofa, carefully hitching his trousers first. "The news will be common knowledge soon enough, Mademoiselle. It seems the Marquis has another heir. He has provided for the child, who has a year to make a claim."

"It serves Jacques right," Lucy said. "I hope they find him — or her — and the other heir will keep him from selling off the forest."

"You would not mind sharing the estate?" I asked.

Lucy shook her head. "They can have the chateau and the estate and welcome. The Marquis left me the Paris townhouse, free and clear."

I glanced at the lawyer, who nodded. "That is correct, Mademoiselle Edmonds. Jacques wanted the townhouse badly, but unless he buys it from Mademoiselle Lucy, it will never be his."

"What will you do with it? You despise living in Paris."

Lucy lifted her eyebrows. "Since when do I need you to tell me what I despise, Ellen? You have always been too presumptuous. Doctor Dubois wants me to go back to Paris for some treatments. He thinks I can walk without braces and throw this damned chair out the window. Also, I suppose I should be closer to the House of Worth."

I smiled faintly. "Well, I'm glad to see you have recovered your spirits, Miss d'Arc." I turned to Betancourt. "Is it true that Lucy can take possession of the townhouse right away, without waiting for this other claim to be settled?"

He nodded. "Yes. That is an outright gift to her, not part of the chateau and estate itself. That is what we must wait a year to settle."

"And if no one shows up to claim it before then, Jacques gets it all?"

He nodded again. "Except for certain incomes that will derive to his sister. Of course, while the property is entailed, they will share in the profits."

"All of this has been very tiring," Lucy announced. "I would like to rest now."

It had been a long while since Lucy had wanted to take an afternoon rest, but this time she'd earned it. After telling Betancourt I would like to see him privately when I returned, I took Lucy to her room.

"You see, things will work out for you," I said.

She looked at me strangely. "What about you, Ellen? Will you be content to leave the chateau and live in Paris?"

"I promised to take care of you, and I will," I said, somewhat crossly.

Lucy knows me too well. My love for Philip must be shining from my eyes like a beacon.

I hoped she wouldn't choose to pursue that matter.

Edouard Betancourt had been a lawyer for many years and had no doubt received many confidences that would have startled a less worldly man. But even he seemed a bit shocked when he read the letters I handed him. He glanced at me, one eyebrow raised.

"Am I to take it that you are the same Ellen Littleton Edmonds?" he asked.

I nodded. "I found these letters only two days ago. They were hidden in the Marquise's trunk for many years. The Marquis had no knowledge of where they were."

"But apparently he knew their content or he would never have changed his will. Very well, Mademoiselle. I take it that you wish to make a formal claim against the estate at this time?"

"I know nothing about the law, M'sieu, but it was the Marquis' wish for me to present the matter to you. He said you would know how to handle it."

Betancourt sighed. "Jacques will not like this."

"When will he have to know?"

"I must tell him immediately, of course. Not to do so would be unethical."

But much safer for me.

"I understand. But please take care to secure these letters. If Jacques should get them —"

Betancourt held up his hand. "Say no more. I have carried documents on my person more than once, and have never lost a single one. Do you have any idea where the young man might have taken himself?"

"He may have gone riding — he went out the door to the stable. He'll probably be back in time for dinner."

"Then I shall see him this evening. Do not look so concerned, Mademoiselle Edmonds. I intend to carry out the Marquis' wishes."

"What result will my claim have on the inheritance? I have no wish to damage the estate."

"There will be no immediate effect, Mademoiselle. After the papers are executed — in several months' time — you and Jacques will jointly own the chateau lands. Jacques will retain title to the chateau itself, but he must give you right of tenancy as long as you live."

"And what about M'sieu Mailley? Will he get anything?"

Betancourt looked faintly surprised. "He will receive a cash settlement and ownership of several of the horses. Other servants will also receive modest bequests."

Philip isn't a servant. As much as I wanted to say the words, I knew I had no reason to defend him to Betancourt.

"One other thing," I said. "I would like to tell Lucy about this myself."

"As you wish, Mademoiselle. But do it soon."

I couldn't wait to tell Philip the good news. Marc grinned and called out something I didn't understand as I hurried past him and across the stable yard. It was twilight and Philip should already have lighted a lantern, but the stable was dark. I tried the door and found it open, but only gloom greeted me.

Moving through the office, I rapped

lightly on his apartment door, then opened it when I heard no response. Like the office, Philip's apartment was empty, and I knew a moment of panic.

What if something had happened to him? What would I do if I lost Philip now? I had suffered too many losses. First my mother, then the marquis —

Philip is out tending to estate business, I told myself. But when I returned to the stable and saw that both his horse and Jacques' were gone, my stomach knotted in fear.

I may have filed my claim at the marquis' urging, but it would only worsen the bad blood between Jacques and Philip.

Returning to the chateau, I found that Sophie had already helped Lucy prepare for bed.

"Did she offer you any medication?" I asked.

Lucy looked puzzled. "No. Why should she? I told Doctor Dubois I had no need of it."

"No matter. But if she does, refuse it. It could be from Jacques."

Lucy shook her head. "I think you are more tired than you realize, Ellen."

"I am tired," I admitted, "but my fear of Jacques is real. And now he has a better reason than ever to try to harm us both."

Lucy drew her brows together. "I despise riddles, Ellen. If you have something to say, do so."

I sat on the edge of Lucy's bed and told her, haltingly at first, what I had pieced together about my parentage. "By filing my claim, I can keep Jacques from destroying the estate," I concluded.

Lucy had listened attentively to my words, but I couldn't tell from her expression what she thought about them. "How kind of you," she said, and I knew from the edge in her voice that, like Philip, she suspected I had come to the Chateau d'Arc with some scheme in mind.

I wanted to grab her shoulders and shake her, but instead I stood and backed away from her bed. "I'm sorry if you doubt me, but it doesn't really matter. Betancourt has the letters and he believes me. Good night."

I had my hand on the door latch when Lucy called to me.

"Lock my door, Ellen."

I looked back at her, but her expression hadn't changed.

"I also fear Jacques," she said.

Although I thought I wouldn't be able to sleep, I locked myself in and prepared for

439

bed. I was still brushing my hair when I heard Jacques in the hall, and from the sound of his conversation with Edouard Betancourt, I knew he'd been drinking.

"I shall speak with you when you are sober," I heard Betancourt say.

Jacques laughed. "See me in a year," he called back.

So he would not be told the news about me this night, at least. And if he had ridden somewhere to drink, it was highly unlikely he would have encountered Philip. I felt strongly tempted to return to the stable, but I dared not venture out in my nightclothes, and I was too tired to dress again.

I would see Philip in the morning. That would be soon enough.

I slept later than I intended, yet Sophie told me Lucy had not yet called for breakfast. I considered asking Sophie about the draught she had given me, but since I was already convinced Jacques had been responsible for it, I knew it would do little good.

"Have you seen Doctor Dubois and M'sieu Betancourt this morning?" I asked, instead.

"Yes, Mam'selle. They had an early breakfast and are on their way to Paris.

Doctor Dubois took the big carriage, since Madame Albert went with him."

"What?" I hadn't had time to worry about her the past few days, much less consider the possibility she would ever leave the chateau.

"It was the Marquis' wish to see her taken care of in a safe place. Doctor Dubois is taking her to some Sisters in Paris."

"What about M'sieu Betancourt?" *Betancourt said he wouldn't leave until he had seen Jacques,* I thought uneasily.

"He left in his carriage shortly after the Doctor."

"I am sorry I missed telling them goodbye. Did Jacques see them off?"

Sophie watched me as if she wanted to see my reaction. "He left when they did, Mam'selle."

"Jacques left? Why did he do that?"

"He said he had to get away and you would know why. Will you take more coffee, Mam'selle?"

"No, thank you."

My mind reeled. My relief that Jacques was gone was tempered by the realization that he probably still meant to retain sole control of the Chateau d'Arc.

I rapped lightly on Lucy's door and then unlocked it. She sat on the side of the bed, half-dressed, and I could tell she'd already taken a few steps to and from the chair where her clothes lay.

"You should have called me to help you."

"I do not intend to be helpless all my life," she said tartly. "Doctor Dubois told me I should begin to practice standing for short periods of time. When I get to Paris, he will help me do more."

"Did you know Jacques left for Paris this morning?"

Lucy's face darkened. "No, my dear half-brother did not bid me farewell. You know, Ellen, we two share no common blood, even though you are the Marquis' daughter."

"I'm sorry about that, Lucy. I'd like to be your sister."

I spoke sincerely, but my words seemed to embarrass Lucy.

"What else would you like to be?" she asked.

"What do you mean?"

Lucy looked at me levelly. "I have seen the way you look at Philip and the way he looks at you. I think you two are in love."

I felt my face grow warm and my tongue seemed tied. "What about you, Lucy? I know you care a great deal about him."

Lucy shrugged. "He was the only man around, and he was always kind. But I knew the only reason Philip might ever marry me would be to get the Chateau d'Arc back, and now the Marquis' will has made that impossible. If Philip marries you, he can still gain some control of the land."

"Philip hasn't asked me to marry him, but I can assure you I would never marry anyone for financial gain — mine or his."

Lucy looked at me as if she wanted to make sure I spoke the truth. "If the Marquis had felt that way, my mother would have married someone else, and all this would never have happened. You have my blessing to pursue Philip if he is what you want. But he had better be armed when Jacques catches wind of it."

I stayed with Lucy until she'd had breakfast, then left her sketching for the first time in several days as I went in search of Philip.

Marc greeted me with a smile, but when I asked where Philip was, he shrugged and spread his arms wide.

"Ask M'sieu Mailley to come to see me when he returns," I said. As usual, I wasn't sure Marc understood, but he bowed and smiled as if he thought it humorous I should want to find Philip.

After the activity of the past few days, the chateau seemed strangely quiet when I came in from the stable, and I was somewhat at loose ends. I felt drawn to the second floor and the room where the marquis had died.

The marquis — I could not bring myself to call him my father, even though I had every right to do so — had the largest chamber on the second floor, and except for the bed, which had been made up, everything had been left as it was.

I walked to the window and opened the drapes, letting in the rays of a feeble sun. The sky was clouding rapidly, signaling afternoon storms. It was a pattern that often happened in the Beauce this time of the year, Philip had said.

Philip. No matter what I started thinking of, it seemed my mind always returned to him. Being in love — truly in love, and not just experiencing a temporary attraction — was new to me. Did he really feel the same way about me?

Seeing the silver hairbrushes and toiletries on the marquis' dresser, I felt sudden tears sting my eyes. He and my mother had known love, but their forbidden passion had led to grief. I vowed to be more careful with Philip.

I was reading in the family salon after

lunch when I heard a knock at the door. I knew it wasn't Philip, since he had the habit of entering without ceremony, but without waiting for a servant to come, I opened the door myself.

Marc stood there, grinning widely, and handed me a note.

"For me?" I asked, and he nodded.

I thanked him, and he tipped his hand to his forehead in a salute. I closed the door and opened the single sheet of paper, which bore the familiar d'Arc crest.

I read,

> Meet me in the summerhouse.
> Philip.

How odd, I thought. The summerhouse wasn't far from the chateau. Why had he not just walked over and suggested we go there to talk?

To talk — or for some other reason? I blushed at my own thoughts. Of course it would make an ideal rendezvous, away from the prying eyes of Marc and the household servants.

I debated telling Lucy where I was going, then decided against it. I would be back by dinner, and no one should need me before then.

I slipped out the side door and hurried toward the summerhouse, my heart beating rapidly in anticipation. I hadn't been back since the day the marquis had taken me there and told me about Lucy's accident. Perhaps it had been the very place I had been conceived. Had the marquis not mentioned my mother thought the cottage charming? But she would, of course. To a woman in love, anyplace she could be with her lover would seem so.

I was so absorbed in my thoughts I was almost upon the cottage before I saw the horse tethered to a nearby tree.

Something is terribly wrong, I had time to think, but I had no time to run away as the horse's owner grabbed me from behind and propelled me through the door.

"Jacques!" I gasped.

Chapter Eighteen

"Welcome, Mademoiselle."

Jacques' triumphant grin turned my stomach, and I felt weak with shock.

"You are supposed to be in Paris."

"The road runs both ways, you know. But for you, my sweet little sister, it is about to end."

"You must be insane! Let me go this instant."

In reply, Jacques tightened his grip, and pain shot through my right arm, still sore where it had been cut.

"You thought you were smart, palming yourself off as the Marquis' long-lost child, but I will not be cheated out of what is mine."

As he talked, Jacques forced me to the love seat. Pinning both arms behind my back, he kissed me brutally. The instant he pulled back, I spat in his face. His momentary surprise allowed me to wriggle from his grasp and run for the door, but I didn't get far before he caught me and held me

447

even more tightly.

His eyes glittered and I saw the madness reflected there.

"What are you going to do?" I asked as he shoved me along the edge of the woods, well out of sight of anyone in the chateau.

"You will see," he growled.

As if matching my situation, the sky steadily darkened and a cool wind began to blow. Thunder rolled across the sky, followed by a flash of lightning. The hour was yet early, but as the storm clouds blotted out the sun, the chateau became an indistinct blur, illumined occasionally by the stabbing probe of a bolt of lightning. Ahead, the dark surface of the lake was broken into miniature whitecaps from the force of the wind, and I realized Jacques must have been taking me there.

When we were still a few feet from the brink of the lake, I screamed as loudly as I could. Jacques struck me across the mouth and pushed me to a sitting position on the ground.

"No one can hear you. Save your breath."

"Why are you doing this? I do not intend to take anything of yours."

"You are lying," he said, his words all but lost against the wind. "Take off your dress."

"I will not!"

My hair had come loose and was whipping in the wind. I could scarcely see Jacques' face, but I hoped he could read the determination in mine.

"Then I will do it for you."

He fumbled with the buttons on my bodice with one hand, still using the other to pin my arms behind me.

"Let my arms go and I'll do it myself," I said, realizing I might as well pretend to cooperate until I saw a chance to escape.

"No tricks," he warned.

"Agreed."

Jacques grabbed my ankles the moment he released my arm, giving me no opportunity to run from him. I slipped first one arm, then the other, out of my dress sleeves, then pulled the garment over my hips until it fell to the ground.

"You are very lovely, you know," he said gruffly. "Now take off your petticoat."

I untied the string around my waist and the petticoat slipped away, leaving me standing in my chemise. The wind gusted, bringing a peppering of rain. I shivered uncontrollably as Jacques pulled me to a standing position and pushed me toward the lake.

"Keep going," he urged when I tried to halt at the edge. "It is unfortunate you chose such a stormy day to take a swim, Mam'selle. But then, you Americans are rather foolish, *n'est ce pas?*"

"No one will think I went swimming."

"No matter. No one has ever thought to look for the Marquise here, either."

"The Marquise?"

Jacques seemed pleased by my surprise. "It seems my dear father drove her to suicide. At least Madame Albert thinks so."

"Madame Albert is unbalanced."

"Perhaps, but she has always wanted the best for me, which is more than I can say for you. Keep walking," he added when I instinctively hung back from the cold water.

The lake was shallow near the shore but deepened only a short distance away. The water was up to my chest when Jacques pushed me underneath it, and although I fought back with all my strength, I couldn't break his hold on me. I felt the pressure as my nose filled with water and my lungs seemed ready to burst, and still he held me down. A roaring filled my ears, and I had an eerie sensation of floating.

So this is what death is like, I thought with odd detachment. What was it Philip said about the marquis? *The end was peaceful.*

But I wasn't ready for a peaceful death —

and certainly not at Jacques' hands. Rather than pushing back against his grip, I dropped my head as far as I could while kicking backward with all my might. My legs made contact with his knees, and in the moment Jacques fought to regain his balance, I surfaced for a deep breath of air, then swam away from him, parallel to the shore.

I gambled that Jacques was not as strong a swimmer as I was, having swum in my uncle's farm ponds from an early age. But when I heard him panting and imagined he was right behind me, I knew I had to redouble my efforts. My right arm hurt too much for my strokes to be very effective, and I feared he would soon overtake me.

Rain began to fall in torrents, blocking the shore from view, but doggedly I kept swimming. I was becoming weaker with every passing moment, and I feared I couldn't keep going much longer.

Through the din of thunder, I thought I heard someone shouting my name — not Jacques this time, but Philip.

I must be imagining what I want to hear, I thought, but then it came again, and this time there was no mistaking his urgent English voice.

"Get out of the water!"

I could scarcely see Philip standing on the shore, but at his command I stopped swimming and cautiously let down my legs to search for the bottom. My toes encountered soft mud and silt, and I turned toward the shore and swam a few more strokes before I saw Philip wading in to meet me, holding out both arms.

"Hurry!" He scooped me from the water just as a tremendous flash of lightning and crash of thunder filled the world. "We must get away from the water before we are struck by lightning."

I looked back at the seething lake. "Where is Jacques?"

"Jacques? I have no idea."

Perhaps he drowned, I thought, sorrow mixed with relief. I knew Philip and I could not rescue him in this storm.

I closed my eyes and allowed Philip to carry me back to the summerhouse. I was soaked to the skin and my teeth chattered with cold, but I scarcely noticed. I was safe now in Philip's arms.

When we reached the summerhouse, Philip set me down, his eyes blazing with anger. "You picked a hell of a time to take a swim, Ellen. It is a miracle you escaped the lightning, not to mention the possibility of drowning."

"I can't b-believe you'd th-think I have that little s-sense," I said through my shivers.

Philip walked into the bedroom and returned with a blanket. "Here, put this around you — and take off whatever that thing is you have on."

I hadn't stopped to think what a sight I must present, with my chemise and pantaloons plastered to my body, and I snatched the blanket away from him.

He turned his back to light the wood in the fireplace, giving me the opportunity to remove my sodden chemise and rub my skin dry with the blanket before wrapping it about me.

"Your clothes are also wet," I said. "Should you not take them off as well?"

Philip turned and looked at me as if he might be having difficulty staying angry. "You would like that, would you?"

"I wouldn't want you to catch cold."

He reached for another blanket. I watched him remove his shirt, but when he started to pull down his trousers, I looked away.

He no longer sounded angry. "Come sit by the fire and tell me what happened," he said, patting the hearthrug beside him.

"Jacques tried to kill me, and he almost succeeded."

A mixture of exasperation and anger sounded in Philip's voice, and he shook his head. "Did I not warn you to watch out for him?"

"Jacques was supposed to be in Paris. How was I to know he'd come back and trick me into meeting him here? And how did you know I was in the lake?"

Philip reached out his hand and brushed several strands of hair out of my face. "You look like a drowned rat," he said tenderly. "I had some business in the village, and then I stopped by the chateau. No one knew where you were, but when I went back to the stable and asked Marc if he had seen you, he told me you walked to the summerhouse."

"That's odd. He delivered a note supposedly from you, asking me to meet you here. He must have known who it was from."

Philip shook his head. "Jacques could have asked him to give it to you without mentioning his name."

"But your name was signed to it and it was unsealed."

Philip gently stroked my face. "Ellen, Marc cannot read French, much less English, but he saw you heading toward the summerhouse. I am just glad I got here in time."

"So am I."

"I will never let you out of my sight again," Philip whispered, his lips against mine. He kissed me, and my response led him to kiss me again, and then again. "Ah, Ellen, you have no idea how many times I have imagined holding you in my arms like this."

"You never did anything about it, though," I reminded him.

"How could I? I was sure you came to the Chateau d'Arc intending to marry a man with money, and I have nothing."

"You should know by now that I'm not a fortune hunter. And as for your having nothing, you have me, if you want me," I whispered against his cheek.

He tightened his embrace. "I want you with every fiber of my being. As much as I tried not to, I have come to love you."

"And I love you, too."

Philip kissed me again, then pulled away to look into my eyes. "We will be married soon." He made it a statement and I nodded in agreement.

"Yes."

Much later, wearing still-damp clothes, we left the summerhouse, hand-in-hand. The skies had cleared and the air smelled fresh.

Seeing its image reflected in the now calm

waters of the dark lake that had almost taken my life, the Chateau d'Arc held no more fear for me. I had been summoned to it as a stranger, but it was with a sense of belonging that I now turned toward it.

"Come, Philip. Let's go home."

Epilogue

Father Campeau smiled at Philip and me from the door of the chapel where we had been married the previous July. "One could not ask for a better day for a christening."

"Little Paul doesn't seem to agree," I said, trying to soothe our son. "I hope it is not considered bad luck for him to cry during the ceremony."

"Surely the chateau will not be affected if its heir adds a few tears to the Holy Water," Father Campeau said. "Are both godparents here?" he added, looking around the small circle of people who had accompanied us to the chapel.

"Yes, Father. Lucy is the godmother, of course, and M'sieu Betancourt has agreed to be godfather."

Philip is such a proud father, I fear he will burst the buttons on his coat, Lucy had said that morning, and I had to agree. I hadn't realized how proud having a son could make a man feel, and I was happy to see Philip's joy matched my own.

Yet my pleasure was mixed with sorrow the marquis had not lived to see his grandson. Nor, I reflected, had he lived to bear the knowledge that his son had tried to take my life, only to lose his own. Fleeing and possibly blinded by the rain, Jacques d'Arc had run into a tree limb at full gallop and broken his neck.

The marquis would be proud of Lucy, however. She stood during the entire christening and could now walk short distances unaided. Soon, she vowed, she planned to dance at the same Paris balls where more and more of her designs for the House of Worth were in evidence.

When the time came for Paul Littleton Mailley to be sprinkled, he wrinkled his little nose — so much like the marquis' that everyone had remarked on it — and looked up with a long-suffering expression, then closed his eyes.

"Such a good baby, yes he is," Lucy murmured, and Philip and I exchanged a smile.

"One of these days you'll come here to christen your own child," I said.

Lucy made a face. "Heaven forbid! I have too much to do to concern myself with such things."

"That will doubtless change, Mam'selle," Betancourt said, taking her arm.

"Perhaps, but only when I am ready," she declared.

"You two go on. We will be along presently," I said.

I had cut a spray of early roses from the garden and now I retrieved them. Philip carried Paul out the rear door and into the graveyard.

I placed the roses atop the marquis' crypt, which had been re-opened the previous July to admit the remains of the marquise, found when the chateau lake had been drained.

"We never would have known what happened to the Marquise had Jacques not told you she was there," Philip said.

"Poor Madeline. I hope she has found some peace."

As Philip and I left the chapel, I realized my life had been richly blessed.

How long ago it seemed since I had been summoned to the Chateau d'Arc! I had changed a great deal, and so had the chateau. No longer a dark place of conflict and secrets, its pink brick glowed in the warm summer sun. The lovely old house, once again rightly known as the Chateau de Mailley, now welcomed us — and its new heir — home.

About the Author

Kay Cornelius grew up in Winchester, Tennessee, and graduated from George Peabody College for Teachers in Nashville. She and her husband spent a year in a French village whose lovely chateau became the model for *Summons to the Chateau d'Arc*, before settling in Huntsville, Alabama. Kay taught secondary English and earned a Master's degree from Alabama A. & M. University. An avid amateur historian, she has researched and written articles for several scholarly and popular magazines, and nonfiction books and biographies for children and young teens. Her published fiction includes several short stories, one novella, and many historical and contemporary romance novels. She and her husband Don, who worked for NASA and Lockheed-Martin Missiles and Space, have two grown children and four grandchildren. They do volunteer work and enjoy traveling. Kay speaks on various topics and conducts writing workshops. In her spare time, she is currently knitting an afghan with twenty different pattern squares.